Overture for Beginners

By the same author

THE DREAMING SUBURB
THE AVENUE GOES TO WAR
ALL OVER THE TOWN
THERE WAS A FAIR MAID DWELLING
THE UNJUST SKIES
FAREWELL THE TRANQUIL MIND
ON THE FIDDLE
THE SPRING MADNESS OF MR. SERMON
TOO FEW FOR DRUMS
CHEAP DAY RETURN
A HORSEMAN RIDING BY
THE GREEN GAUNTLET
COME HOME, CHARLIE, AND FACE THEM
GOD IS AN ENGLISHMAN

THE AVENUE STORY *(Omnibus)*

NAPOLEON IN LOVE
THE MARCH OF THE TWENTY-SIX
THE RETREAT FROM MOSCOW
IMPERIAL SUNSET

THE ADVENTURES OF BEN GUNN

FOR MY OWN AMUSEMENT

Overture for Beginners

by

R. F. DELDERFIELD

HODDER AND STOUGHTON

First printed 1970
ISBN 0 340 10628 x

Printed in Great Britain for Hodder and Stoughton Limited St. Paul's House, Warwick Lane, London E.C.4, by Ebenezer Baylis and Son Limited, The Trinity Press, Worcester, and London

Contents

FOR ANNE OF PEPLOW;
VIVANDIÈRE AND CHEER-LEADER,
1943–1970

Apologia for so much Rambling

In the preface to his delightful *Vice Versa* Anstey cites the story of the Greek father who, observing a vast gathering at the funeral of his little daughter, apologised for bringing so large a crowd to so small a corpse. The disclaimer is applicable here.

After forty years at the game I am a compulsive scribbler. Just as, short of reading material, I will study a bus ticket, I cannot sit still for long without plying the pen or typewriter. Two years ago, in an idle moment between writing two sagas (each of which turned the scales, according to the *Daily Mirror*, to several pounds) I set down a few chapters of autobiography and called the book *For My Own Amusement.* It was no more than a collection of impressions gathered over the years whilst serving time as a schoolboy, a reporter, an airman, and a professional writer of books and stage plays. I was astonished at the response. People in my own age group wrote from all over the world, some to renew acquaintance but others to add their comment on various aspects of life as it was lived by most of us throughout the 'twenties, 'thirties and 'forties. Incidents and people I had mentioned in passing seemed to have had as much significance to them as to myself, a dedicated collector of the bizarre and eccentric. By this means I learned a great deal I had not known about my own past, in itself a singularly interesting experience.

I am therefore encouraged, in another spell between two bouts of fiction writing, to try again and rake over the first few decades of this restless century in search of what I called, in *For My Own Amusement*, 'Butterfly' moments; that is to say, those brief passages of one's life when, for one reason or another, time is caught and spread out for inspection, a moth under glass.

This book is really an expansion and extension of three predecessors. Apart from *For My Own Amusement*, which was written from the standpoint of a man in his mid-fifties, my adventures into autobiography include two other books, *Nobody Shouted Author* and *Bird's Eye View*, both written getting on for twenty years ago. The former was a collection of sketches, the latter a chronological account, but in neither did I venture to take more than a cursory look at my backgrounds, my times and, above all, myself. Life has changed since then, for me and for everyone else in Western Europe.

Few need to be reminded that the pace of life in the late nineteen-sixties is stunning. Styles and attitudes in all spheres of existence are changing so rapidly and so finally that it is very difficult indeed for those of us born before August 1914 to strike some kind of balance between developing into the fuddy-duddy or that most pitiful of creatures, the breathless, balding 'adjustor', who spends himself in attempts to adapt to the fashions of succeeding generations. All we can do, I suppose, is to accept the fact that we, in our late fifties, are already as far distant from the period of our own youth as our parents were from the era of Beau Brummell. All the guide-lines have been cut. The format of politics, science, religion, education, culture and even the law itself has changed, and perhaps the one consolation of being a survivor of two world wars and the intervening slump is to look back over one's shoulder and admit, by and large, that the experience was well worth having. I wouldn't care to go through it again from here but I would gladly do just that if I could return to my original starting-point, a few weeks before the loss of the *Titanic* destroyed the confidence of the Edwardians in their own infallibility.

Searchlights on the Ceiling

Ask anyone who cowered under aerial bombardment in World War Two, particularly the Cockney who survived the winter of 1940–41, and the V.1 and V.2 onslaughts in 1944–45, what he thinks about Zeppelins and he will probably tell you they were cigar-shaped objects that made a few abortive flights over London in 1915–18 in order to unload a few small-calibre bombs. He would, of course, be right.

In his interesting book, *The Zeppelin Fighters*, Arch Whitehouse, who made a definitive study of Zeppelins, tells us that, in the three-year period under review, German Zeppelins made 208 raids on Great Britain, dropping a total of just under 6,000 bombs, killing 528 people and wounding a further 1,156. Comparing these figures with Britain's civilian casualties of the Second World War he adds, very sensibly, ". . . the people killed were just as dead as their descendants who perished in the rubble of London during the Great Blitz". I concur, having been on the receiving end.

• • •

The house occupied a corner site between Fort Road and Reverdy Road, in Bermondsey, S.E. It was probably early Victorian and was built of that yellow-greenish brick so popular during the period of the South London population explosion when, for the first time in the long history of the capital, materials could be hauled to a site by rail from anywhere in the country.

It was blitzed in 1940 and when I went back, in 1945, rosebay willow-herb was sprouting on a pile of rubble and about the boles of three stunted trees my brother told me he had planted in 1909. The house looked much smaller than I remembered. It was difficult to believe that five of us, plus a deaconess lodger, had lived there through the final glimmer of what people now call The Edwardian Afternoon. But for me the ruin had poignancy and I was sorry the *Luftwaffe* had singled it out for demolition, leaving next-door and next-door-but-one untouched.

There it was, a heap of brickdust, slivers of slate and splintered woodwork, crowned with the weed that thrives on chaos, but it was that other war I remembered as I poked about looking for clues.

My first conscious experience was that of witnessing the frantic terror created by Zeppelin attacks and one should not forget, in assessing their effect upon people, that this was the first time in the human story that a civilian population was bombarded from the air and that London, and all other areas attacked, was absolutely defenceless against such attacks when the reign of terror began. The author of *The Zeppelin Fighters* made another interesting observation. Reluctantly approving the terror policy submitted to him by his warlords, he tells us, the German Kaiser issued strict instructions that raiders "were to avoid bombing Buckingham Palace, Westminster Abbey and museums". He made no reference to hospitals and orphanages, but perhaps this is not surprising. As Mr. Chips said at the time, *Genus hoc erat pugnae quo se Germani exercuerant*—this was the kind of war in which the Germans busied themselves. They seem to have enjoyed it immensely over the last two millenniums.

The earliest Zeppelin raids that I recall were those of the winter of 1917. By then residents in south-east London had perfected the kind of drill they were to practise on a much larger scale twenty-three years later. There were modest anti-aircraft defences, many of them mobile. There was a small night-fighter force. And there were shelters of a kind for whose who wanted them. Most people did not want them but sat tight and hoped, and my father was among that majority.

Warning alerts were still extraordinarily primitive. At first policemen cycled the streets blowing whistles, calling attention to a placard slung round their necks and worn as medieval malefactors wore legends describing their crimes. Later on, red lights were affixed to lamp standards and maroons were fired, a novelty that almost caused my father's arrest when my brother Bill, who played the base drum in the Scouts, brought the entire residential section out in the streets by beating his drum in our reverberating cellar.

To a child of five an air-raid was a compelling but not necessarily a frightening experience and I recall one raid very vividly. I was lying in bed waiting for my brother to come upstairs and watching the reflection of searchlights on the ceiling. Outside I could hear two girls talking to two young men and their flirting voices were carefree and punctuated by laughter. Then one of them shrieked, "The red light's up!" and a moment later the street outside was full of tumult as pedestrians began to run for shelter.

For me, however, air-raid drill began smoothly, as always. I was wrapped in an eiderdown and carried downstairs into the kitchen but this time there was a difference. *En route* there was a frenzied beating on the front door and my father, opening it, admitted a young woman who fell over the threshold, vomited and then fainted. I watched my father douse her with water and I can still see the pallor of her face that I now associate with deathbeds, a yellowish pallor framed in a mop of dripping hair. When she recovered we all assembled before the fire and I was given a scribbling pad and pencil to occupy my attention. I drew, as I recall, aeroplanes, tanks and armoured cars. It seemed to me that these were the everyday appurtenances of life, just as khaki was the colour worn by nearly all the young men I saw in the streets.

There were many other raids of this kind and occasional facets of them are stark and clear. Sometimes my mother, her nerves at breaking-point, would burst into tears when anyone spoke to her, and sometimes I would watch a daylight raid (it must have been by Fokkers rather than Zeppelins) and witness the mad rush past our windows towards the shelters. Perhaps my very first introduction to the law of self-preservation was to see a muffled coster pause, dart over the crossroads outside and bawl at his wife, lumbered with three small children, "Come on, Liza, or I'll go wivaht yer!" Chivalry is at a premium during bombardments.

We heard many horror stories of devastating strikes. An aerial torpedo, the first ever fired over London, had demolished a row of houses in Albany Road, off the Old Kent Road. A scent factory, being used as a shelter, had been the scene of a direct hit. But there was one moment of triumph before we vacated the area and moved out of range in the spring of 1918.

Wrapped in the inevitable eiderdown I was held up to the landing window and told to look at an orange rag floating down the night sky. It was one of the last of the Zeppelins, shot down by our expanding defence force that now included young men flying what we should now consider mobile banana crates from a Home Counties base.

It is difficult, at this distance, to decide who demonstrated more courage—the numbed German Zeppelin crews, flying on their forlorn missions and often not knowing whether they were bombing Cromer or Croydon; or the leather-helmeted youngsters plunging about the sky in open cockpits, hoping that probing searchlight beams would cone on a Zeppelin before their fuel was used up.

And as well as one moment of uncomprehending triumph there was a moment of blind, unreasoning fear, of a degree of terror that I do not recall having experienced before or since. It was during a daylight raid by Fokkers or Gothas, and I had just been released from the local kindergarten when a flight of aircraft passed overhead, far too high to identify as theirs or ours, although this did not prevent a young pessimist standing close by from shouting, "Germans! I can see the black crosses!" I did not wait for corroboration. Growing up, born as it were in the teeth of a gale of propaganda in which black crosses signified evil as surely as the swastika, I fled, amazed at arriving home without having been overtaken and impaled on one of those Prussian spiked helmets that were, at that stage in the war, coveted trophies by enterprising frontline infantrymen.

. . .

Wavering beams on the ceiling, exposing cracks in the plaster and the leering wolf in the Red Riding Hood fire-screen; the rumble of 'our' anti-aircraft gun, said to chase Zeppelins all over London; a chalky-faced stranger vomiting in the hall; boots crashing on the pavement and a flaming rag in the sky. Perhaps a fitting introduction into the world awaiting us all in the winter of 1917–18, and somehow its images have remained sharp and clear when most of those of another war are blurred or mellowed. Yet one is tempted to ask, after more than half a century of this continuing idiocy, what military advantage was ever gained by plastering civilians with high explosive, and whether words like Guernica, Coventry, Warsaw, Rotterdam and Dresden are not indictments written by our generation into a document that contains our collective death-warrant. For there is, to a Londoner in his sixth decade, a tenuous link between his earliest memories and the present revolt of the young. It is tempting to dismiss a student riot seen on television as a display of adolescent exhibitionism and mass hysteria but one should, I feel, look for the mainspring of the demonstrations. In my own youth we grumbled but few dared to rebel. The nuclear stockpile wasn't there but the dole queue was and its threat was more immediate. So if the present generation can do anything to improve, even marginally, our social and political system, so that their children's first recollections are more tranquil than mine, then I for one will forgo middle-aged cynicism, take up their slogans and even (suitably disguised) carry one of their bellyaching banners across Grosvenor Square.

Bulldozers in Arcady

Why do we equate suburbs with dullness? With boredom and personal defeat? How did the adjective 'suburban' acquire the status of a calculated insult? After all, three-quarters of us in the Western World live in suburbs of one sort or another, and many of them are pleasant, even fragrant places. Some are built with taste and all are capable of exhibiting tremendous vitality. The people inhabiting them are almost always decent, hard-working folk, concerned with minding their own business, improving their standards of living, paying their taxes and, what is so often overlooked, maintaining their ancestral links with sodbreakers in tiny, lovingly-tended gardens. Why else would they pour into the open on Saturday afternoons and Sunday mornings, with sleeves rolled up and tools in hand to trim the privet, tie back the loganberry trailers and contribute to that pleasantly muted song of the suburbs, the intermittent whirr of lawn-mower, the snip-snip of shears and the steady chink of spade?

One of the few contemporary Englishmen who finds the suburbs rewarding is John Betjeman, and no one will ever do a better job of crystallising their elusive charm in verse. Being of John's generation I find it easy to share his enthusiasm, for the songs he sings are already nostalgic, telling as they do of corners of England that may soon be banished as finally as the meadows of eighteenth-century Staffordshire and South Lancashire. Already the writing is on the wall. Gaunt and featureless blocks of flats and offices are replacing rows of terraces and tiny, zealously-maintained green patches in the outskirts of our cities. The corner shop, if it has not already gone, will soon become a supermarket, with closed circuit television keeping watch on potential thieves. The parks and recreation grounds, where lovers still embrace one another on municipal seats and children sail yachts in municipal ponds, will probably be reclassified by artful bureaucrats seeking more land to build more universities. And in those universities young men and women will be trained in sciences that will make the English suburb as archaic as the village green. Soon, I suspect, bulldozers will advance into Arcady and when England is either a scorched desert or a clinical hell of tarmac, chromium, plastic and computerised thought, a few elderly survivors will dream of suburbs, as a few of the very old now dream of village communities in the era before the planners decided that our untidy lives needed drastic reorganisation.

Before anyone is amazed that I should confuse the suburb with Arcady let me explain.

• • •

In the spring of 1918, when the people living inside the old perimeter of London were beginning to falter on account of air-raids, those who could moved further out, seeking dwellings in areas they assumed were less vulnerable. In fact once there, they were no less likely to be killed by a stray bomb or a flying splinter of anti-aircraft shrapnel. The poor, bemused devils in the Zeppelins and aircraft of that period were not often in search of a specific target and, even when they were, their chances of finding and hitting one was seven million to one. It seemed logical, however, to assume that one would be safer in, say, Hounslow, than in Hammersmith, in Croydon than in Camberwell, and one of my numerous uncles had fled twelve miles south at the height of the raids and bought a terrace house in Ashburton Avenue, off Shirley Road, in the parish of Addiscombe. It was he who persuaded my father to follow and catch an early train into the city each morning, so we moved out to the very same avenue.

To a child of six the translation from Bermondsey to the then rural district of South Croydon was as final as the movement of a succeeding generation of evacuees from Stepney to Somerset. The only difference was that I did not travel with a label round my neck giving my name, school and destination.

Perhaps no area in outer London has changed more dramatically than Croydon has changed over the last half-century. Today its southern boundary is a wilderness of housing estates and shopping centres but in the spring of 1918, when the British army was battling to plug the gaps torn in its line by

Ludendorff's final offensive, Addiscombe was as pastoral and peaceful as is most of the West Country peninsula today. Ashburton Avenue was only five minutes' walk from the ruins of the old military academy set up by the East India Company before the Indian Mutiny compelled the Crown to take over that part of the Empire. The quiet residential roads were named after Mutiny personalities—Generals Havelock, Outram, Nicholson and Campbell, all of whom had been educated at the Academy. The houses in this area were a good class of property, detached residences set back from the road, and often four-storied. Further out, towards the straggling villages of Wickham, Shirley, Addington, Down, Cudham and Westerham, where the farmland of Kent merged into that of Surrey, the countryman was unchallenged. Thatched cottages leaned on one another, interspersed with ancient pubs and shops that smelled of bran, candles and lamp-oil, and on every side stretched hundreds of acres of ploughed fields, studded with tufted copses. In the pastureland fat cattle grazed and chaffinches flirted in thickets and, beyond was the green twilight of the Archbishop's Woods, with its huge deserted mansion fronting a lake.

It was Wonderland to me. My experience of unspoiled country was limited to an occasional weekend in Kent. I had never seen an English spring move across field and coppice, scattering a carpet of yellow buttercups and scarlet campion, and the only wild birds I had ever seen were house sparrows and starlings. To explore there, to cross Farmer Still's meadows, to stand under his giant oaks that were growing when Edgehill was fought, to birdsnest in hazel thicket and pick my first bluebells under flowering chestnuts, was the most enriching experience of my life. In those days nobody I knew owned a car and the long war had done much to discourage holidays, so that I was seeing these things for the first time and at a period in development when impressions were strong and lasting.

But although my imagination was deeply stirred by the rural aspects of the shift the social implications had an even stronger effect. It was here, at that time, that I came to sense and ultimately to understand, the subtle undercurrents of the English class system, something that had not impinged upon me in Bermondsey, where we all seemed to belong to one rowdy family. The suburb had a scent and the suburb had a song but it also had a *tone* and that owed nothing to bullfinches, hawthorn, honeysuckle, whirring lawn-mower and the chink of spade. To those who settled there from more congested areas, it had, however, a curious sense of security, of having arrived, of having progressed to another, loftier plane, and it is very difficult to convey this sense of social uplift to someone who has not experienced it. It had to do with the jaunty way the commuters (the word was unknown then) set out for Woodside Station on the old South-Eastern and Chatham Line, and with the presence of so many private schools that were called, for a reason I have never been able to discover, 'Colleges'. It was to be found in the galaxy of private music teachers, the competitiveness of local rose-growers, in the curtains in the bow-windows and the fact that everyone had not only a back but a front garden. Suburbs like Addiscombe were not merely suburbs. They were also frontiers.

One could stand by the pregnant red pillar-box at the junction of Ashburton Avenue and Shirley Road with a definite sense of having penetrated to the furthest limits of the Big City. To the north and west lay the stale, labyrinthine streets of the largest city in the world. To the south and east was the Garden of England that had not changed much since Wat Tyler's men staged their protest march against the mandarins of Richard II. It always seemed to me that London Wall was in the wrong place. It should have cut clear across Shirley Road to mark the difference between town and country.

Here, among the borderers, there was a strong sense of community and this is not to say that the menfolk forgathered in local pubs, or the womenfolk called on neighbours to borrow cups of sugar. Camaraderie, in the true sense of the word, did not exist but we Avenue dwellers were all conscious of having a great deal in common and an obligation to conform. Do not imagine for one instant that this obligation was in any way irksome. On the contrary, we revelled in it and went out of our way to emphasise the subtle distinctions between the ranks of the carefully graded society in which we found ourselves. No one, apart from the deliverers of coal and the emptiers of dustbins, ever appeared on the pavements collarless, and even the tradesmen who called on us for orders knew their place and used the prefix 'sir' or 'madam'. There was very little gossiping over the garden fences and virtually no casual dropping-in, of the kind one sees in contemporary TV soap operas like *Coronation Street*. This curious sense of exclusiveness was even more apparent among the children. One was strictly enjoined 'not to play' with the village children, who were collectively termed 'Street Arabs'. Gentle pressure was exerted to seek one's companions among 'nice boys', in an income-group approximating one's own, and even the games were heavily prescribed. One never saw, for instance, the children of the suburb playing at marbles, and all the time I lived in the Avenue I never came across a hopscotch pitch chalked on the pavement. If one needed room to expand one went along to the Rec—Recreation Ground—and this was a kind of suburban Royal Enclosure set aside for us. The village children were seldom seen there and if they appeared they were never invited to join our games. Cricket, rounders, tennis and an occasional Punch and Judy show were available behind the tall brick pillars of the Rec, but highcockolorum, a boisterous game played in school playgrounds, was left outside. Taken all round we were fearful snobs.

One would have thought that such an atmosphere was mentally crippling but somehow it wasn't. I have never since lived in a community that was as safe and ordered and neither will I again. Nor anyone else for that matter. One knew and accepted one's place to the last decimal point. Children attending the local 'Colleges' did not mix with those attending elementary schools. One raised one's cap to adult neighbours, washed carefully behind the ears, and learned to speak civilly but rather distantly to shop assistants. At the same time one took no liberties whatever with the children who lived in the big detached houses and had nannies and the use of the family Humber and telephone. The gulf between them and us was as wide as that between us and the children who picked wild flowers and offered them for sale at a penny a bunch, who stood watching the stream of traffic returning from the Derby and shouted, "Chuck aht yer mouldy coppers!" My brother once picked up one of those mouldy coppers. My mother insisted that he threw it back.

I often wonder, looking back, what a foreigner would have made of it all. I never met one, or even glimpsed one in the Avenue, but they must have appeared there from time to time, to return home as baffled by the English class system as they are today. No one along our terrace could have been earning, at that time, more than seven pounds a week, and I am certain most of them earned much less. But this in no way prevented them from patronising, as only the people of the suburbs can, those who lived a hundred yards closer to the heart of London on approximately the same income.

There was no written code of behaviour. No one ever prescribed in as many words what was done and what was frowned upon, what could be worn on weekdays and on Sundays, what slang was permissive and what words were not accepted as slang by decent people, when to pull down the blinds for a funeral and when to lift aside the lace curtains for a wedding. Among those who dwelt there were Anglicans high and low, Free Churchmen of every known sect, and a minority torn by Bradlaugh's 'honest doubt'. They were not given to gossip, but somehow, as though circulated by code-notes on a hundred parlour pianos, all that transpired along the length of the Avenue became common knowledge between two successive sunsets. Trevor Sinclair, of Number Nine, had won a scholarship to Charterhouse. The 'new' people at Number Nineteen were engaging a maid. Audrey Follett's wedding had been put forward at Number Forty-six, the result, no doubt, of not getting her indoors by ten, and in these circumstances how could anyone risk taking a chance in the Avenue? One slip and it was snakes-and-ladders right back to base, and who, in their senses, would face that hazard after the effort it had required to get there?

. . .

I have been back several times in the last few decades and on every occasion the place seems to have sloughed off a little more of its identity. I may be wrong but I have a feeling that the spurious but highly prized gentility of our suburb was destroyed by an assortment of factors. By the onslaught of the *Luftwaffe*, by the creation of the Welfare State, by the ball and chain tug of our economic malaise, by the loss of the Empire and also by the forest of TV masts that now weave a crazy pattern along the rooftops of the crescents and closes. A majority, perhaps, will view this demise as a significant social advance but I am not convinced of this. The egalitarianism that has replaced it is as featureless as a Government White Paper and for the incurable romantic the suburb had a flavour that has disappeared as surely as flavour disappears from the pre-packed meal. Whenever I wander up Shirley Road today, and poke about among the new roads between the frontier pillar-box and the Rec, I seem to be remembering a time as distant as Agincourt but the song of the suburb, although considerably muted, is still to be heard. A whirr of lawn-mower at Number Twenty-three. The slow castanet of hedge-clippers at Seventy-three. And the scent of the suburb lingers too for those who inhaled it fifty years ago. Clipped privet and full-blown cabbage rose and melting tar in the sun on the few occasions the sun seems to shine there nowadays. For that is another secret the children of the Avenue knew so well but seem, somehow, to have forgotten. The ordered procession of the seasons that rotated, in a thousand chests of drawers. Cricket-shirts and cotton frocks from Easter to September. Mufflers, hairy gloves and galoshes from early October to March.

For Your Own Good

Not long ago, when I was being interviewed on the *Late Night Line-Up* programme of B.B.C.2 the interviewer asked me if I had any exceptionally strong views on any particular subject outside the general sphere of my work as a professional writer. I told him I had—just one. It concerned the apparently eradicable belief among the British that corporal punishment in schools is an aid to the process of education. This is something concerning which I have always held strong views and my failure to impress them on most of my contemporaries depresses me for, in most other respects, I still consider the British to be far ahead of any other race in their assessment of human rights. This, as I see it, is one of their few blind spots, and I look forward to the day when Parliament legislates against those who persist in the archaic notion that to beat children is to improve them.

One of the most glaring errors practised by Western legislators in the second half of the nineteenth century, especially in industrialised countries like Britain, France and Germany, was that of herding infants into barrack-like buildings at the age of five to begin, what was euphemistically called their education, and subjecting them thereafter to a system of instruction based on fear. Fear of the freely applied strap, rod and ruler and, what was worse, fear of humiliation and ridicule.

Mercifully the drive to bend and shape a child's mind to the rigid precepts of unimaginative mentors has slackened very considerably in the last twenty years. Schoolmasters and schoolmistresses are no longer the pedants and bullies they were a generation ago and compassion has crept into the schoolroom like a fugitive out of the rain. The man who consistently flogged children for their own good, and the even more common wisecracking ironist, has been all but eliminated from educational establishments and most children are no longer urged forward under the threat of physical punishment. At the same time the basic creed of the educationist has not changed as much as it should have done and there is still a strong tendency among them to equate textbook knowledge with intelligence and moral stature. Examinations, if possible, have become even more vital to the child's future than they were fifty years ago, and if there is a faultier measuring-stick to determine the true potential of a human being I would be interested to hear about it.

Real education, of the kind in which the advanced nations stand in such terrible need today, is not often to be found in a school textbook. It really has little to do with the kind of information fed to children by various media in a majority of school periods. Books that would help a child to discover the world through his or her own eyes are plentiful but they are not recommended with much enthusiasm. One of the saddest trends in British schools during the last decade has been the constant efforts of narrow-headed fools to banish religious training from the curriculum on the grounds that it will prejudice the pupil! What is the next move in this extraordinary campaign by progressives? A public bonfire of the Gospels?

. . .

When I attended my first school, in the winter of 1916–17, the Victorian cult of self-help had passed its apogee. Well-meaning but short-sighted sociologists had taught the preceding generation that all the problems bedevilling mankind at that period could be solved by education and perhaps, broadly speaking, they were right. It depended upon the kind of education applied and this, unfortunately, was not very well understood when W. E. Forster's Elementary Education Act went on the statute book in August 1870.

At that time, of course, the great majority of children in the West were illiterate and their illiteracy condemned them to a life of servitude. It was seen that if the nation was to hold its place as the major industrial power of the world it would need millions of recruits for the offices and counting-houses of the giant business enterprises that were mushrooming in all centres of population, and that an ignorant work force was not equipped to compete with industrial nations elsewhere.

A very promising start was made, at least in some of the new schools. My mother attended one of the first London elementary schools and in later years the standard of her education frequently astonished me, especially when I reminded myself that she went out to work at thirteen. She wrote a good legible hand and could perform, what were to me, prodigies of mental arithmetic. She knew, and carried to her grave, the substance of many of Shakespeare's plays, as well as the verse of poets like Gray, Wordsworth, Goldsmith and especially Tennyson, who still had ten years to reign as Poet Laureate. She acquired, before she left, a taste for Scott, Thackeray and Dickens, and she told me that Dickens was one of the standard authors at the school she attended.

My father was less fortunate. He also attended (until the age of about twelve when he too went out to work) one of the first elementary schools in London, but it seems to have had a good deal in common with Dotheboys Hall. At my mother's school there were teachers of discernment but the disciplines of my father's elementary school were more like those that prevailed in the galleys. One of the standard punishments, he recalled, imposed upon under-nourished mites of the Thames-side street, was to hold a stack of writing slates above the head and earn a flogging if it fell below a certain level.

It may seem astonishing to a more enlightened generation to learn that teachers who relied upon these methods of keeping order were commonplace in British schools at that time. Chaplin writes of them in his autobiography, and any elderly man who attended these pioneer Council schools (and many of the private schools) could verify the fact. What I find remarkable is the notion you could assist a child's mental development by free use of the goad of fear that persisted into the 'twenties and 'thirties of this century.

There is a hidden streak of cruelty in the British character that is far less obvious than that frequently demonstrated by their ancestral cousins, the Germans. Ordinarily the British are kindly compassionate people, but one would never have suspected it had one attended state schools in the second decade of this century. Here, all too frequently, reigned men and women whose methods of maintaining discipline were vicious but the really frightening thing about this lust to control a class by the threat of inflicting pain, humiliation and misery, is that it dies so hard a death among the general public of to-day. Recently a popular TV personality asked his audience to vote on the question of whether or not they believed in thrashing children. An overwhelming majority shot up their hands with a kind of glee and it was obvious that they considered a progressive schoolmaster, holding an opposite view, an object of ridicule. Every now and again there is a press exposé of scholastic torture that would shock the Kremlin and the Congo into prompt action, but the legal abolition of the cane in our schools is almost as far away as it was when I was a child, and this despite the fact that almost every other nation has stopped beating its children.

I attended two state schools, the first as an infant, the second as a child of nine. At the infants' department the cane was in the offing (for five-year-olds!) but I never saw it used, although I am quite sure it was.

Discipline, however, was rigidly maintained. We were compelled to sit with arms folded on the desk and chatterboxes were silenced by having sticking-plaster slammed across mouths. Slow-learners were exhibited as fools. There were dunces' caps and frequent banishments 'to the corner', but I do not look back on that red-brick building with horror, notwithstanding the gloomy, cavernous impression it made upon me, or the memory of the hysterical efforts of an ageing spinster to control a class of sixty children. As long as one behaved as a robot one was not punished. This could not be said of my second elementary school, where I spent two wretched terms four years later. The six months I was there rank among the unhappiest of my life.

This place, as I have since learned from observation, and from discussion with men of my own age, was not in any way singular. On the contrary, it was typical of the kind of establishment common at the period and as such a disgrace to the legislators of the post-World War One period. Neither was it peculiar to London, for my wife attended a similar school before going on to Manchester High School. Down in easy-going Devonshire there still lived a headmaster whose Wackford Squeers' antics had been checked by members of the local School Board who concealed themselves in a stationery cupboard in order to witness his brutality. This fiend, I was informed, always began the school term by flogging a random group of boys and liked to pick them from among those who had plump posteriors. He announced, as he went merrily to work, "This is what you can all expect if you don't behave yourselves!"

Years later, when I was a reporter and had this same man in my sights at the Petty Sessional Court, there was an interesting sequel to his career as a headmaster, then a magistrate! A former pupil returned from Canada after a long absence and was greeted by his old mentor with great affability. Ignoring the proffered hand, the emigrant said, "All I recall about you, mate, is that you were a bloody swine and a sadistic bully. I'd drop dead before I shook your hand!"

As to my own experiences, they left me with a hatred of cruelty to children who, in these circumstances, are quite defenceless. 'Mr. Short', in the *Avenue Story*, is based on a man I met there. This headmaster would have made an admirable recruit for the concentration camp guards who, in the nineteen-forties, became the personification of savagery all over the world. I was to meet one or two others who reminded me of 'Mr. Short' at subsequent schools, but they were mere apprentices in the art of instituting terror compared with this wretch. They still exist, although today they are far more vulnerable to public exposure. They will continue to exist until a nation that has abolished the flogging of criminals has the courage to ask itself why, when it prohibits the beating of vicious men, it stubbornly refuses the same protection to its children. Or why, indeed, it does not face up to the fact that the impulse to hurt someone has nothing to do with the process of correction and never had.

Progress, slow progress, has been made in England and Wales in this field, but it looks as if the last stronghold of the scholastic sadist will probably be Scotland, where the educational symbol would sometimes seem to be the tawse. The only escape route from poverty, some Scotsmen will tell you, is via education, and therefore, if necessary, education must be beaten into wee laddies with the strap. It is an odd belief, that persists to this day among a sizable minority up there. Do they suppose that the Scots race will cease to contribute to the arts and sciences of the twentieth century the minute the tawse follows the cat-o'-nine tails and the thumbscrew into the museum? Possibly they do. Interrogation by torture was not abandoned in Scotland until long after it had been struck from the legal code south of the Tweed and obstinate English prisoners were sometimes sent north in order that their interrogators could take advantage of the fact. Perhaps the time will come when recalcitrant children will be sent over the Border to make the acquaintance of the tawse.

. . .

Corrective methods on one side, some very notable progress has been made in the last few years concerning methods of imparting information to children, but here again educationists, with many notable exceptions, are not much given to pioneering. It would seem to me that far too much time is still wasted in schools in what should be a mere offshoot of education, that is to say, the preparation of pupils for examinations of one kind or another. The front was even narrower in my day. Hundreds of hours were devoted to subjects likely to benefit the few rather than the many, and the broad aim of education—to produce a kindly, intelligent, useful human being, was all but overlooked. To me, and I admit to being an eccentric in this respect, this is what schools are for, and something to this effect should be inscribed in letters of brass over every schoolmaster's desk. Personally I look forward to the day when the humanities take precedence over economics and to the introduction into schools of a system where the premium is on the formation of character rather than examination passes, but perhaps I am wishing for the moon. I do not know what proportion of time is still spent in the average British school on subjects like geometry and algebra but I hope that it is less than in my schooldays, when whole vistas of time were taken up with specialist information of this kind while two periods a week were devoted to history, the only science available to us of showing where we went wrong and are still going wrong as human beings compelled to live in one another's pockets.

The teaching of English had a fair showing in the timetables of forty years ago, but in six of the seven schools I attended far too much time was devoted to what was then called 'parsing', and no more than one period a week to the art of learning how to enjoy the work of men like Blake, or that splendid generation of poets all but destroyed on the Western Front. I think of them particularly, for it was years after leaving school that I made the acquaintance of Wilfred Owen and Siegfried Sassoon, to say nothing of the novelist, Richard Aldington, then at the height of his fame. Why? Was there nothing in their work that would have helped young men to know and understand the challenge of Hitler in 1932, or tackle more successfully the problems of the 'fifties and 'sixties? The ideal teacher, to my way of thinking, is a bit of a stick-in-the-mud, who clings, with fearful obstinacy, to standards and methods that have little to do with the demands of 'A' and 'O' levels, or that idiotic and now discredited Eleven Plus, a man or woman who sees his or her main task as one of joining with parents to turn out any number of decent fathers, decent husbands, good wives and good mothers, people, let us say, who would prefer to tell the truth on a thousand a year than win a place in the supertax bracket by selling dubious insurance or even more dubious packaged holidays. He or she would lay stress on such old-fashioned virtues as honesty, compassion and tolerance, and some would have a way of making English literature and English history do much of their work for them. The best of them, I should like to think, would be the counterpart of the fast-disappearing family doctor, who knew the history of all his patients from the moment he yanked them into the world to the time when they came to him as middle-aged men with problems that were not strictly medical. He or she would be more of a counsellor than a teacher but what they imparted would remain in the minds of their pupils and, with a little luck, filter into the national ethos of the future. There were such teachers, even in the days when the unpleasant rhythm of the cane was the sound most often heard from the classroom. I had the good fortune to encounter several and today, I am happy to say, they seem to be proliferating among the younger recruits for the profession.

It is difficult for those of us whose education ended in the 'twenties to have much patience with the more violent section of the Student Revolt but one area of their manifesto we should applaud. They want more say in the substance and system of their courses and I see no good reason why, at university age, they should be denied it. When I look back on all those wasted hours with Euclid and his ilk I share the latter-day students' sense of frustration. One of the few gleams of sunshine on the newsfronts of recent years has been the refusal of the young to take the wisdom of their elders for granted. Another is the occasional experiment in the system of teaching children at infant level where the relationship between pupil and teacher is fostered by the mutual respect of the latter for his or her charges as sensitive human beings plus a ready appreciation of individuality. As a taxpayer I would be happy to see millions of pounds used annually to enlarge careful experimentation in the educational field at primary level for it is here, not in the universities, that repose the chief hopes of finding satisfactory solutions to the mounting problems of a technological age.

A Baptist Bonus

I never mentioned The Baptist Bonus to anyone and there is a logical reason for this. My association with the Baptists lasted five and a half years, from the time I was six, until I was rising twelve, but it was not until I was in my middle fifties that I was even aware of that Bonus, how it was bestowed and how it accumulated. It is an odd, quirkish story but it has a place in these confessions.

The Avenue, in those days, had two aspects. Its weekday, workaday aspect, and its Sabbath aspect. The changeover occurred, for me at all events, at first light on Sunday, and again twelve hours later when Sunday, according to Greenwich, still had an hour or so to run. The only thing in the Avenue that was not involved in this weekly metamorphosis was its architecture.

Long before dawn on Monday mornings the Avenue assumed its familiar pattern of sights, sounds and smells. Fathers hurrying to catch the first Workman's Train could be heard striding along the pavements. The postman rat-tatted. Milk cans rattled. The smell of frying bacon could be sniffed in back bedrooms. Soon every Rip Van Winkle in the crescent was astir, rubbing his eyes and wondering, distractedly, where he had been and what he had done since Saturday night. The steel rims of tradesmen's one-horse vans grated on tarmac. Children erupted from almost every house in the long curve, blazers flying loose, perhaps a smudge of marmalade on chins and, where garter elastic was beginning to lose its snap, a concertinad stocking. Turbaned housewives appeared on windowsills, backs to the street, as they put a guardsman's polish on their glass and, here and there, according to the time of the year, a husband on holiday (or on the Dole) set to work on privet that never despaired of breaking the bonds of the neat, looped chains slung between the brick pillars of entrance paths.

No such domestic scenes disturbed the heavy silences of the Sabbath and that libellous eighteenth-century traveller, who once declared that the English were a race without benefit of religion, should have spent at least one Sunday with his back propped against our red pillar-box. Had he done so he would have sung a very different tune.

The scene was not so much muted as sterilised. Everyone who appeared on the pavement wore a Sunday suit, a gleaming collar and highly-polished boots. No one ran, skipped or raised their voice. The tails of the dogs drooped and the chirp of the birds was faltering and intermittent, as though they feared, by introducing a single note of gaiety into the crescent, that they would forfeit Monday's cake crumbs. The silence, both before and after the brief exodus to church or chapel, was that of a well-run prison before the introduction of 'association' and this was fitting, for in a way we were all doing time, sentences that would expire when the footsteps of the last neighbour, homeward bound to brisket of beef after evensong, had ceased to clatter on the flagstones.

There were well over a hundred houses in the Avenue and almost as many families so that we could muster, perhaps, two hundred and fifty children under fourteen. It may be hard to believe in this day and age (as far removed, ritualistically, from the time of which I write as is the era of the Tudors) that of this total at least two hundred attended one or more church services and one Sunday School session every seventh day, and I do not include the few Jews and Roman Catholics who lived among us. Their approach to Sunday was at variance with ours and on this account we half-thought of them as damned well in advance. The Jews had paid their tribute the day before, whereas the Roman Catholics made their obeisance before we had rubbed the sleep from our eyes, and thereafter were licensed to treat Sunday as a holiday weekday. This boon was not for us. Anglican, Wesleyan Methodist, United Methodist, Primitive Methodist, Congregationalist, Baptist, Presbyterian and Plymouth Brother, we all went through the motions with a sullen resignation that made the approach of Monday, school notwithstanding, a dawn to be faced with the utmost fortitude. If I sound prejudiced in this it is because I was even more unfortunate than most. My family was spiritually divided down the middle and the strain of arranging Sunday's domestic programme put a keen edge on everybody's temper.

Just as my mother, a high Tory, cancelled out my father's Radical vote at every Parliamentary election between 1918 and 1953, so she sought, throughout all her days, to offset the possibility that my father was worshipping a bogus God. She would have dearly loved to have been received into the Church of England but somehow, I never discovered why, she never was. She therefore made the best of a bad job by walking two miles to worship among the Congregationalists. My father was much less dogmatic. The freest of Free Churchmen in all England, he would attend any Nonconformist service that promised to be convivial and declamatory, and the moment he settled in the suburb he poked around and finally opted for the local Baptists, like a wine-taster opting for a particular vintage. He had no basic objection to my mother's preference but considered it a violation of the marriage vows if she attended morning service and was not on hand to prepare the Sunday roast.

I have it in mind that my mother preferred the evening service but she hated cooking and although, almost invariably, she gave in, and did her duty by the rest of us, she did it with scant grace and wore a heavy frown through Sunday morning and well into the afternoon. She was also inclined to become testy during the inevitable scramble to find clean underclothes. This was the first, range-finding skirmish in the Sunday guerrilla war and inevitably enlarged itself into a shouting match, with my father hopping about waving his soap-encrusted cut-throat razor and declaring that once again we would be late and make a spectacle of ourselves.

Now this, in itself, was uncharacteristic of him. Ordinarily, on weekdays that is to say, he did not give a damn about drawing attention to himself, indeed, he often went far out of his way to make certain that he did, but on Sundays he was never the same man. It was impossible to see him as the rip-roaring extrovert he was from Monday to Saturday. A heavy and hopeless gloom engulfed him and it was as well to keep out of his way. He was not much given to cuffing but every cuff I collected throughout my childhood and boyhood was administered by a hand momentarily detached from *John o' London's Weekly*, *The Methodist Recorder* or some other Sunday reading.

I suppose a number of factors contributed to his mood. One was the necessity imposed by protocol of doing without Sunday newspapers. As a political animal he devoured newsprint and no one ever succeeded in persuading him that Sunday papers were written and printed on a Saturday. Another factor was the obligation to walk everywhere as a silent protest against the employment of public transport servants on the Sabbath, thus depriving them of a chance to worship. A third was his three-inch Sunday collar. A fourth, and possibly a key factor, was the obligation to keep his voice down. All these handicaps combined to play such havoc with his nerves that sometimes, on a Sabbath evening, I could identify him with Abraham on the point of sacrificing Isaac to Jehovah.

I often think our weekly departure for chapel must have scandalised neighbours who adhered to a more rigid time-table. The Baptist chapel was only fifteen minutes' walk away but we never, but once, arrived there on time. My father would always leave the house ahead of us, with strict instructions to follow in a matter of seconds, and these instructions were usually reinforced by threatening gestures all the way down to the pillar-box where he turned the corner at a slow trot. Trot and gestures were in themselves violations of Sunday protocol, but he probably saw them as the lesser of two evils.

My brother would leave next, taking care to keep father in sight but not to catch him up. On weekdays he always wore his school cap at a rakish angle but on Sunday my father saw to it that it rested squarely on his head, the peak level with his fringe. It gave him an unfamiliar and rather suspect look, as though, notwithstanding an outwardly pious aspect, he was the kind of boy who kept a catapult to fire at cats when nobody was looking. I would set off at the tail of the procession, to lose sight of both of them until I saw them waving and prancing on the steps of the little church, while the strains of 'From Greenland's Icy Mountains' proclaimed that, yet again, the service had begun without us. The one occasion when we were early was the day we arrived exactly one hour before the opening hymn, my father having forgotten to put the clock back at the end of official summer time. It was the only time I ever heard him laugh on Sunday.

Sometimes, even now, I try and rationalise my disinclination to attend those services but it is not an easy thing to do. The root causes were so subtle and so various. One was the secret fear of being caught out by God, in a silent revolt against Him and all His works. Another was an instinctive distaste for the chapel itself, with its green, distempered walls tricked out in gold lines and the maddening complexity of its focal point, a stencilled text that ran clear across the wall behind the pulpit. The text announced 'Hallowed Be Thy Name' but the sign-writer had attempted to execute it in Gothic script so that the individual letters were difficult to isolate and spell out. Any attempt to do so blurred the vision and induced a kind of biliousness. Then again there was the preacher himself, who wore a fixed, catlike smile, even when he was quoting Isaiah. But more daunting than any of these factors was the approach of the moment when 'The Dear Children's Hymn' would be announced, and I was required to rise and warble through seven verses of 'All Things Bright and Beautiful' or 'Courage, Brother, Do Not Stumble', not solo exactly, for there were other penitents ranged behind me, but aware of the fact that one day, during an epidemic for instance, I might be the only child present. It was a moment not to be contemplated.

I was always greatly relieved when this ordeal was safely past and I could put my hot penny into the offertory plate, compose my thoughts, and slide into my sermon coma until the benediction. After that there was only one hurdle to be dodged. The preacher's handshake at the exit.

We went to Sunday School in the afternoon as a matter of course and among the regulars was a cousin of mine, a lucky dog with an agnostic father, who was spared the ordeal of a morning service and was therefore good recruiting material for the Devil. So reckless was he, in fact, that he regularly spent his collection money on chewing-gum at a machine near Woodside Station. No one was more surprised than me to learn, some forty years later, that he had not only survived to become an executive in an oil-distributing company, but had reached retirement age without catching leprosy or being destroyed in an earthquake.

Sunday School followed a set pattern, an improving address by the Superintendent, a hymn, a prayer, and then dispersal to classes, where we mulled over a Bible story in the hope of extracting the moral, much as a kernel is drawn from a nutshell.

All in all, it will be seen, I derived no spiritual benefit whatsoever from my long association with the Baptists, unless one counts a weekly reinforcement of belief in the power of Jehovah to punish beyond the grave. Yet a very important by-product did emerge and was to have a vital bearing on the course my life took long after I had moved over to the Congregationalists and, ultimately, to the Anglicans.

I like to think of it as a Divine Afterthought. I like to believe that God really does work in a mysterious way, and gives full value for money so long as you are prepared to give Him extended credit. After all, I had done my part. I had spent six years trying to decipher the Gothic lettering of that gilded text.

It came about in this way.

As a family we were necessarily involved in the social life of the church and this included an occasional weeknight concert that at first promised to be almost as dull as a service. Amateur conjurers conjured, amateur baritones bellowed 'The Cornish Floral Dance', amateur contraltos lifted clasped hands and rolled their eyes, and there were recitations. I contributed one of these myself, a poem about a club-footed slum child with a drunken mother, who was translated to glory by instant conversion. I could hardly have chosen a more responsive audience. The very certainty proclaimed in the theme was in harmony with all the threats and promises levelled at us from the pulpit at the conclusion of 'The Dear Children's Hymn'. The poem was called 'Tommy's Prayer' and the final verse, all I recall, ran:

> In the morning when his mother
> Came to wake her crippled boy
> She discovered that his features
> Wore a look of shining joy.
> Then she shook him (somewhat roughly)
> But the cripple's face was cold.
> He had gone to join the angels
> In the streets of shining gold.

My ego was so inflated by the thunderous applause I received that I unwisely gave an encore at a friend's Christmas party. It broke it up very effectively, with everyone sniffing as they groped for their gloves and galoshes.

The ability to hold an audience, however, is not the bonus to which I refer. This was something more subtle and, as I say, I did not acknowledge it for nearly half a century. It had to do with a man I never met, a professional elocutionist who, by some happy miracle, was booked in at the Baptist church concert on two or three occasions when I attended. His name was John Torceni and I am making a guess at the spelling.

He was not, as the name might imply, a foreigner but a thickset Englishman and my father, who had often heard him perform, was very enthusiastic regarding his talents. All the way to the concert he kept repeating, "He's great! Wait until you hear him recite! He's great! Marvellous! Terrific!" but my father said this sort of thing about all kinds of people, including our preacher, so it is not surprising that I reserved judgement.

. . .

I don't know what Torceni was paid to appear, as star turn, on that makeshift stage. The Baptists were not well endowed and it could not have been more than a couple of guineas, plus his supper and a return railway ticket from an inner suburb. Neither was he, in the outward sense, the least impressive, being short, plump and nearly bald, with a volatile, rubicund face, an *actor's* face, that had absorbed too much make-up over the years. Or is this the benefit of romantic hindsight? Might he not have been another amateur, who worked as a clerk or warehouseman or shop-walker by day and earned extra money giving recitals in the evening? I never knew the least detail concerning his background. I never spoke to him then or later and he remains, for me, a name and a kindly face. That, and a beautifully pitched voice with the power to focus my attention as few people have done before or since. I remember he came downstage modestly, taking short steps and looking uncomfortable in evening dress and old-style dickey that was a bad fit.

He began, I recall, with the episode of David Copperfield and the waiter, and when the polite applause had spent itself he acted the story of two children who ran away to Gretna Green to get married, were intercepted and hauled back at the first stage. Then he recited a poem about a trio of soldiers in the American Civil War, and having warmed up on these items he gave us a haphazard selection from the works of Kingsley, Tennyson, Conrad and Goldsmith. I have never rediscovered most of the passages he selected and cannot swear to the authors. They remain for me the lost opium-shop of De Quincey that assumed actuality for no other reason than to trap and enslave me. For by then, after he had held the stage for upwards of forty-five minutes, I was drunk. Hopelessly and gloriously drunk on great draughts of words, so that it seemed incomprehensible to me that I should have ever hankered after the professions of heroes in *Boy's Own Paper* serials—a Mountie, an explorer, a pirate or the like. I knew then that whatever I did would have to do with words and phrases, with the great rolling sentences that came tripping off John Torceni's tongue, conjuring up scenes and situations and characters capable of painting the bilious-green walls of the chapel the colours of the rainbow. I knew then that in some manner I would have to spin English words on a thread and that no other occupation made would make the least appeal to me. Meantime I could have sat there without food or drink until the same time tomorrow, without so much as rearranging my buttocks on the uncushioned pew where, for so many Sundays, I had awaited the announcement of 'The Dear Children's Hymn'.

I say I knew this, and I did, for I never afterwards wasted thought on any other career. What I did not know was that the decision was not my own, that it had been made for me by the rubicund little man in a dress suit that looked too large for him and would have sat more comfortably upon the shoulders of Copperfield's waiter. And this was to remain hidden from me for a very long time, until chance dropped it on the floor of a television studio, when I was older than Torceni was when I first heard him recite. It was then that I understood with great clarity the role John Torceni had played in my life and how much I would have enjoyed meeting him and recalling our mutual flirtation with the Baptists.

. . .

They were giving me the usual half-courteous, half-cynical treatment on a late night programme. Why had I become a writer? How had it all begun? At what age did I make the decision and so on. And because these stock questions cannot be answered in the way audiences expect I suppose I answered flippantly or absent-mindedly. I said, "It was because of an elocutionist called John Torceni . . .", and as I said this I understood that it had validity, that it really was so, that it was Torceni and no other who had decided on my behalf how I was to spend my days. In other words, the wrappings had fallen away from the Baptist's Bonus and as I peered at what was beneath them I wondered if John Torceni was still alive and decided, sadly, that this was improbable.

He was dead and had been for many years, but he touched me again for all that. About a week later a letter reached me, forwarded by the B.B.C. It was hardly more than a note written on lined paper and giving a North London address and said, without preamble, "I heard the broadcast and your admission of how you became a writer. My John would have been very pleased. As you can imagine, he loved writers, all kinds of writers." It was signed, "Mrs. Torceni".

Digger Beau Geste

Most of us, at least those among us who seek satisfaction in lasting personal relationships, have a private Beau Geste. A former school-friend, paunchy but wise, a favourite, elderly relative who was free with tips when we were young, or possibly someone who is no more than a well-observed acquaintance who, for us at least, embodies the virtues and characteristics of our childhood heroes; someone with the courage and élan of, say, Rupert of the Rhine, Robin Hood, King Arthur, Grace Darling or Mrs. Pankhurst. I've had one all my life—my eldest brother Bill, and it seems to me, whenever I measure his claims against the also-rans, that his head-start is a strange and wonderful thing, for we have met but once in a period of almost half a century.

We were parted, casually it seemed to me, one dank January morning in 1922, and it would therefore seem natural if his memory had grown dim as I chased him along the years but this is far from being so. There he is at sixty-eight, the Beau Geste of the Antipodes, as real, solid and dependable as the next-door neighbour whose lawn-mower one borrows on Saturday afternoons, a man who would be first on the scene if your house caught fire. In these circumstances do time and distance matter?

I am sometimes puzzled by the anxiety some parents show concerning what they call 'the age gap' between successive children in a family. They seem to view it as a potential obstacle to the development of an amiable relationship but let me reassure them. Bill missed being a Victorian by a whisker of twenty-one days, whereas I did not appear until the third year of her grandson's reign. Neither one of us has ever been conscious of an age gap and for my part how could it be otherwise? Seniority is obligatory in a Beau Geste.

. . .

I remember him first as a grave-eyed, knickerbockered sixteen-year-old, with the patience and inclination to teach me how to tell the time by the kitchen clock. Perhaps this earliest memory of him prejudiced me in his favour, mildly that is, as an adult prepared to perform a service without the impatience five-year-olds expect from senior members of the family. It may have been so, but on the whole I think not, for very soon after that he passed into legend and, once I was able to read, became indistinguishable from the hell-raking heroes of Henty and Ballantyne. From then on, throughout the eternity of childhood, Bill and his exploits, relayed to me through family gossip (some of which was not intended for my ears) continued to expand until he filled my horizon, stepping clear across the frontier between reality and the bonafide storybook world, where bandoliers take the place of school satchels and the tinkle of scales on the upright piano is drowned in the rattle of the Maxim gun.

Too young to enlist, he signed on as a steward on a merchant ship out of Rotherhithe and my father, for reasons best known to himself, made no effort to stop him, letting it be understood that his eldest son had 'run away to sea' thus forfeiting his patrimony. I have learned since that this was one of my father's self-delusions and that he actually went on board the vessel and discussed Bill's prospects with a laconic captain. At all events, Bill sailed, in the U-boat winter of 1916–17, and no one was much surprised when he turned up a week later, having been torpedoed off Falmouth and set adrift in an open boat.

And now begins the near-hopeless task of separating fact from hearsay, for the curious thing about my memories of my brother's early career is that every verifiable move on his part is swaddled in romantic fiction and even regular access to him by mail has not enabled me to discard details he himself has forgotten. Forty years passed before I was able to run down the salient facts on this, the first of his adventures. He was awakened by the torpedo explosion and, forgetting he was in a bunk, stunned himself when he sat upright. On this account he was the last to leave as the vessel settled down but the U-boat commander was a 'good' German. He gave them biscuits, wine and sailing directions. Twelve hours later they were picked up by a British destroyer.

Beau Geste he must have been for he at once signed on again, this time in a convoy bound for South America and West Africa and here fact, fancy and family chit-chat become so involved with one another that I have never been able to separate them to my satisfaction. He was missing and assumed drowned. He had been chased by a Spaniard with a knife along the quays of Buenos Aires. He caught malaria off Dakar. He was home and having malaria in our spare bedroom. He owned a six-chambered revolver and a single-shot pistol. He met a girl in a tree at the village of Leigh, in Kent, and formed an attachment for her on the basis of a mutual admiration for Ethel M. Dell's *Way of an Eagle.* Scraps of unverifiable information concerning him drifted into the house like ambiguously-worded telegrams and were bandied about the fireside. Bill was here. Or there. Bill had done this. Or was thinking of doing that. Is it surprising that a six-year-old saw him as Sexton Blake with a dash of D'Artagnan, or that hard facts concerning his odysseys should have been so difficult to check?

Then, very suddenly, the picture cleared and I saw him briefly in the flesh, a tall, gangling, sunburned young man in a merchant sailor's double-breasted reefer, advancing at a run down the breakwater at Bognor years before it earned its Regis and grabbing me by the hair as I floundered in deep water. And again, that same summer holiday, sculling up the Arun to give us tea at The Black Rabbit. But long before I could come to terms with him as a bonafide brother he disappeared again, this time into the Royal Flying Corps, and immediately the tide of legend began to flow south from a flying training base in Scotland. Bill was driving an ambulance. Bill had sawn a wounded pilot out of a tree. Bill was in charge of a motor rescue boat and lifting inept pilots from the drink with a boathook. Bill had sent home a souvenir propeller-hub with sawn-off blades that would do very nicely for an umbrella stand in the hall.

Then, as always, he appeared again in yet another uniform, the cross-over, high-buttoned tunic of the R.F.C., and suddenly the war was over and they were going to hang the Kaiser, squeeze Germany until the pips squeaked, and build homes for heroes to live in.

It did not seem unreasonable to assume that Bill qualified as one of these heroes, that he would marry the girl he met in the tree and become as sober and workaday as everyone else along the Avenue, and I suppose I assumed something like this would happen. It never did, of course. Beau Gestes visit suburbs from time to time but they never settle in them. He took a job as a butcher in Peckham and for a year or so was half-integrated into the family although, for me, he still lacked the substance of everyone else in the crescent and only became real at odd, unexpected moments.

I would sometimes come upon him in the narrow hall, standing with his back to the door and looking not troubled exactly but vague and pensive, as though he was trying to remember why he was there and not in Patagonia or the Arabian Gulf. Then with a wink in my direction, he would drift into the front room, sit down at the piano and play ballads or ragtime by ear but expertly and tunefully, so that few would have believed he had learned the trick in half a dozen lessons from a dipsomaniac professor in Southwark Park Road years before he went away to sea.

He had a preference for heroic themes and would play '*The Golden Vanity*' (that sank upon the Lowland Sea), or crash out a series of heavy chords as an accompaniment to a narrative poem about Mad Carew, a subaltern of Katmandu, stabbed to death after stealing the green eye of an idol for his Colonel's daughter. Strong stuff always, with the smack of Imperialism about it, so that watching him through the crack in the door I was conscious of his insubstantiality again and would see him not as he was at that time, a bored, underpaid ex-serviceman, but as one of the characters in his ballads, the bo'sun of *The Golden Vanity* perhaps, or Mad Carew, despoiler of Indian temples.

The girl he met in the tree was now a regular visitor and whenever she stayed with us she occupied Bill's tiny bedroom over the porch. On these occasions he shared our room, leaving early, usually before it was light. When this happened I would hear the furtive chink of coins and after he had gone I would reach out and run the tips of my fingers across the cane-bottomed chair beside my bed. Balanced on the broad arm there was always a small pile of pennies and halfpennies. On only two occasions did he speak sharply to me. Once, when I awakened him by crossing the bedroom on my heels, he called me a baby elephant. On another occasion he sent me to the grocer's for a tin of pears and I brought peaches because, as I freely admitted, I preferred them. This time he called me a cheeky whippersnapper, who had no business to consider his own preferences. On both occasions I burst into tears. It is a dreadful thing to earn a rebuke from Beau Geste.

Then he was off again, this time to Australia, and there was, for all but me, a terrible finality about his latest journey for Australia, in 1922, was the far side of the moon. Distance notwithstanding, I was not equipped to judge the prospects of ever seeing him again. All that had happened, in my view, was that he had withdrawn once again into the storybook world, where he really belonged, perhaps in pursuit of bushrangers. If so then the best of them had better look out!

News of him trickled back to the Avenue from time to time and it had the same unlikely elements as the rumours that reached us during his prolonged absences during the war. Bill had joined the South Australian police. Bill had been shot at by armed convicts on the run from Yatala gaol. Bill patrolled a bottomless lake shaped like a leg-of-mutton. Bill had lent five pounds to an emigrant cousin and had no prospects of getting it back. And then, imperceptibly, the pattern began to change and tidings concerning him assumed an almost mundane pattern, of the kind that might concern someone living next-door-but-one. Bill was married to an Australian girl called Freda. Bill was a father and I, to my stupefaction, was an uncle.

I was fourteen then and able, I suppose, to get him into a less distorted perspective but although elements of sobriety began to invest him from here on he never did assume the come-day go-day aspect of folk going about their normal business, leading normal workaday lives, changing jobs, getting older, dying and getting buried in the cemetery down the road. The aura of Rupert and Robin Hood did not altogether fade and even baldness, seen in mailed snapshots, did not succeed in detaching the Galahad halo. Neither did I ever once entertain fears concerning his survival. Tidy suburban cemeteries were not for him. Not so long as there were vacancies in Valhalla.

From time to time we exchanged letters but what satisfactory communication can be established between a home-based schoolboy and Beau Geste, faraway and presumably fighting it out in Fort Zinderneuf? Things continued to happen to him in a way they never happened to any of us, and in the end the Australians themselves must have acknowledged this for they passed a law in the State Parliament to make him Police Commissioner of Tasmania, the first man who was not Tasmanian-born to occupy the post. In this capacity he supervised a State Visit of the Queen, recalling, perhaps, that he would have been a subject of her great-great-grandmamma if my mother had had a sense of history and advanced her confinement by three short weeks.

Then the undreamed of happened. Shortly after my father's death in 1956 he wrote saying that he was attending a world police conference in Lisbon and flying on to Britain for a holiday. He asked if I would meet his flight at London Airport.

I wondered how I would recognise him. Thirty-five years had passed since I had heard him slip quietly into my bedroom, stack his loose change on the cane-bottomed chair, and steal away to Tilbury Docks and exile. I should not have doubted. Any fool can single out a Beau Geste. He came lunging out of the crowd around the Customs counters, hand outstretched, a broad, home-from-sea grin on his sunburned face, trilby hat pushed back at an impossible angle on a head that was not so bald as mine. I would not have been much surprised if he had not emptied his pockets of loose change and disappeared again, leaving me to imagine that his brief appearance had been at one with all those comings and goings in my childhood. The only thing about him that had changed in any way was his accent that recalled Australian airmen I had consorted with during the war, that and a rather macabre impression that my father had recrossed the Jordan radiating a rare tolerance acquired during his brief sojourn among the Blessed.

We found a taxi and trundled through London traffic to Paddington and then west towards the peninsula where, forty years before, he had stepped ashore from a destroyer after the first of his adventures. We talked and communicated easily and naturally, as though he had been off somewhere on a brief holiday and wanted to catch up on local news. Nothing about him was strange or unfamiliar and this, I suppose, is not surprising for he had been there all the time, popping in and out of the pages of every book of adventure fiction I had read during the interval. In one sense he was real enough inasmuch as I could touch him and hear him speak. And yet, in another, he was not, for I could not rid myself of a sense of unique privilege, of making a four-hour railway journey in the company of Robinson Crusoe, Don Quixote, Long John Silver, Huckleberry Finn, Ghengis Khan, Marco Polo, Richard the Lionheart and Peter the Whaler, and this was to persist until the moment of his departure.

When the moment came for parting, and his brown, amiable face became an indistinct blur beyond the end of the platform, I found myself stroking the leading edge of the porter's trolley beside which we had stood when we shook hands. Why, I wonder? Did I expect to find there a neat stack of pennies and halfpennies?

The Far Side of the Railway Poster

I

Almost every family in the Avenue spent an August fortnight at the seaside. Residence in our part of the suburb conferred that privilege upon you and you lost caste if you did not take advantage of it. The 'high-income people', that is to say those earning in excess of four hundred a year, went to ostentatious places like Cornwall and the Norfolk Broads, and took very good care you heard about it and scrutinised their Brownie snaps on their return home, but the more modest among us settled for resorts in Kent and Sussex advertised by posters displayed the length of the old South-Eastern and Chatham Railway—Brighton, Worthing, Littlehampton, Folkestone, Broadstairs and the like.

The posters were a colourful feature of every halt on the Charing Cross–Addiscombe Line and it never occurred to me, during the long, leafless winters, that the resorts they advertised were slightly oversold. To me the posters had veracity. Here, it seemed, the sun never ceased to shine and the piers probed almost as far as France. Sometimes, but not often in those watch-your-step days, a coy bathing beauty, wearing a decorous one-piece costume was featured but the emphasis was usually on the family and the miles of golden sands awaiting the kiddies.

Whenever the annual holiday approached I was sick with excitement and I never recall returning home disappointed although, like every other child along the crescent, I hated turning my back on the sea and letting myself be reclaimed by those labyrinthine streets and housing estates that, even then, were advancing south and south-east at the rate of over a mile a year.

It can be imagined, then, how I reacted to my father's bland announcement, in the late autumn of 1923, that we were to sell up almost at once and actually *live* beside the sea. I don't think I should have been more astounded if he had let fall the news that, from Christmas onwards, our address would be Buckingham Palace, S.W.1.

My mind raced at once to all those railway posters and I made a rapid mental rundown on possibilities. Bognor or Broadstairs? Littlehampton or Hove? Not that it mattered, for every poster on the line advertised a marine Elysium. As things turned out, however, we were not going to any of these places, or to any resort that I had heard of up to that time. We were removing, Father announced, with an almost indecent lack of emotion, to a town situated at the mouth of the River Exe in Devonshire, and when I looked even more thunderstruck he asked for my school atlas and pointed it out to me.

There it was, in insignificant print—Exmouth, the London side of the Exe estuary, some twelve miles south of Devon's county town, Exeter. Measuring the distance with my eye I judged we should be about a week getting there.

My impressions of Devonshire at that time were necessarily conventional. I had heard about the cream and the cider. I knew that everyone down in that part of the world was a farmer and walked about in a felt, crush-on hat and a smock, with a long straw in his mouth. I assumed that the sun shone there indefinitely, just as it did at Bognor, and that inland, no matter in which direction one travelled, one was certain to cross trackless moors studded with granite boulders, or vast forests of oak and beech, of the kind seen in the second act of the Christmas pantomime. I communicated these reflections to my father and he did nothing to modify them. In his way he too was an incurable romantic. Why else, at fifty, should he throw up his job at Smithfield meat market and invest every penny he possessed in a weekly newspaper, a printing office and a stationery shop?

We set out on Christmas Eve, stowing ourselves into the crowded eleven a.m. from Waterloo. We could just as easily have gone before or after the Christmas rush but my father was not a planner in that sense and simply left as soon as the last trunk had been roped. It seemed, as I had anticipated, an interminable journey, and it was nearly dark when we caught the branch line train at Exeter and ran south alongside the wide estuary to the sea. Not dark enough, however, to resolve doubts concerning the authenticity of those posters.

To begin with sleet was slashing the carriage windows and who ever heard of sleet within smelling distance of the sea? For another thing the tide was out, exposing miles of gleaming mud-flats dotted with unsavoury-looking flotsam and I had an uneasy suspicion that, even in daylight, the miles of golden sands were a fiction as far as this stretch of coast was concerned.

It was too late to explore when we detrained and hauled our luggage the hundred yards or so to the impressive, three-storey building that housed printing-works, shop and living accommodation, but what little I saw of our new home before being packed off to bed promised bonuses one would not necessarily associate with permanent lodgings at the seaside and this in itself was reassuring. There was a flat roof reached by a short flight of stairs that ended in a movable trolley shifted with one's shoulders. There was a cavernous loft over the printing-works, with a trap-door through which a spread of machinery, not unlike that in the famous picture depicting Caxton seeking the patronage of Edward IV, could be glimpsed. The authentic smell of Fleet Street rose from the cogs and belts and flywheels, prompting the most extravagant dreams in a mind forsworn to the service of printers' ink. There was a cellar stocked with thousands of shop-soiled mourning cards and a stockroom where, had my mother not been on hand, I could have helped myself to a sackful of Christmas presents to compensate me for those already mislaid in the migration. I went to bed reserving judgement, lulled to sleep by the strains of the British Legion band playing 'Once in Royal David's City' in the War memorial enclosure across the road.

2

I had the waterfront to myself that first, unforgettable morning and I wonder now if the Exmouth foreshore would have made the same impression on me had it not been Christmas morning, when everybody else was cooing over their Christmas gifts. The tide was ebbing now, ripping down the river at what seemed to me a prodigious rate and pointing the line of marker buoys out to sea where the channel ran between the sea wall and half-exposed sandbanks; then on under red cliffs to the open sea.

It was utterly unlike any seaside I had visited or heard about and it did not occur to me to make allowances for the fact that it was mid-winter and all the seasonal trappings were packed away in the Council's storerooms. The sea-front curved east from the toy dock for more than a mile, dunes on the left, beach on the right, and the river here looked as wide and impressive as Mark Twain's Mississippi. There was a lifeboat house and a look-out mound, a captured tank and guns, town trophies of World War One, and a string of forlorn, wooden shelters, half-filled with blown sand. In a way it was a parody of the railway posters, a ghost resort that had once, perhaps, been teeming with city holiday-makers before it was engulfed in some natural disaster, like the destruction of Pompeii. It gave me a queer sensation of being an only survivor.

In the dock, forlornly at anchor, were three Continental coasters, some of the very last of the vessels dependent on sail and I stared at them unbelievingly. They were extraordinarily like the pictures illustrating the *Hispaniola* in my copy of *Treasure Island* and I yearned to board one and satisfy myself that it had a sparred gallery, an arms-rack and a tarpaulin-shrouded stern-chaser aft. I paddled around here a long time and then went along between the timber yard and the single rail track that led back to the town. On the way I had another surprise. Abandoned on a waste patch of ground was a genuine 'Royal Mail', not unlike the Deadwood Coach, and I could not imagine what it could be doing there bereft of its driver and horses. It was still in good shape and looked as though it had been held up and sacked by Sioux the day before yesterday. Then, down by the tideline, I saw the bag.

It was a heavy, hessian bag, carefully sealed with cord and weighing, possibly, five pounds. It seemed to me a prodigious stroke of luck that I should find a treasure-cache the first day I set foot on the beach and I went to work on the fastenings, first with my fingers, then with my penknife. When I had removed the cord I took a careful look around before lifting it and carrying it under the sea-wall. I knew all about treasure-trove and was not inclined to share my good fortune with His Majesty's Receivers of Wrecks. Carefully I upended it on a weed-covered slab of rock. Out rolled a dead cat in an early stage of decomposition.

3

It was a community that grew on you, yielding its confidences grudgingly as though, for a season or so, you were on probation. It had nothing whatever in common with the suburb. Back there, notwithstanding the tightly-prescribed social code you were obliged to observe, you never really lost the sense of belonging to a vast, anonymous city. Here, in a town of eleven thousand inhabitants, who lived mainly by taking in one another's washing, you might have set foot in a new country and adopted a fresh nationality. You were no longer an Englishman or a Britisher but an Exmothian. Your loyalties belonged right here, enclosed by the English Channel on the south and the pine and bracken country to the north. And as if this was not enough to ensure your provincialism you were boxed in by two other frontiers, the tidal estuary in the west, the brick kiln in the east that marked, with its pointing stack, the urban district boundary between you and that of your nearest neighbour, the legendary town of Budleigh Salterton, subject of so many music-hall jokes and allegedly populated by retired admirals, lieutenant-colonels, ex-Indian Civil Servants and their army of helots.

Architecturally the town was not typical of a West Country community. Its core had been built by Regency speculators, cashing in on the new cult of sea-worship set in train by Prinny when he took his rakish court to Brighton, but expansion followed the railway boom and almost all the dwelling houses and public buildings had been built in the last two decades of the nineteenth century. A few years later, in the Edwardian decade, a better class of property grew up in the open section of the town where it nudged Budleigh Salterton. We too had our aristocracy, although one had the impression that the majority of the folk who lived in what we called 'The Valley' had made their pile in trade, laid no serious claim to being gentry, and would have been blackballed *en masse* by the real gentry in Budleigh.

Down near the river a large housing estate had been built on a partially-reclaimed marsh. It was known by the slightly derisory name of 'The Colony' and consisted of a dozen streets of narrow, redbrick houses, far less permanent-looking than the terrace houses of the Avenue. The tradesmen, who were the activists of the town, occupied a group of more solid-looking shops and houses in and around the town centre, whereas the roads leading to the sea front were given over to landladies who made two-thirds of a living out of the short summer season.

It did not take an observer long to decide that Exmouth had been a laggard in the race among British coastal towns to transform themselves from fishing village or watering place into resort. There was, even now, a half-heartedness about its drive to attract visitors, as though it had never made up its mind whether or not it wanted and needed them. In the season any number of token gestures were made. An orchestra was installed in the windswept bandstand to play popular sheet-music and excerpts from Gilbert and Sullivan operas. Strings of fairy-lights were slung precariously between the ornamental lamp-standards. A few forlorn donkeys plied between widely-spaced refreshment huts. Jerseyed longshoremen offered trips in the bay on the few summer days when the water looked calm enough to attract customers. Back in the public gardens a marquee was erected to house a seasonal concert party that returned year after year and became, as it were, honorary residents, for its clientèle was largely Exmothian. It is among local quirks such as this, I think, that one must look for the real ethos of the town and of all towns like Exmouth. Outwardly they exist for holiday-makers but actually the reverse is true, or was true then. It always seemed to me that only natives, the householders and ratepayers that is, exerted any influence upon it as a community and every one of these, including the landladies and those of the seasonal workers who did not migrate in winter, regarded the summer visitor in the way a settled and self-satisfied family might regard an unsuccessful cousin, home from the Colonies and faced with a long leave on an inadequate salary. He was tolerated, fed, and given houseroom but sent out to amuse himself the moment weather permitted. In the meantime he had to take good care not to get under anyone's feet.

This became more clear to me when the spring advanced and

the force of the south-westerlies, that seemed to rattle the windows nonstop from October until March, moderated to some degree, so that residents could peel off their jackets and attend to the annual ritual of erecting their beach huts, where they spent almost their entire leisure-time from early May until the last week of September.

There was absolutely no nonsense about this annual chore and it was carried out with the attention to detail that would be demonstrated by a good regiment digging in against an enemy attack. Sand was levelled, spirit-levels were used, and hut sections carefully bolted together, after which the shack was lovingly painted. Then, from coastguard station towards a point near the dead end of the esplanade, the shanties curved in an unbroken rank, effectively cutting off all view of the sea, so that you could walk the length of the promenade without ever knowing you were at the seaside if you ignored the occasional glimpse of blue and gold between huts and where steps led down to the beach.

The Exmothians regarded these huts as summer palaces and gave each one of them a jaunty or a cosy name. One of the delights of the early part of the season was to learn these names by heart as you walked east, taking furtive peeks at the ruffled surface of the Channel. Some of the names had an ironic ring – 'Farenuff', 'Dunworkin', 'Dunroamin', but others proclaimed the owners' indisputable right to his patch of which 'Yrusb' is a fair example. Others still had a deceivingly mild title, like 'The Hermitage', 'Downalong' and 'Restawhile', but all, one way or another, underlined the fact that the beach, every gritty grain of it, belonged to those who had weathered out the winter here and the use of any part of it by strangers was, like a soldier's leave, a privilege and not a right.

It was the same with the annual carnival. Some of the progressives once staged a carnival in high summer, thinking it might be an attraction to visitors, but it was a disappointing failure. The visitors got in the way and would not enter into the spirit of the occasion, so that soon the Carnival Committee reverted to the customary date in October, when the strangers had all gone home and we could make fools of ourselves in private.

Exmouth, at the time of which I write, was a boom town for

joiners. Set an Anglo-Saxon down anywhere in the world and he will at once busy himself founding clubs and societies. In the early nineteen-twenties Exmouth was the most organised community in my experience.

There was hardly a human activity that lacked its quorum of devotees, its headquarters, its President, Vice-Presidents, Chairman, Hon. Secretary and Hon. Treasurer. There was a golf club, a cricket club, a rugby football club, and an association football club; an archery club, two bowls clubs, a miniature rifle club, a cycling club and a lawn tennis and croquet club. There were bridge clubs, a multiplicity of women's clubs, a Temperance club, an amateur photography club and a wireless club, and this in the days of crystal sets! There was intense political activity during and between elections, with a strong Conservative Association and a Liberal following that ran them dangerously close at the ballot boxes. Whoever you met was sure to be on the committee of one or more of of these organisations and after a time you learned to identify residents by their sparetime pursuits. You could walk down the main street any day, winter or summer, and be certain of seeing window-bills advertising gatherings of cage-bird fanciers, sea-anglers, yachtsmen, philatelists or water-colourists, and almost every conversation you overheard concerned these things and little else unless a local election was in progress.

Exmothians took their local politics seriously enough but the Town Clerk (paid at that time around six pounds a week) exercised the real power of executive and stood no nonsense from any of us, least of all the elected representatives. The town was very strong on amateur dramatics, notwithstanding the fact that we had four cinemas featuring Hollywood professionals but the pseudo-gentlefolk living in The Valley, who did not take much active interest in town affairs generally, had monopolised this sector and it was a closed shop to the rest of us, unless you were content to stand around holding a spear, or make your sole appearance at rise of curtain dusting props or answering the telephone while the audience settled down.

The Operatic Society was more democratic but the Old Guard usually shared the leading roles among themselves, relegating all but the most talented newcomers to the chorus. All in all, it will be seen, there was a tremendous amount going on, particularly out of season, when once the town had stopped catering for visitors and could reassume its natural rhythm of sale-of-work, annual meeting, sporting tournament, whist drive and half-crown hop at the Church Hall (one-and-six at the Church Institute).

Occasionally there was a gala event, the visit of a warship, a conference banquet, a British Legion or Women's Institute rally, or a ten shilling supper dance where everyone was obligated to shake the mothballs from their dress clothes and young men wearing dinner-jackets were politely turned away. It seems astonishing that so much activity could be generated for nine months at a stretch by a mere eleven thousand people but it was so, and far from seeming parish-pumpy and ignoble it always struck me as the reverse, as though we were all members of one gigantic family, dedicated to leading interesting, assertive lives.

This was certainly true of the younger set, one small group excepted. Almost all of us attended the same local Council and Church Shools and moved on, at about eleven, to the co-ed Secondary School, so that we grew up, a thousand strong, knowing one another's Christian names and family backgrounds. It made for unshy matings and a relaxed atmosphere at dances and Christmas parties. It also tended to encourage early and generally successful marriages, particularly if the bread-winner had a secure economic footing in the town. The only exceptions to this rule were the younger folk who lived in The Valley, the sons and daughters of wealthier folk, who had attended boarding schools and were thus at a disadvantage. They tended to hang together, at least the males did, roaring about in tiny sports cars from which the baffle plates had been removed, and usually seen with yards of scarf festooned about their necks. I often felt a little sorry for the Valley maidens. They looked very lonely when they drifted down to change their book at Boots, but few of us would have risked a snub by inviting them to dance the Charleston at the Annual Hospital Ball, the only big social event they attended.

The rest of us, as we passed from childhood to adolescence, and from adolescence to young manhood or womanhood, tended to forget the world outside, glimpsed across the estuary, or eastward beyond Keeper's Cottage, on the road to Budleigh

Salterton. We knew, of course, that things happened out there from time to time. We read London newspapers and some of us had wireless sets, or watched the newsreels between silent features at the cinema, but whatever it was it did not trouble us much, nothing like as much as Biafra and Vietnam disturb small-town dwellers today. Even the antics of men like Lloyd George and Stanley Baldwin seemed irrelevant, as though they were taking place in Stamboul or the Orkneys, whereas a front-page crime like a trunk murder did not seem nearly so immediate to us as, say, a local solicitor's bolt with his clients' funds, or a milkman's conviction for adulteration.

Life in the Avenue must have prepared me for rapid assimilation into such a community for I was thinking of myself as an Exmothian, and nothing else, within a month of that Christmas Eve journey along the mud-flats. I wonder if, but for the war that shook so many of us loose, I would have had much curiosity about the rest of the world. Now that I have seen and savoured a few slices of it I am inclined to think I got the worst of the bargain.

The moments I recall from that period of my life have a sparkle that is not solely a legacy of youth. It comes, I feel, from a sense of belonging and participating and also, to a degree, from a sense of permanence that seems to have departed not only from Exmouth but from every centre of population in the Western World. I do not know why this should be so. Viewed as a whole, young people living in this kind of community today enjoy better housing, have far more money to spend, have a longer expectation of life, better health and a much higher standard of living than they enjoyed forty years ago. But somehow they are not as happy or, if they are, they take great pains to hide the fact. Their expressions, when you see them enjoying themselves, remind me a little of the fixed grins on the faces of families depicted on the railway posters that once plastered the stations of the old South-Eastern and Chatham Line. They seem, on the whole, unaware that so much fun is still to be found on the far side of the hoarding.

Bastion of Privilege

Was it Julian Grenfell, Sassoon, Robert Graves, or one of their frontline contemporaries who took his first, appalled look at the glutinous battlefield of Passchendaele in 1917, and exclaimed, "Great God! It's worse than School!" Whoever it was, the remark is revealing, and I wish someone would use it as a counter-broadside during one of those perennial debates aimed at abolishing public schools, establishments that Left Wing politicians still regard as bastions of privilege.

As stated, I attended seven schools between 1917 and 1928 and only the last of them was 'public' in the sense implied. I enjoyed my time there enormously but this is not to say that I ever thought of myself as privileged for having worn its cap and blazer. Indeed, there were occasions when I thought the exact opposite, looking over my shoulder at feather-bedded day-school boys, much as the under-privileged of Paris looked through the locked gates of Versailles at pampered nobles. For whatever one can say for or against public schools, one is obliged to admit that a mercurial temperament and a tough hide is needed to enjoy such privileges they have on offer. It was said of mine that its pupils made excellent soldiers. Nothing worse was likely to befall them on active service.

It was not the intention of my father that I should complete my education at this type of establishment. As a fiery radical, who had been storming bastions of privilege all his life, he bracketed public schools in his mind with breweries, stately homes, episcopal palaces and the Cavalry Club, but he could never be bothered to study handouts and when it became imperative for me to leave the Exmouth co-ed school he handed me a sheaf of brochures and told me to take my choice. It was typical of him, as was his scornful dismissal of the incident that brought about an abrupt change of school.

This incident was known at the time as the 'Brickworks Affair', and its inflation into a tiny local scandal illustrates the vast distances we have moved in half a century towards the establishment of a permissive society. Today the 'Brickworks Affair' would not crease the forehead of the most exacting headmaster or parent, involving as it did no more than a little innocent horseplay between the sexes on the way home to tea. It was very different then, however. Any overt expression of the sex urge between adolescents was apt to be regarded as a prelude to debauchery. When it became known that a dozen of us were exchanging pledges and kisses in the disused kiln five minutes' walk from school one might have judged, from the resultant uproar, that the boys had opted to train as White Slavers and the girls were earmarked for the streets.

When it blew over, and staff and parents were satisfied that there was no likelihood of an abrupt rise in the local birthrate, my father came to the conclusion that the best way to insure his leisure against interruption throughout what remained of my adolescence, was to put distance between us. That is how, in brief, I came to qualify as a potential enemy of the militant Left, likely, indeed almost certain, to man the wrong side of the barricades when the October Revolution was launched.

This long-anticipated event, it appeared, promised to coincide almost exactly with my enrolment in the junior ranks of the oppressors. The General Strike took place during my first term at West Buckland but it proved a mild upheaval and taught the British what they should have known, i.e. that the prospects of a Continental-style revolution in England are almost as unlikely as that of teaching them how to make carnival, how to transform Sunday into a public holiday, or how to win a war and come out of it more solvent than the vanquished. There are certain spheres in which the average Briton is less likely to succeed than the Australian aboriginal and making a revolution is one of them. He will master the trade of hotelier long before he understands how to overthrow an elected government.

I had, of course, many preconceived ideas about life at a public school and all of them stemmed from books published in the latter half of the nineteenth century. *Tom Brown*, of course, was one, and three others were *The Bending of the Twig*, *The Hill*, and *The Fifth Form at St. Dominic's*. These were buttressed by a weekly injection from the late Frank Richards, the prolific recorder of the japes at Greyfriars and St. Jim's in

The Magnet and *The Gem*. The stage background built by these industrious carpenters took a severe battering before it was replaced by a more solid structure. The process occupied, I suppose, the better part of a year during which I learned, albeit slowly, that a dormitory feast seldom expanded beyond the furtive sucking of a few acid-drops, that fat boys were not necessarily butts, that the smoking habit, far from being confined to bounders and weeds, was considered a manly accomplishment, and that the luxury of a study, enjoyed by Tom Brown from his first day at Rugby, could not be anticipated until one had plodded all the way from second form to sixth.

The school buildings occupied a western spur of the Exmoor plateau, six hundred feet above sea-level. The nearest market-town was six miles distant, the nearest railway halt two miles, the nearest village a mile and a half. All three were out of bounds.

The school had been founded by a muscular Christian, himself a pupil of the famous Doctor Arnold but it was not to Arnold that he looked when he approved the architectural lay-out. I have it in mind that his inspiration went back somewhat further in history, say to a Spartan barrack for defaulters, and he apparently overlooked the fact that Sparta enjoys a Mediterranean climate. The wind charged through the stone corridors like an army of howling Cossacks and in my time there was not a stitch of carpet or, for that matter, a fibre of linoleum. Knotted wood, slate and granite enfolded us, and there was never room for more than three at the classroom heating-pipe alcoves. It was said by those who did not qualify for these places that to lean against them was to court constipation but I never put the theory to the test. At fourteen I was a medium-sized boy but West Buckland catered for farmers' sons and there were at least three hulking Jan Ridds in each class.

The full force of these disadvantages did not strike me until my second term, for I joined the school in April and we had a long hot summer ahead of us. Soon after the commencement of the autumn term, however, I raised a splendid crop of chilblains and became resigned to dying young, possibly of exposure.

The headmaster, a very genial soul, had inherited the Spartan tradition. At sixty-plus he was still playing in the scrum of junior games and on one occasion had a game suspended for half an hour while we combed the trampled mud for his false teeth. He had a number of eccentric beliefs and one in particular was responsible for implanting in my mind the belief that I was unlikely to survive my first winter on the moor. The bath-house was situated in a vast covered playground on that side of an open quad furthest from the dormitories. Boys were required to make their way there in pyjamas and dressing gowns. As a preventative against catching cold on the return journey the headmaster instituted a system of cold douches, supervised by a prefect. I was warned of this in advance but dismissed it as terror propaganda, fed to all new boys. It was even so, however, for on stepping out of the bath I was steered into another where the prefect in charge baptised each boy with three large pans of ice-cold water, "To close the pores," he reiterated, quoting the headmaster.

I have dwelt on the cold but there were times when the over-privileged were tortured by heat. It was pleasant to lie all day long on a rug in the shade of the plantation watching, without seeing, important cricket matches, in honour of which two dull periods had been cancelled. One dozed, or read *Monte Cristo*, to the accompaniment of scattered applause and self-conscious cries of "Oh, well *played*, sir!" but summer idylls such as this were not to be had for nothing. Our contribution, as juniors, was enlistment in rolling gangs charged with the task of keeping the pitch in good order for the Somerset Stragglers or Devonshire Dumplings. It was the kind of labour performed in the Peruvian silver mines by the enslaved Inca.

For specified periods throughout summer terms teams of eight conscripts dragged a horse roller up and down the level turf between the wickets, two members of the team supporting the shafts, where the horse should have been, the other six pushing to maintain momentum. The overseer, a prefect or a cricket colour, pretended to push but had more important obligations—to keep the bondsmen at their work with a cricket stump.

One way and another there was not much time for waiting one's turn at the heating-pipe alcoves. Everyone in authority had been indoctrinated with the spirit of Henry before Harfleur. Someone was always around, winter and summer, to ensure that our sinews were stiffened and our blood summoned up by prolonged sessions of violent movement within a ten-mile radius of the naked ridge.

West Buckland, then and now, was a famous running school. In the autumn and Lent terms there were, in addition to bi-weekly rugby games, early morning P.T., Saturday penal drill for defaulters, and a weekly Cadet Corps parade, a series of testing cross-country events, eight in number, over the tracks and folds of moor and pastureland. They were not the usual, easy-going jog-trots of my day-school days but highly competitive events, averaging three to four miles out and upwards of two miles in. On the outward course whippers-in kept gasping and stitch-tormented laggards closed up. On the home run it was every man for himself, the honour of his house and St. George, or possibly St. Phaidippides with a postscript from Marathon. After one of these events your calves ached abominably and usually to no purpose, for only the first forty into the quad scored points.

If, on a Wednesday or a Saturday half-day you were, through some oversight, not actually participating in a field sport, you were under an obligation to watch a First Fifteen game against a neighbouring town side or visiting team. Bad weather (and up there a blustery day on the plain was a tornado) was no excuse for frowsting in a classroom with a P. G. Wodehouse. Gauleiters flushed the small fry into the open and thereafter patrolled the touchline as official cheer-leaders. Every now and again, as you struggled to shorten your neck against the storm, a cricket stump would prod you in the small of the back and a senior would growl, "*Cheer*, you bastard, *cheer*!" It was as well to respond with the high-pitched and plaintive cry of "Come *alonggg*—school!"

Years later, when Fleet Street split its sides at the expense of the Fascist claques, lining the streets of Rome and Berlin to applaud Mussolini and Hitler, I often wondered if the commentators were men who, as boys, had been numbered among the privileged. If so, they must have forgotten those Banshee wails flung into the wind along touchlines throughout the length and breadth of England. But I never did forget those occasions, having served claque-time myself. I am still astonished when I catch a glimpse of a football-match crowd on TV and reflect that here are men, aye, and women too, who are eager to pay for the privilege of shouting encouragement to players.

The diet at West Buckland in the mid-twenties was equivalent to that served to indigent prisoners in the Debtors' Ward of the Marshalsea, a century before. It included porridge (sugarless if you were low in table seniority), murky toast, strips of meat that would have passed for the boucan eaten by eighteenth-century pirates, potatoes—warts and all, lashings of cabbage, cindered hard-bake, thin custard and scrape, the sole, official issue at six o'clock tea unless you bought extra at the tuckshop. Tuesday was a red-letter day. We had a sausage apiece for breakfast. So was Thursday, but then it was fishcake, and on Saturdays an egg. There was no issue of jam at the final meal of the day and the tea, served in large jugs, was unsweetened. Somehow the privileged thrived on it but the regular arrival of tuck-box parcels may have accounted for the fact that, according to my reports, I grew an inch a term.

I seem to have forgotten penal drill, reserved for classroom defaulters on Saturdays. This was a kind of mobile field punishment, organised on Army lines and I was not to see its like again until, in 1941, I escorted a prisoner to an R.A.F. detention barracks. Each penal mark awarded during the week earned a defaulter fifteen minutes' drill consisting of alternate bursts of hefting an eight-pound First World War rifle and doubling round the quarter-mile circuit of the school buildings. It was an excellent substitute for more conventional training and some of our best athletes emerged from the penal squad, where the same faces appeared every Saturday afternoon.

It might be imagined from the foregoing that life at West Buckland was a purgatory, that growing boys could hardly wait to kiss their hands to the place and scramble aboard the train in search of less strenuous servitude elsewhere, but this is very far from being the case. One or two new boys drifted away after a term or two and were seen no more, but the great majority of my contemporaries can be seen swilling beer and swapping stories at the annual Old Boys' gathering at the school each Whit Monday, when a bar is set up for them in order that they may lubricate their reminiscences. On these occasions they are shown the many improvements in fabric, diet and home comforts, by a new generation of masters, but they are not impressed. It sometimes seems to me that they equate the installation of Aga cookers, a gymnasium, a fire escape and new lavatories with the dissolution of the British Empire. I can only assume that the Anglo-Saxons are a masochistic race, or perhaps the answer to the deeply-rooted affection we all feel for that gaunt huddle of buildings on the Exmoor ridge can be found in *Tom Brown*, particularly in that early part of the book, where Tom reflects on the compensations of the discomfort of an all-night coach ride up to Rugby . . . "the consciousness of silent endurance, so dear to every Englishman, of standing out against something and not giving in".

My own attachment for the high, isolated plateau where I spent the better part of my adolescence is less complicated. I remember it as a series of discoveries, some of them magical, a few frightening, but all of them absorbing to someone with a predisposition to translate observation and experience into word pictures. To cite them all would fill a book but I can recall a few outstanding ones. Bluebells, covering the steeply-angled slopes of a North Devon woodland and a late afternoon sun playing hide-and-seek with the course of the Bray; the pleasant sound of ball snick-snacking on willow, capped by the harsh but somehow reassuring clamour of the school bell swung by a jolly, buck-toothed boy called Shaw, killed in a Lancaster bomber in 1942; the massed pit-pat-pat of rubber shoes—'stinkers' as they were called—on the surface of Exmoor farm-tracks as we ran, two hundred strong, across the folds of the moor; school entertainments, made by us for ourselves alone, including the annual Gilbert and Sullivan opera; a few microscopic triumphs, such as running second in the Senior steeplechase; and rather more egregious failures that provoked laughter, always laughter, that seemed sometimes to have taken permanent residence among all that stone, slate, knotted oak and the ineradicable smell of boiled greens; strings of improbable nicknames and faces to go with them, 'Juicy', 'Bummy', 'Romeo', 'Daffy', 'Waso', 'Bouncer' and 'Legweak'; 'Buster', 'Gobber', 'Tightass', 'Stalliio', 'Beaky', 'Bo' and 'Puddleduck', some of them dead within ten years, and their official names added to an earlier list on the stone cross at the head of the east drive, a majority alive, balding and paunchy with, here and there, a grandson at a greatly enlarged school that has finally rid itself of the smell of boiled greens.

These things and a sense of belonging that was more intimate than the community tug exerted by my home town, an easily detachable segment of life that can be framed in the memory, to hang there until an impersonal nurse draws a sheet over the bed and goes out, closing the door.

Enter Inez

There are certain aspects of the national scene that are so intrinsically English in thought and texture that it is almost impossible to visualize them outside the geographical confines of, say, the seventeenth-century frontiers of England. One such endowment is village cricket. Another is Morris Dancing. A third is the weather gambit in conversations between strangers. A fourth the pact of silence in railway compartments. But none of these, I think, are as esoteric as the Gilbert and Sullivan opera.

I have no doubt that, from time to time, and with the active encouragement of expatriates, professional and amateur companies perform *Iolanthe* in places like Wick, Llandrindod Wells and even Ballynacally, but I am persuaded that attendance at such a performance would leave one with the impression that the locals were not concerned with Mr. Gilbert's libretto and Mr. Sullivan's tinkling tunes so much as with guying the English. It is well known that when the operas were first performed in the eighteen-seventies they were taken down in shorthand and exported without benefit of royalties. In a sense the authors are still victims of this act of piracy, for I cannot but feel that any performance of their work outside the English shires must be a kind of parody. Gilbert and Sullivan operas not only need an English cast, they cannot be relished as they deserve by any but an English audience, and a provincial audience at that.

I was introduced to these delightful entertainments at the age of eleven, when my music-teacher encouraged me to learn excerpts as a variation to the standard 'pieces' we Avenue children practised *ad nauseam* on our upright pianos. Their gaiety and sparkle were so apparent to me that I fairly wore the Bechstein out with fumbling interpretations of 'The Sun Whose Rays Are All Ablaze', 'When Frederick Was A Little Lad', 'Tit-Willow', and the like. I was then taken to see the local amateurs' presentation of *The Pirates of Penzance* and was tremendously impressed, for until then the word 'opera' had made no appeal to me, conjuring up visions of busty women warbling their sorrows and dying men hanging on to their notes to the very brink of the grave. In terms of dullness, operas matched the books of Thackeray, the comedies of Shakespeare, Algebra and Mensuration. The music, the libretto, the strictly stylised stage business and, above all, the ponderously underlined jokes, disposed of my prejudice overnight, so that I was wildly excited on learning, during my first term at West Buckland, that the school operatic society was already auditioning for the Christmas production of *The Gondoliers*, due to be performed in the dining hall on three successive nights towards the close of the autumn term.

It seemed that Gilbert and Sullivan had been long since embodied into the school's tradition and an unbroken succession of their operas had been presented there for a generation. We had no girls, of course, if one discounts the Second Form mistress who was stuck with a leading role whether or not she could sing a note, but we had a surfeit of chubby, pink-cheeked trebles, who could be disguised as fairies, peeresses, sailors' doxies and teetering Japanese maidens. I had small hope of being enlisted in this troupe, if only on account of my spectacles, lack of experience and ineradicable Cockney accent. The headmaster, however, who was producer and chief motivator of these occasions, possessed a kind heart and noticed my disappointment at the audition. With the best will in the world, he admitted, he could not see me tripping along in a bonnet on the arm of a gondolier but was willing to try me out in the part of Inez, the aged nurse, who makes a single appearance at the very end of the second act in order to identify Luiz, the royal changeling.

I was, I recall, speechless with gratitude, for Inez, with lines of her own, was reckoned a cut above the chorus. True, she remained on stage no more than three minutes, but everyone was obliged to pay strict attention to her announcement for it was the climax of the entertainment.

I sang the lines and was given the part, the music master undertaking to coach me in certain vowel sounds in order that the audience did not leave the hall with the impression that Inez had been born within the sound of Bow Bells.

I did not find the long waits in the wings tedious. Sitting there, awaiting my nightly cue, I soon learned every word and every trill of the book. I could have prompted any one of the cast and, if necessary, corrected their gestures. By the time Christmas approached I was probably more familiar with the piece than its authors had been the night after their initial triumph at the Savoy, in 1889.

When the costume hampers arrived from London I was delighted with mine, a voluminous green silk skirt, innumerable petticoats, a lace mob cap worn over a heavy grey wig, an apron and a crooked stick as the badge of extreme age. The only fault I could find in the outfit was the size of the wig, designed for a roundheaded adult. During final rehearsals it tended to slip forward over the lenses of my glasses so that we had to fix it at the back with a strip of adhesive tape. The mob cap, however, was securely pinned and moved with it, so that I did not think the misfit would be noticed from the auditorium.

Neither was it at the dress rehearsal, witnessed only by boys, although hints reached the make-up man that, concerning me, he ought to employ his ingenuity to bridge the gap between fourteen and eighty. He did his best, experimenting on me for half an hour before rise of curtain on the first night, adding a wrinkle here, a pouch there and blacking out most of my teeth. I don't know whether he was satisfied with his work but I knew that I was. The reflection in the fly-spotted swing-mirror reminded me instantly of Garghoul, the wizened old witch in *King Solomon's Mines*.

There was, unhappily, no accommodation behind stage for dressing-rooms. Robing and make-up had to be carried out on the top floor of the headmaster's house, immediately adjoining the hall, and to reach the stage the chorus, and bit players like myself, had to descend three flights of slate steps, cross the open forecourt, enter the dining hall by a back door and climb a step-ladder into the wings. The only real difficulty this presented lay in timing, particularly for me, due to appear within minutes of the final curtain when the entire company were safely on stage. Thus I was left to nurse my stage fright in isolation as the second act unfolded and it seemed very lonely up there, with a south-westerly competing with the strains of the music coming up the stairwell. I stood on the landing listening, reckoning to allow myself a good five minutes to descend, cross the forecourt, pick my way through the clutter behind stage and take my place in the wings for my entrance.

I must have miscalculated the passage of minutes or the place in the score, for suddenly I was seized by a dreadful panic that I would miss the entrance and the consequences of this were too awful to be contemplated. Without bunching my skirt and petticoats I dashed down the slippery stairs and the next thing I recall was retrieving wig and cap at the foot of the first flight and wondering who had been base enough to hit me over the head with a pickaxe handle. Having fallen head over heels down a flight of fifteen slate stairs my confusion was understandable. Not only was I stunned and winded but bleeding at both knees.

I must have sat there several minutes, canvassing my system, nursing my wig and cap, and trying to recollect the reason for the urgency of my descent. Then, with a sense of doom, it came to me on the strains of the music below, and I realised the climax of *The Gondoliers* was approaching with the certainty I associated with Judgement Day. Every note, every word, brought me that much closer to absenteeism and it seemed to me preferable to die here on the landing than go down in school legend as the new boy who had ruined the 1926 opera. I must have negotiated the remaining flights and crossed the forecourt by instinct. Perhaps the sleet driving in from the moor revived me, for I recall the tremendous surge of relief when, on reaching the wings, I picked up the lilt of the chorus and realised that I had minutes in hand. Kindly hands took the outsize wig and cap I was still clutching and placed it firmly on my head but no one bothered with the tab of adhesive tape. Seconds later I was on stage, leaning far more gratefully upon the stick than any authentic pensioner but able to point, with quivering finger, at the changeling Luiz, and identify him for the benefit of the assembled company and two hundred schoolfellows perched on tiers of dining tables in the body of the hall. I croaked my lines and heard the weighted curtain swish down. I edged forward with the dramatis personae and made, not a curtsey but a low bow. It was my ultimate misjudgement that evening. As the curtain rose again its corner-weight brushed my forehead, whisking wig and mob cap into the orchestra pit, but

I did not associate the gale of laughter with myself. It was the due, I thought, of Messrs. Gilbert and Sullivan.

The following year, my voice having fortuitously broken whilst practising the tones of the toothless Inez, I made the male chorus in *H.M.S. Pinafore* and was among the company invited to open the new Town Hall at Dulverton with a gala performance. The occasion was not without incident. The scenery, designed for our dining hall, was a poor fit and during a vigorous sailors' hornpipe one of the largest flats, representing a turret and an eighteen-inch naval gun, fell on us, dispersing us as effectively as a broadside. We crawled out, raised the turret and carried on. Judging by their applause the audience accepted the mishap as an unrehearsed piece of stage business but the shame of the moment lives with me yet and prejudiced me against further personal involvement in light opera. From then on, and with increasing enjoyment as I grew older, I was content to sit and watch, and as a reporter with a large provincial beat I had more opportunities to indulge myself than did D'Oyly Carte in his heyday. I suppose I must have seen *The Mikado* thirty times and its runner-up *The Pirates* almost as frequently. Ordinarily it was a chore I never sought to evade but honesty compels me to admit to a qualification as regards the addiction. Whenever I am in the stalls, witnessing the second act of *The Gondoliers*, and the moment is approaching when Inez is due to make her arthritic way down left to centre to identify the changeling, I rise and steal away, as though to catch the last bus. The fear that she will muff her entrance, and leave us all in permanent suspense, is too compelling to be endured. I prefer to leave, taking her timely appearance on trust.

Under the Cloche Hat

I

West Buckland, like every school of its kind, was necessarily a monastic establishment. Ordinarily we did not so much as exchange speculative glances with an eligible female from the time we boarded the train at our nearest main station, until the moment we were dumped there thirteen weeks later, on the first day of the holidays.

A very great deal has been written concerning the enclosed aspect of public school life, with emphasis on the sinister atmosphere segregation of this kind is likely to produce. In the interests of truth I have to state that I saw no evidence at all of homosexuality during my schooldays. Maybe I was lucky. Or maybe it was so exposed on that high, windy ridge that romantic friendships withered in the Exmoor downdraught before they could mature. There was, I recall, a little innocent ragging about associations between seniors and juniors, but I would take my oath they fell far short of the charges levelled at larger, more famous schools in the last few years, mostly, I suspect, by memoir writers and novelists with a hopeful eye on the best-seller lists. A majority of the two hundred-odd adolescents with whom I shared this period were hard at work cultivating more conventional relationships through the post with schoolgirls encountered during the holidays, and there was often a pooling of experience arising from a communal recognition of handwriting when letters in a girlish hand (sometimes in scented envelopes) were flipped the length of the breakfast table when mail was distributed. A little blonde who was writing regularly to me would use a large, blue envelope with heavy gold edging and the entire house grew interested in her, supposing her to be a person of some consequence on this account. Her letters usually arrived on my plate spotted with prefects' porridge.

The secretive among us would make great efforts to evade this kind of publicity but there were others who took pleasure in boasting of their conquests, displaying photographs and sometimes reading their letters aloud. I sometimes wondered if this happened at girls' boarding schools, and the unworthy thought did something to moderate the tone of the protestations I despatched to various quarters of the realm.

In the main, I think, we idealised women. Jokes and quips of the cruder variety were usually reserved for masters' wives, or the odd young woman, buxom, red-faced and broad of beam, whom we met in the farmyards within easy walking distance of the school. We tended to think of girls our own age as fragile, ethereal beings, like the heroines in paintings by the Pre-Raphaelites, and in this sense we were a long way behind the times. As I was to discover within a few months of leaving school, the girl of the nineteen-twenties was anything but ethereal but the discovery, once you adjusted to it, was a relief. They were, in fact, a lively, vivacious, captivating, capricious breed, and the collective word for them—'flapper'—suited them very well.

The high noon of the flapper lasted for about a decade, from the early 'twenties until the early 'thirties, after which the genus suddenly disappeared, like the unfashionable bosom of the period. Somehow the flapper was unable to survive the frenetic period of the mid and late 'thirties, when Hitler went on the rampage, and the young became gloomily obsessed with politics.

Few under twenty gave a damn about politics until the Slump of 1931. All through the 'twenties the teenagers I met were content to live each day as a separate existence, and this despite a shortage of jobs and a standard of wages that would bring industry to a standstill today. Rightly so, I might add, for everywhere one looked in those days one saw injustice and inequality of the kind that threw a shadow over the late Victorian and Edwardian eras. Despite this, however, there was an air of flirtatious triviality, and a zest for the passing moment, that seems to have deserted us all in an era when the young enjoy licences that would have appalled their parents forty years ago. Whenever I hear that protest song, the one that fathered so many successors, I am tempted to add a verse beginning, 'Where has all the gaiety gone . . . ?'

. . .

I remember them all so well, those cloche-hatted flappers, epitomised by the Hollywood 'It' girl, Clara Bow, on whom the latecomers modelled themselves. They were the first generation in the West who could walk abroad wearing make-up without being regarded as tarts, the first to have made available to them a supply of cheap, ready-made garments that had dash, style and individuality, the first, probably, who would cheerfully date a boyfriend without thought of marriage. They were thus social pioneers but pioneers without a specific goal or a cause, and this made any kind of association with them exciting, colourful and inconsequential. Their skirts, after 1926, were nearly as brief as the micro-mini-skirt of the late nineteen-sixties, and they had, as a rule, pretty, twinkling legs, even if their shape as a whole was odd by today's standards, losing its sex-appeal an inch above the bottom to become rather squarish and sexless as far as the shoulders.

This, of course, was due to the abdication of the pinched waist and the bosom, so dear to their mothers and grandmothers. From around 1926, until the early nineteen-thirties, there wasn't a waist or a bosom to be found outside a graveyard, where they were the prerogative of smug-looking angels perched on expensive marble tombstones. The popular dresses of the period fell in a straight line to the hips, and if your appraisal of a flapper had been limited to her middle section you might just as well have been looking at a boy.

This boyish look was emphasised by the frantic shearing of tresses that began about 1924. First the bob, considered recklessly daring by its innovators (I knew a girl who cried all night after submitting to the scissors), then the shingle, that removed nearly all the hair from the back of the head, and finally, in 1926, the Eton Crop, that was not so popular as its two forerunners. Later on a reaction to the Eton Crop introduced the pageboy bob, with hair combed straight down and curled under in a roll, and a year or so after that the long bob, the last individual hairstyle of the genuine flapper. In all the styles the fringe was popular and sometimes the Victorian kiss-curl, added as an afterthought. Long boots, when they became popular in the mid-sixties, were reckoned kinky but they were no more than a revival of the 'Russian' boots worn by many of the flappers and wholly approved by the male. Within this overall framework, however, there were many sub-styles that had their day, sometimes quite a long day. One, I recall, was the pinafore frock, usually worn with a beret. Another was the bolero. A third was the sunray skirt, with its galaxy of pleats.

The flapper had absolutely no pretensions about being devious, intelligent or ambitious, and herein, I think, lay her charm. She was content to be feminine and made the very most of her physical endowments, with no specific aim other than to attract a man physically and encourage him to make the running. Looking back, their renunciation of all other designs seems at one with the Victorian girl but this was the only thing they had in common with their grandmothers. They knew and cared nothing about what was going on outside the world of sheet-music, the fashion houses, scandal in high places and, to a degree, the internal combustion engine. Very few of them bothered with books or newspapers but they devoured an avalanche of twopenny magazines and usually had one protruding from the outer flap of their patent leather handbags. They used a great deal of slang and the words they used sound very archaic today. A film was a 'flick' and a fast operator was 'mustard' who 'qualified for the Wandering Hand Society'. Words like 'topping' and 'spiffing' signified their approval but I do not recall their equivalent for 'square' or 'grotty'. Mostly they left their sentences unfinished for want of a terminal point, their enthusiasm boosting them from one subject to another in a series of short, breathless rushes. In short, if you were looking for a soul-mate among them you were wasting good mating time. They believed vaguely in God but would have shown embarrassment if you mentioned Him or His works. Parsons made them giggle. They were inclined to switch on an aggrieved expression if you tried to test their political opinions, as if politics were slightly indecent in mixed company. They were all excellent ballroom dancers but very few of them could drive or swim, although they enjoyed pillion-riding and prancing about beaches in skirted, one-piece bathing costumes. In every way they went to great lengths to proclaim their new freedoms but there is a curious contradiction here for they responded warmly to old-fashioned courtesies on the part of the male and were overwhelmed if you sent them flowers or a poem or a thinly-disguised Valentine card. A verse or two of homemade poetry, composed in their honour, was almost certain to advance your cause and they were alert to good manners and chivalric displays in public. For all that there were very few fools among them and the great majority knew precisely how many beans made five when it came to dispensing favours after dark. I would say that they occupied a position exactly halfway between their Victorian ancestors and the young women of today who proclaim their sex liberation almost nightly on television.

2

She was walking slowly along the esplanade on a Good Friday reconnaissance, grey beret perched at a provocative angle over her right ear. Her dark hair swept in a smooth curve down the other side of her face, the 'Pola Negri' or 'Vamp' style, that was in vogue about the time I quitted the Exmoor monastery and began to look about me and see what I had been missing up there. I had not had sufficient time to learn the conventional gambits so she willingly helped me out, as flappers usually did with beginners. She approached me and demanded to know the time.

We went down the slipway and along the deserted beach, exchanging titbits of information about ourselves, and she gave me careful instructions where to be at a certain time in the vicinity of her home that same evening, adding that I was not, on any account, to show myself but was to use the cover offered by her father's macrocarpa hedge.

This throws into relief a curious technique the flapper used on these occasions. She liked to pretend to herself that she was still lumbered with a chaperon, that watchful parents were jealously concerned for her honour, as though she was contemplating elopement with a fortune-hunting scoundrel. It was pure fiction, of course. Even in the mid-twenties the new freedoms were beginning to have an impact on parents but the pretence added spice to assignations.

I met her at the appointed hour and we walked out of range of the macrocarpa, exchanging rather formal kisses modelled on the silent film close-ups we had studied, and endearments borrowed from the same medium. Then she did a curious thing that went some way to erasing the Pre-Raphaelite image I had of young women up to that period. Solemnly, almost ritualistically, she shed one of her beaded garters, presenting it to me as a keepsake and a reminder of our first meeting and doing it so artlessly that it would have seemed preposterous to put an improper construction on the gift.

It was, as I see now, a typical flapper gesture, proclaiming not wantonness but liberation and I accepted it clumsily, wondering anxiously where I could conceal it when I arrived home. I wish I knew what became of that green, beaded garter. It would qualify as an interesting period-exhibit now that garters have followed the farthingale.

Betty, the first of them as far as I was concerned, had her declaration of independence, symbolised by her beaded garter, but they all had something original to offer. That is to say, they did not rely exclusively on their charm, plus a few shillings' worth of cosmetics, a 'Pola Negri' hairstyle, and an off-the-peg jumper suit or pinafore frock. They put as much imagination into the business of projecting themselves as a modern commercial concern buying time on television. They each had a gimmick.

The word was not in circulation in those days but it must have been on the etymological drawing-board for it is by their individual gimmicks, woven into the pattern of their several personalities, that I distinguish them one from the other. What they had to sell was very marketable at that time – gaiety, infectious optimism, and any number of lighthearted embraces and stylised end-of-film kisses. Seldom much more but we, their escorts, did not quarrel with this. It was that kind of society in the late 'twenties. We weren't out looking for trouble and a deep emotional involvement meant trouble on an impossibly low budget, so that although we were well aware the flappers were leading us up the garden path we did not hold it against them when they slammed the summer-house door.

Muriel's gimmick (I wrote of her at some length in *For My Own Amusement*) was a shy, downcast glance that passed for modesty among those but slightly acquainted with her, but she had something far more practical in reserve. It was her mother's hard, shiny, imitation-leather couch, a mute but extremely vigilant chaperon on the occasions you were invited into the front-parlour after a dance at the Church Hall or Institute. I swear that couch was human. As long as you conducted yourself like a gentleman it stayed neutral, but at the least show of ardour it projected you straight on to the floor, the rapid movement inevitably reducing romance to farce. Muriel was, of course, well aware of this and exploited the propellent properties of that couch shamelessly. So, I think, must Sweeny Todd have regarded his barber's chair, an ultimate in secret weapons.

Gwen was more sophisticated. She could play ragtime and although she was very pretty, and fairly forthcoming under the stars, my tenderest recollections of her were not, as one might imagine, the moments we danced together, or sat out in the Plantation, but the occasions when she asked you into the house, sat down and rattled off 'Old Nebraska', 'Valencia' and 'Swannee' on her upright piano. She had a way of looking at you over her shoulder as her fingers skimmed the keys, and although her glance might be said to have contained promise, it was veiled in mockery. She was using that piano to keep you at arms' length. In my mind's eye I can never picture Gwen without her walnut piano, just as I can never see Muriel out of range of her slippery couch.

Cis and Kathy had colour fixations. I cannot recall Cis ever appearing in anything but pink, or Kathy wearing anything but royal purple. Cis was one of the few flappers who did not succumb to the beret but went right on wearing a cloche hat beyond the turn of the decade. They were usually of pink straw or velour and they suited her very well for she was a dainty little brunette, with fine brown eyes. The hat acted as a kind of arbour from which she could survey you without committing herself. Kathy always looked regal in her purple dance-frocks and was more dress-conscious than most flappers. She was an expert dancer and anxious to teach you all the latest steps, showing the greatest forbearance when you steered her into a collision or stood on her toes.

Perhaps the most authentic flapper I ever consorted with, however, was Esther, who insisted on spelling her name Esta. Esta had gone to tremendous pains to absorb the 'Pola Negri–Theda Bara–Clara Bow' techniques, for she somehow succeeded in combining the nonchalance of the vamps and the allure of the famous 'It' girl. The circumstances of our first meeting are typical of the way Esta went about things. She was standing on the pier, propped against one of those machines that stamp names on strips of tin. Her dark hair ('Bible-black' Dylan Thomas would have called it) was Marcel waved, and the undulations were exposed by the extreme tilt of the almost inevitable grey beret, in her case worn so far back on her head that it was in danger of falling into the sea. It was an obvious ploy on my part to set the pointer, stamp my name, and then pretend to ignorance as to how one extracted the strip of tin from the machine. When, in her estimation, a sufficient number of seconds had elapsed, and she had subjected me to a careful and expressionless scrutiny, she reached out very slowly, pulled the ejector lever and smiled. It was the smile of a tolerant mother indulging an enterprising three-year-old. It was also the beginning of a very rewarding holiday.

Esta had set her heart on a Decca gramophone and to get it she was obliged to assemble a thousand Kensitas coupons. That first day she enlisted me in the crusade and I smoked Kensitas, much against my will, for close on a year, after which she wrote and told me she was deeply committed to a boy working in Germany and the correspondence between us must now cease. I could never decide whether this decision on her part was dictated by the fact that she was in love or by the arrival of the long-awaited Decca gramophone.

3

I was relatively inexperienced then and still had a great deal to learn about flappers and flapper techniques but I was an earnest pupil and I enjoyed my work. One of the first things that impressed me about their techniques was the gap between promise and performance. The flapper pulled out all the stops except the essential ones, so that one never lost the impression, even in the company of the boldest among them that, whilst they worked hard at persuading you they regarded mother's advice and the gipsy's warning as old hat, one was left in no doubt that they had pondered and approved both. This provided them with a kind of yardstick to measure the dishonourable intentions of every man in the world and rarely failed them in an emergency. They would, for instance, never venture beyond a couple of small ports, or one glass of rough cider, and they had a way of classifying their escorts into categories, all the way down from the too ardent to the impossibly dull. For someone who had spent three years in the exclusive company of males it was a testing apprenticeship and conclusions about the way in which the feminine mind worked were hard to come by. Gradually, however, one learned by trial and error and it was an enriching experience, particularly for someone like me, bent on earning a living by writing fiction. And because I still live within a few miles of the parks, lanes, beaches, cliff walks, sea-front shelters and front-parlours where all these encounters occurred forty years ago, there has been for me a rewarding bonus. Every now and again, in a surge around a Christmas counter, in a supermarket, on a station platform, or in a crowded café, I see a face I can identify, the face of one of those adorable flappers, and a glimpse of any one of them leads me to contemplate what the newspaper and TV pundits call The Generation Gap. It occurs to me then that this too is an illusion, for the gap is so certain to close that there is no profit whatever in making a song and dance about it. For there they are, these quietly-spoken, well-dressed, carefully corseted grandmothers, buying toys or cereals or raspberry sundaes for grandchildren, or seeing grown sons and daughters aboard the London train. Sometimes we exchange greetings or a half-smile but not often, for our associations were brief and none of us were concerned with putting down roots at that time. It is best, I think, to savour the past without exhuming it, to hear behind the clatter of café china and the hiss of the departing Golden Hind, the toot of saxophone and the click of heel-taps on frosty pavements, when these elegant matriarchs were bobbed and shingled and babbling happily about topping bands and the spiffing time they had had at the British Legion dance.

It is in the frame of the dance hall that I remember them best as they were when I had hair on my head, for it was there that their spirits soared like champagne corks and promised romantic ecstasies through an eternity of youth. The one thing that puzzles me about them is the location of the moment in time when their transformation began, when they stopped being flappers and began to train as matriarchs. Perhaps it was the day the last notes of the Jazz Age were drowned in the diatribes of the Führer and the vapourings of the Duce. Or perhaps it was the day they fell in love.

4

As I say, the cult of flappery did not long survive the Great Slump. Pola Negri and Clara Bow passed into legend. Tilted berets, cloche hats, bobs and shingles went out of fashion, to become symbols of the Charleston era. Skirts came down below the knee, to remain there, alas, for a whole generation and then soar again like the end of a long night. But here and there a lonely flapper survived, recognisable by her glances, her mixture of pertness and archness and, above all, by her techniques in beguiling men. It was my destiny to meet one in dramatic circumstances on a warm summer night in the year 1941, by which time the flapper had become almost as dated as the Victorian masher.

I was hitch-hiking back to an R.A.F. camp in the Midlands after an unauthorised weekend leave. Because I had no pass the time-factor was important and traffic was disappointingly light. To increase my anxiety, some idiot in the Tewkesbury area inadvertently rang a church bell and church bells in those days signified invasion. There I was, forty miles south of my station, without a pass and likely to qualify as a deserter when Nazis parachuted into the shire. At last a car stopped and offered me a lift to within a mile or two of my camp and I scrambled in very gratefully. It was driven by a young civilian and his passenger was a very pretty girl whose angled beret reminded me of happier days. The young man was one of those motorists out to prove something—perhaps a belief in their own immortality—by driving at high speed on sidelights but it was a brilliantly moonlit night and we made good progress until we ran between a belt of trees into deep shadow. Here, before he could switch on his masked headlights, we collided head on with a herd of cows straying on the highway.

The impact was savage. One cow was killed and another injured. The car was badly damaged and the driver and myself stumbled around in a dazed condition, wondering how to set about clearing the road. For a few moments neither of us were much concerned with the girl, but then we saw her, wandering unconcernedly around the wreckage. She was humming snatches of a currently popular musical comedy song and seemed totally detached from the incident, as though she had been a spectator rather than a passenger in the car. "The radiator has taken a frightful beating," she announced, cheerfully. And then, "Silly cows."

Her detachment was fatal to the driver's self-control. He blurted out that the car had been borrowed from his father's garage without permission and that the wounded cow in the ditch was not alone in needing the service of a humane-killer. I thought the girl would be touched but she wasn't. All she said in reply was, "There's a lane there leading to a farm. These will be that farmer's cows. We'll roust him out and get some transport. It's getting a bit late, isn't it?"

Her self-possession hypnotised me. I went with her down the lane beyond the trees and into a brilliant patch of moonlight where she stopped and fumbled with her handbag. "Derek's sweet but upset," she said. "Could you hold this a moment?" and I found myself angling a pencil torch and a hand-mirror whilst she applied fresh lipstick. Comment and action were so typical of the flapper that I felt myself whirled back to 1928 and was not in the least surprised when she tucked her arm cosily through mine, squeezed my hand, and drew me on towards the farm buildings. I wasn't sure what was expected of me. It seemed to me hard on Derek that he should wreck his father's car and lose his girl-friend to a stray airman all in one night, and a moonlit night at that, but I soon discovered she was far more concerned with her strategy than with me. She said, as we knocked on the farmhouse door, "Don't say a word about the cows. Not yet."

The farmer appeared with his pyjama jacket tucked into his trousers and she flashed him a smile that would have compensated any man alive for the inconvenience of being dragged from sleep at two a.m.

"We've had a slight accident," she said, "back on the main road. Nobody hurt. Could we use your 'phone?"

The man said he would brew some tea and as soon as he had disappeared into the kitchen she lifted the receiver and asked for a number. It struck me as curious that she should have the number of the local policeman so pat but not nearly so odd as her greeting when the callee came on the line. She said, in a soft, dear-old-bean voice, "*Keith*, darling? Sorry to spoil your beauty sleep but I'm in a jam. I've pranged about half a mile south of the 'Haymaker'. Be a cherub and fetch me, there's a dear." She listened for a moment and then replaced the receiver. "He'll be along in twenty minutes. I'll see to the tea while you ring the policeman. Tell him to bring a butcher with a humane-killer." She drifted away while I made the call. The policeman was less co-operative than Keith.

I suppose, until then, I had misjudged her, assuming that I would be the one to explain to the hospitable farmer the true nature of the accident back at the spot where Derek was contemplating suicide. When we had finished our tea, however, she said, equably, "Thank you. That was lovely. It was cows, straying all over the road. Black and white cows. They materialised out of nowhere . . ." The farmer did not wait for her to finish. He shouted "Jesus Christ!" and was gone in a flash. We heard his gumboots thumping on the surface of the lane and when the sound had died away she said, in the same equable voice, "Poor Derek. He seems *so* upset. Come along then, I shall insist Keith runs you back to camp. What a lovely night, isn't it?"

She tucked her arm through mine in the cosiest manner and we went out and down the lane to the main road. Lights and figures were bobbing about and there was a continuous rumble of conversation. Keith arrived five minutes later and the girl and I jammed ourselves into his two-seater. Derek did not accompany us. He had business with the policeman and said good-bye ruefully. The girl blew him a kiss. Another typically flapper gesture.

The Mandarins

In the early summer of 1929, with the world slump just over the horizon, I joined the staff of *The Exmouth Chronicle*, my father's weekly newspaper, as general reporter and sparetime ledger clerk. Times were hard and my starting salary was five shillings a week, plus a withheld thirty more for board and lodging at home.

It seems, looking back, a modest sum, even for those pinch-penny days, but my father had not learned the knack of adjusting to the passage of years. To him the value of money was static and had he owned a vineyard he would have paid for labour at the rate of a penny a day, citing Holy Writ as a precedent. I was seventeen then, and he had gone out to work at twelve for about the same weekly sum as I received. His views concerning money survived another world war. Even in the early 'fifties it was difficult to persuade him that five pounds a week did not put a man in the supertax bracket.

At that time father was fifty-five and his obsession with the game of bowls coincided with a conviction that forty-three years of steady toil is as much as can be expected from a human being. He opted out, transferring the paper to me as though it had been a bicycle that required to be kept in reasonable running order, and I like to think this was a manifestation of faith in my latent ability as a journalist. Doubts regarding this, however, continue to linger in the mind. More probably he never gave a thought to the dangers and complexities of placing his destiny in the hands of a youth so utterly lacking in experience. The prospect of a libel suit had never cost him a moment's sleep. He had been walking hand-in-hand with libel and slander ever since he entered local politics at the age of twenty-one. By 1929 he and they were boon companions.

I learned by trial and error, the only way anyone can learn to be a newspaperman, and sometimes the element of error brought me within hailing distance of disaster. More often, however, it brought me into conflict with the local mandarins for, whereas it was easy to learn the rules of evidence whilst attending sessions at the local Magistrates' Court, it was very difficult indeed to acquaint myself with the sensitive areas of the fifty-odd individuals who ranked as mandarins. They all had an Achilles' heel and it was essential when interviewing them, or reporting their speeches, to know what would enlist them as patrons and what would incur their wrath. I soon learned to identify them and set about studying them in detail, a technique now discernible among stalwarts who interview national mandarins on television. In those days, however, there was little in common between Fleet Street men and small-town provincials like myself. The Fleetstreeter could be, and often was, very cavalier with human material, basing his style on story value. The provincial-based reporter had to live with the people he wrote about and I was never able to convey this sober fact to London news-editors, who sometimes employed me on local stories that made national headlines.

I recall one occasion when an agency sent me to interview the son of a millionaire, whose father had just died in the Channel Islands, leaving a relatively untaxed fortune. The beneficiary, not unnaturally, refused to confirm that his father was a selfish capitalist, who had made his money in Britain and then escaped to Jersey to ensure that it did not find its way back to the Chancellor of the Exchequer, but he knew me by my Christian name and consented to give me an interview on the plans he had for building a model farm. In the morning an account of the interview, cunningly slanted to coincide with a newspaper's initial policy-line, made original reading, particularly for me, the alleged source. The dead millionaire was pilloried once again and not a word concerning the model farm appeared in print.

For the next few days I waited for the mine to explode and sure enough it did, at a local charity ball, where the new millionaire was the principal guest. We met one another in a crowded dressing-room and pointing a derisory finger at me he roared, "Look at him! The Yellow Press lapdog! A scoundrel who would sell a fellow-townsman for thirty pieces of silver!" It took me nearly a year, and the offices of several mutual friends, to get on speaking terms with him again, and talk him

6

into subscribing to our local relief fund for the Gresford Colliery disaster.

Confrontations of this kind were rare but during my apprenticeship period it was all too easy to tread on a mandarin's tail and start a chain reaction. The only certain way of avoiding trouble was to familiarise oneself with the full range of local eccentricities and foibles, to discover what made each mandarin tick and write accordingly.

In one of the best of his many short stories about English provincial life the novelist H. E. Bates describes a journalist's endeavours to examine, run down and expose the true character of a local worthy. The story is called *The Late Public Figure* and has, for me, great authenticity. The journalist's discoveries in this particular case were unflattering, and I would not like to imply that all our local mandarins had feet of clay. But the comparison is there nonetheless, for each one of them had a public face and a real face. If, like me, you sat at their feet for more than a decade, you could while many tedious hours away making guesses at the thoughts that were passing through their heads whilst the rhetoric poured from their mouths. You could do more than this. Soon you could see them as they had appeared to their schoolfellows forty-odd years before, how they were regarded by their families, and then make a guess at how much they were likely to tip waitresses who did not know them. The sum total of these informed guesses was rewarding, for sometimes you could assess them as fallible human beings instead of self-inflated figureheads, comic turns, or the platitudinous old bores that they sometimes seemed in public. As the years passed I mellowed towards them and when, one by one, they died, I was genuinely sorry. A Micawber, a Pickwick or a Quilp had been lost to me. Here and there, as I grew older, I made friends with survivors for, by then, I had come to understand that they did what they did, not, as I had once assumed, from motives of self-aggrandisement, but from an instinctive desire to serve that lies buried in most Englishmen, particularly Englishmen rooted in the shires.

. . .

I can think of three who seem to me fairly representative of the kind of men who ran our town in those days and I see them as standard-bearers for one or other of the sectors of town life I chronicled, day in day out, for twelve years. There were many such sectors but those of local government, good works, and the Church were three of the most important and often overlapped from my point of view.

There were, at that time, eighteen urban district Councillors who conducted a monthly public meeting round the horseshoe table, presided over by the Chairman, our substitute for a mayor, and guided in their duties by the Town Clerk, with some assistance from the Town Surveyor and the Chief Financial Officer. The Councillors were divided into what I always thought of as progressives, who wanted the town to expand, and diehards, mostly retired residents, who opposed all changes. Collisions between these factions provided me with a monthly headline. Tremendous heat was generated round that horseshoe table from time to time and the controversies, at this distance, look absurdly parochial. Should the railings round the Strand Enclosure be removed or strengthened? Should the tank and guns remain on the esplanade as a permanent reminder of the town's contribution to victory in 1918? Should we change over from gaslight in the streets to electric power?

The dynamic champion of change on all these occasions was the one member of the Council who proclaimed himself a working man, a van-driver by profession, and an unrepentant Socialist in days when British Socialists were suspected of being financed by the Kremlin. His name was Bert Humphries and he was a delightful character from my viewpoint, for he provoked any number of civic shouting matches, with the Chairman banging away with his gavel in a vain attempt to restore order and dignity to the chamber. Bert, however, did not have a spark of malice in his make-up and was always prepared to shake hands with all his opponents after the meeting. Chubby-faced, given to extravagant practical jokes, and inclined to corpulence even as a young man, he was Devon born and bred, and possessed a curiously offbeat West Country accent. He was the only man in town familiar with political theory and threatened us with the arrival of a Socialist millennium by 1940, at the latest 1941. Snatches of his genial rhetoric return to me: ". . . Milyons of workin' men won't be denied their rights . . ." "Here we are, back where we started out, time o' the universal franchise . . ." and sometimes, egged on by a sense of innocent fun, he would exaggerate his dialect, beat his chest and bellow, "You all know who I be! I'm 'Pudden' Humphries, born in the shadow of the gasworks!"

From the first I believed Bert to have a future in the national Socialist party and I was right. After countless *mêlées* in the Council chamber, exchanges that he always described, with his broad, schoolboy grin, as 'spuddles', after innumerable victories on behalf of the locally oppressed, he gravitated to Union officialdom and became a West Country organiser on behalf of the Transport and General Workers' Union. He survived all his onetime opponents and attended all their funerals, genuinely regretting their demise, for he esteemed them not only as fellow townsmen but as targets. He was, I suppose, an old-fashioned Socialist even then, for his ultimate loyalty was to his home town rather than Transport House. I recall some of his elaborate practical jokes, as when he organised the erection, on an open field facing a row of select, detached houses, of a huge board painted with the legend, 'Site of Hi-Wun-Lung's New Chinese Laundry'. It was accepted at face value by all the residents who at once organised a petition and presented it to the estate office officials responsible for administering the land in question.

I was once the victim of one of Bert's practical jokes. He bribed a boy to bring in a small ad., offering for sale a parrot owned by a local sea-captain. The bird was alleged to be a non-stop talker, answering to the name of Polly, who turned out to be not a parrot but the sea-captain's garrulous wife of the same name. The captain, whose address was given, was extremely abusive when the paper went on sale and Bert, hovering in the background, delighted in the blasphemous threats he directed towards me and the staff of the *Chronicle*.

A mandarin cast in a very different mould was Major Arnold, a small, shuffling, walrus-moustached ex-regular officer, who somehow got himself elected to both the Council and the Magisterial Bench. The Major was the most uninhibited elder among our city fathers and some of his antics, performed with a curious innocence, set the town in an uproar. His election address was a minor classic and I wish I could quote it in full but I recall only that it began: "I was wounded at Dargai. They got me through the liver in the first rush. Vote for the old soldier who has fought and bled for his King and country . . ."

The Major was not a success in the Council Chamber. Mostly he looked as though he was asleep, and dreaming of Afghan rushes and Sikh counter-attacks in the Swat Valley, but he was a never-ending source of entertainment on the Bench, for he contrived to give the impression that all the business conducted there was make-believe, that cases could be shrugged off when it was time for a chota peg, or when sounds of something more entertaining drifted into the court from the street outside. I remember once, during a long and intricate motoring case, when a dozen witnesses were resolutely engaged in a lying-match concerning speeds and skidmarks, the skirl of bagpipes was heard and the Major, who had seemed to be sound asleep, braced himself and suddenly vacated the chairman's seat. A witness, understandably baffled by this abrupt movement, stopped in mid-sentence, and the eyes of everyone present followed the Major's purposeful shuffle the length of the magisterial dais to the window, where he drew aside the curtain. "Dagenham Girl Pipers!" he announced, with the slow smile of a gratified child and then, shuffling back to his seat and nodding at the witness, "Carry on, carry on!" It was only after the gale of laughter had subsided that I recalled that the Gordon Highlanders had played a prominent part in the battle for Dargai in Victoria's Jubilee year and that the Major had gone down in the first rush.

The Major often employed this sort of gambit to relieve the deadly tedium of the petty sessional court and we were always pleased to see him slumped on the Bench. One day an application for an affiliation order had occupied us throughout the morning and part of the afternoon, the respondent resisting all attempts on the part of a shoal of witnesses (including two Peeping Toms and a mother-in-law elect) to saddle him with the paternity of the child. I am inclined to think the Major missed even the spicy bits concerning waving grass, the parlour couch and the alleged exchange of whispered endearments, but he opened his dormouse eyes as the respondant's solicitor announced, "That's my case, Your Worship," and sat down. The Major then blinked three times and said, aggressively. "We find defendant guilty. Any previous convictions?"

Bert and the Major qualified as light relief in the routine of filling an eight-page newspaper once a week but there were mandarins whose long, rambling speeches, and sustained avalanche of platitudes, sometimes kept us imprisoned in hall or committee room for two hours before we could extract from the meeting a single paragraph embodying the decision. By far the most long-winded of these was the wealthy owner of a chain of stores who had retired from business to devote himself to good works. He was earnest, plump, pale and beaky, so that he looked like a benign owl when he was pecking through his notes and he covered a very wide front indeed. Wherever you went in search of copy he was sure to be there, usually in the chair, and as he was a generous subscriber to dozens of local causes we were obliged to suffer him gladly, especially if the causes he supported brought printing orders into the office. I recall him particularly because of a certain irony that attended his funeral.

The cortège started out from his home, a large house at the top of a narrow drive that gave on to a busy and equally narrow thoroughfare. I ran a hooded Austin Seven in those days and its engine had as many eccentricities as the mandarins. For a reason I cannot recall, all the local pressmen, with myself at the wheel, were late for the funeral, and having no opportunity to beat the cortège to the lych-gate we decided to join it at the house. Turning into the drive, however, I had carburettor trouble and stalled the engine at the very moment the hearse was setting off. There was no room to pass and low, grass-covered banks made it difficult to push the car off the road, so the press was instrumental in delaying the man who had so often made it miss its deadline.

There were perhaps a score of residents who popped up at almost every annual general meeting and hardly one among them who did not enjoy indulging in a long, prolix waffle. They were there as figureheads, however, and left the real work of the movement to the honorary secretaries, a terse, efficient breed, as impatient as we were to push on to the relevant part of the agenda. We, the secretaries and the press that is, would sometimes commiserate with one another by eye-rollings and gestures of despair, as the figurehead rambled on and on, pottering among anecdotes that lacked a punchline, and groping for well-worn phrases to thank honorary auditors and scrutineers. It is interesting to recall that this rarely happened when the meeting was convened by women and chaired by a woman. Women's meetings were refreshingly business-like and cut most of the corners, the Chairman silencing the wafflers from the platform. I have always held that if Parliament was made up entirely of officials picked from Women's Institutes and Townswomen's Guilds, we should solve most of our social and economic problems in a single session. They have a way of sifting the relevant from the inconsequential and are not much given to self-glorification.

One prominent townsman to whom I looked for a steady supply of news did not qualify as a mandarin, inasmuch as he never concerned himself with public affairs but concentrated manfully on a business that was, in a sense, everybody's business. He was our most prominent local undertaker, whose detachment from the local junketings was impressive but spine-chilling. To look at him,to see him going softly about his work, helped to restore one's sense of proportion but it also reminded one that time was flying and that nothing mattered much, not even the disputed switch from gas street-lighting to electric street-lighting. Death was out there waiting for all, that is, everyone but Jabez, who had somehow wrung the secret of immortality from the gods and would be on hand to make a tidy job of the youngest and healthiest among us.

Perhaps his detachment encouraged this belief, that and his trick of measuring the most pompous of us with his expert eye. He invariably referred to his customers as 'parties', as though he was conducting mass burials at one or other of our churchyards, and it was some time before I could persuade myself that his approach to his work was in no way disrespectful but traditional, for he came from a long line of local undertakers. Jabez had some interesting theories about Death. He would call sooner, he claimed, if one was unfortunate enough to possess a short, thick neck but could be kept at bay a long time if one was reluctant to invest in life insurance. It was his experience, he declared, that parties with short, thick necks rarely reached the allotted span and usually came his way well in advance of it. Similarly, parties known to be heavily insured had a way of dropping off soon after the first big premium was paid, almost as though they had been nudged by avaricious relatives.

He would sit on my office table when he came in with his bi-weekly list of departures and chat cosily about his associations with the deceased, so that his profession would shed its natural gloom and assume the aspect of a learned profession, deserving a long and arduous apprenticeship. He was never surprised by death, not even when it struck haphazardly among the able-bodied. It was as though he had been privy to what was about to happen and it had, in a way, been arranged for his benefit. Yet he was a craftsman and spared nothing to do his customers credit. He could convert the most modest funeral into an event of great dignity and sometimes mild hilarity, for he was not merely the undertaker on these occasions but a family counsellor, who gave advice both before and after the event. He could also be relied upon to recall all manner of amusing stories about the dear departed. Nobody ever challenged him or his decisions. He was the local Diogenes, dispensing wisdom from an enormous vat of experience.

Jabez must have been a wealthy man by the time I met him but his dislike of ostentation extended to his way of life and dress, especially his dress. All the years I knew him he possessed but two suits. One was informal, and worn during preliminaries, the other was his gala attire for the actual interment. Both must have been bought at least twenty years before our first encounter for the informal suit, that had once been grey, was now dark green, and the trilby hat that went with it was a defeated ruin that had weathered countless south-westerly gales as he cycled about his business in the high season of the trade, between mid-December and late February. His graveside clothes were cut from more lasting material and had withstood the weather fairly well but the nap had disappeared from his topper that had weathered a shade of black one might look for in the feathers of an elderly crow sitting out a shower. In either suit, however, you could never mistake him for anything but an undertaker, for he had a long, measured stride and held himself very erect, a gait and posture acquired during the hundreds of miles he had walked between lych-gate and grave, chapel and family plot.

I grew very fond of Jabez but this did not prevent me from

transporting him, root and branch, to one of my early novels. He appears there as he appeared to me under the somewhat Dickensian name of Sleek.

I had a bad moment on this account. A few days after the appearance of the book on the bookstalls I saw him striding purposefully towards me with an unfamiliar gleam in his eye. A sore conscience made me wonder how I could possibly excuse myself for conferring upon him, without his prior consent, a different kind of immortality, that of the printed word stowed away in the British Museum, where at least one copy of every author's work must survive. I had under-estimated human fallibility. Clapping me on the shoulder he smiled his thin, wintry smile and congratulated me on what he described as "a rare pen portrait of 'X' ", naming a rival and less distinguished local undertaker.

From that moment I have never been over-worried about the possibility of libel. There exist, here and there, a few Englishmen prepared to accept the mantle of the scoundrel in fiction and sue. But no promise of damages will tempt an Englishman to don the motley, climb into the ring and consort with clowns.

Jabez was not immortal after all. In the fullness of time he died, just like everybody else, but to me at least his death was an affront, a welshing on the part of the gods who had promised him immunity. He was, however, a ripe old age and long past his work, so it seems superfluous to add that his neck was long and thin and that his passing did not occasion so much as a tut-tut at the head offices of the giant insurance corporations.

Budleigh Salterton and Mrs. Simpson

I

One of the most profound social changes that has occurred in Britain over the last quarter-century concerns the public attitude towards divorce, particularly divorce in high places. If anyone denies this let him reflect upon the tremendous impact caused by what has become known, in history, as 'The Domestic Crisis', leading up to the abdication of Edward VIII, in December 1936.

It was a mere thirty-four years ago, less than what passes for a generation, and yet the heat it generated, the fury and self-questioning it occasioned at the time, was stupendous, dividing as it did any number of families, and splitting the country into two camps who, for a month or so, glared at one another as though on the verge of carrying the issue to the point of physical violence.

I touched on this in my saga of the suburbs, *The Avenue Story*, where an elderly spinster, who had revered Edward through his long period as Prince of Wales, assaulted a neighbour with her shopping bag during an altercation on the subject in a grocery store. I do not think I exaggerated. People did get tremendously steamed up about it and the emotional wounds caused by the abdication, that came as a great shock to a British public almost completely in ignorance of the mounting crisis, were not healed until George VI and Queen Elizabeth had restored public confidence and won international respect by the tactful way in which they set about filling the vacuum. As a journalist pounding a small, provincial beat I was probably more aware of this than Fleet Street men, who were naturally more concerned with day-to-day headlines and were thus able to put the abdication behind them in a week or so.

One of the main reasons why the crisis generated so much controversy, I think, was the action of the British press in contriving, with remarkable success, to keep the public in ignorance of the situation long after it became general knowledge elsewhere. This, of course, was done in good faith and designed to spare the parties concerned acute embarrassment, but it was folly for all that. It had the effect of multiplying the force of the explosion many times over when, at last, the silence was broken, and those members of the public who had seen saucy references to Mrs. Simpson in American and Canadian papers, could no longer dismiss them as examples of transatlantic fantasy in bad taste.

I can recall the circumstances in which I came to hear about it, some time in the early autumn of that year, when a friend sent me a Canadian newspaper with a headline that ran, *Will Teddy Marry Wally?* Until then I had never heard of Mrs. Simpson and when I showed the newspaper to friends they regarded it as so nonsensical that it hardly merited perusal.

In ordinary circumstances, I suppose, a story as sensational as this would seep into the public consciousness and perhaps it did in more sophisticated circles. But nothing like that happened in places like Budleigh Salterton, the town on our eastern border, allegedly populated by scores of retired admirals and major-generals, with a sprinkling of mahogany-faced Indian civil servants who had migrated there at the expiration of their service abroad. Budleigh Salterton, I'll stake my wig, had no inkling of what was brewing. It went right on preparing for Edward's coronation in May of the following year and Wally, whoever she was, was not spared a thought, even by the tiny minority who read overseas newspapers.

Then, like a thunderclap that strips every slate from the roof and brings out all the local fire-brigades, the story broke and we were plunged into a mad welter of rumour and counter-rumour, involving not merely the King and Mrs. Simpson, but Mr. Ernest Simpson (whoever he was), the Queen Mother, the Prime Minister, the Archbishop of Canterbury, the Bishop of Bradford (who unconsciously leaked the news in a sermon) and the entire British establishment.

It was appalling. Nothing remotely like it had occurred since George IV had refused to admit his wife to the Coronation over a century before. People went about their business with dazed, incredulous expressions, exchanging views about what was likely to happen and half-believing, *wanting* to believe, that it was all a gigantic hoax on the part of Fleet Street and the B.B.C. Lesser scandals had always been relished to some extent, the subject of sly innuendos in the bridge clubs and on the golf course, but there were no fringe benefits to be extracted from this fantastic sequence of events. It was all far too personal, for most people living in the British provinces in 1936 had come to regard Edward, Prince of Wales, as a kind of Sir Galahad who used a sportscar instead of a horse, someone they saw as the very embodiment of British tradition, with a pleasing dash of modernity about his temperament.

It is difficult, at this distance, to convey to a later generation the extent of the popularity Edward enjoyed as Prince of Wales. It was more embracing than that enjoyed by any member of the Royal Family today, much as the Queen, Prince Philip and the present Prince of Wales are liked and respected by a vast majority of the British people. He was at once a fact and a legend. Young and old identified with him, were interested in everything he did and said, and saw him as someone endowed with the ability to blend past, present and future. He was a symbol of continuity to the elderly and a lively promise to those of his own generation. He did everything and went everywhere. He hunted, and came an occasional cropper over a hairy fence. He travelled by air. He walked bareheaded in London. He knew, from personal experience, every corner of the Empire. He showed a very real concern for the plight of the unemployed. He was known to dislike protocol and flunkeydom and would run contrary to it whenever he saw an opportunity. He dressed informally, used slang, danced well, enjoyed visiting night clubs and somehow, to those who remembered his amiable face on toffee tins during the First World War, he never stopped being young. Those among us born during his father's reign looked to him to occupy the throne for the rest of our lives and were not in the least concerned whether he married or went through life as a bachelor. He had plenty of brothers, the line of succession was secure, and we liked him for his vitality and informality. He was a fixture, like the Houses of Parliament and Westminster Abbey and at that time, with Hitler and Mussolini rampaging across the Channel, we were in sore need of a fixture.

All this blew up in our faces overnight. One morning he was there, as rooted as the oak in which his Stuart ancestor had hidden, the next he was a royal cork, tossed about by people we didn't much like or hardly knew. It was all very chastening and uncomfortable, as though we had come down to breakfast one morning and learned, via the milkman, that the head of the family has absconded with his blonde secretary and was said to be making for Buenos Aires.

2

My own family was split on the issue. My father, a great traditionalist despite strong radical convictions, was outraged by the whole sorry business, whereas my brother and myself, whose job it was to present a local interpretation of the crisis to *Chronicle* readers, were King's Men from the outset. We took the view, a view upheld by a small but vocal minority, that, Mrs. Simpson notwithstanding, we did not want Edward to stand down, and that Parliament and the Dominions would be well advised to find some kind of compromise. My mother, another traditionalist, took my father's side in the argument and I imagine acrimony of this kind was present at millions of breakfast-tables from Pentland Firth to the Longships Lighthouse. I would not like to give the impression, however, that the battle was joined between Victorians and Edwardians on the one side and Georgians on the other. This controversy was unique. It had no kind of precedent and protagonists were left to sort themselves out and align themselves as best they could. Churchill and Beaverbrook, of course, were regarded as potential champions of the King's faction, whereas the ubiquitous Baldwin, and His Grace the Archbishop, emerged as the figureheads of the King-Must-Go faction. It seemed at first as though the King's Men were holding on to the initiative during days of mounting confusion and they found themselves in strange company. Mosleyites (and left-wingers who abominated Mosley) were seen bearing placards that read *We want the King and not Baldwin* parading up and down Whitehall, and every point of view put forward by leader-writers was solemnly debated in saloon bars, public vehicles, shops and on the kerbside. The most extravagant forms of compromise were mooted but in the end they crystallised into that of a morganatic marriage. It was this, however, that succeeded in widening the gulf, for that section of the public siding with Baldwin could not swallow the fact that Mrs. Simpson would have not one but two divorces behind her if she became the morganatic wife of a man ruling over the largest empire in the history of mankind and who was also, through no fault of his own, a royal Peter Pan.

I first became aware of the strength of this undercurrent when I elected to take a sample public opinion poll in one corner of my beat. I should have known better than to choose Budleigh Salterton but it happened to be a Thursday and Thursday was my day for visiting Budleigh Salterton.

I must admit to being shocked by the reception I received from this section of my regular subscribers. By merely asking the question—were they for or against the King—I somehow converted myself into a target for the abuse that would have been directed at Mrs. Simpson had she taken refuge in Budleigh Salterton instead of Fort Belvedere, the mock-Gothic retreat of the King at that time. Mrs. Simpson herself tells how, during her flight to Cannes, a man seeing her car pass down a street in Lyons screamed, "*Voilà la dame*." I am persuaded that the arrival of Wallis in most parts of the English provinces at that time would have provoked similar epithets and possibly demonstrations.

As an opinion-sounder, designed to test the local strength of the Churchill-Beaverbrook faction, my private poll was a failure but it taught me something important about the worth of popular adulation. Budleigh Salterton, at that time, was probably the most throne-loving township in the country, with the possible exceptions of Sandringham, Windsor and Cheltenham, but I can see now why its verdict was so unanimous. It considered itself, collectively, to have been the victim of an outrageous practical joke. Its older inhabitants (long since laid to rest alongside what the brash newcomers to Budleigh Salterton describe as 'The Curry' of earlier generations) never forgave Edward or Wally and would growl when their names were mentioned, but the middle-aged and younger sectors soon mellowed. If the Duke and Duchess of Windsor appeared in the High Street now they would probably be greeted with respectful hurrahs.

For my part, however, I was equally unforgiving. It seemed to me at that time, and still does for that matter, that the British did not emerge very creditably from the Domestic Crisis, demonstrating as they did a most uncharacteristic vein of hysteria. Up to that moment Edward's life had been devoted to public service and it has since been admitted by historians that he made a spectacular success of his job. His post-war imperial journeys alone were of very considerable value to the economy. He had always seen himself as a bridge between the sedate but hypocritical era of his great-grandmother, and the more relaxed era of the 'twenties. I never recall hearing a slighting word spoken of him until December, 1936, if one excepts an unemployed Welsh miner's refusal to sing 'God Bless the Prince of Wales' at a local concert. Yet the things said of him during the ten days of the Domestic Crisis were not merely critical. Many were spiteful and some were scurrilous. Men and women, who until then, I had always looked upon as tolerant and kindly neighbours, talked of him in a way they might have referred to an infamous scoundrel, caught in the execution of a shabby crime. To live through it all was an unpleasant experience at the trusting age of twenty-four. To record it, as I did in the course of my work, was to understand that there are times when British moral righteousness deserves the cynicism of Continentals. The historian, Macauley, was very discerning when, in the middle of the last century, he drew attention to this curious quirk in the national character, this sudden and inexplicably violent access of puritanical rectitude that is capable of flaying a man alive and enjoying the exercise. For a week or a fortnight the British public dance on the corpse and then, feeling rather foolish, they return to their cricket and their crumpets beside the fire and promptly forget all about him. Such a demonstration helped to send Edith Thompson to the gallows. A little more than a decade later another moral explosion (this time spiced with leeriness) delivered the Reverend Davidson, sometime Rector of Stiffkey, to the lions. In the early 'sixties we saw it again in the Profumo case, but on each of these occasions there was some kind of justification for a public outcry. We know that Edith Thompson played around the edges of murder even if she had no real intention of committing it, whereas Davidson, guilty or not, behaved like a fool over a long period of time. Profumo made the mistake of deceiving Parliament and the nation. But Edward VIII deserved, to my way of thinking, something better of the people he had served so well and for so long. At the very least he should have earned their spontaneous sympathy and not their execration. Unwise and headstrong he might have been but his own account of his life, up to the moment he left these shores on the appropriately-named *Fury*, makes it abundantly clear that his patriotism, and his deep regard for his heritage and what it entailed in terms of duty, were never in question, then or later. A majority of Saltertonians of that time thought otherwise and their attitude was not singular. You would have found the same sentiments in any market town or resort and even in the cities. A few people openly championed the fallen idol, and rather more sympathised and held their peace. But a majority fell over one another in their eagerness to cast the first stone. It is curious that all this occurred less than four years before the period Churchill described as Britain's finest hour.

A Shower of Namedrops

I

When my father acquired *The Exmouth Chronicle*, in the autumn of 1923, its format resembled those old copies of *The Times*, announcing the victories of Trafalgar and Waterloo. The front-page layout had not changed since its foundation in the eighteen-seventies, being devoted almost exclusively to advertisements, imploring people to try Doan's Backache Pills, or keep baldness at Bay with Doctor Pilkington's hair restorer. The sole relief offered the eye from these closely-printed columns was a block measuring about eight inches by six, depicting Exmouth as it had been about the time Prince Albert died. Crinolined ladies carrying precisely-angled parasols were seen walking sedately along the esplanade, accompanied by stovepipe-hatted escorts in pegtop trousers. A few yawls and wherries sailed in the estuary, and a circular bathing machine (it was still there in 1923) established the fact that the town had already launched itself as a resort.

My father banished the block in order to use the space more profitably but otherwise he made no changes in format or general presentation. Six years later my brother and I persuaded him to go over to front-page news and streamline the journal, using banner headlines for the more sensational news items, and boxing titbits of special local interest. In a few years we hoisted the circulation from around fifteen hundred to six thousand, reckoning to sell two papers to every three houses in the area. Revitalising the *Chronicle* was fun and a good deal of that fun stemmed from the column 'In Town This Week', a feature devoted to the most notable of the town's visitors.

The idea for the column originated, I think, from a brief encounter I had with Sir Arthur Conan Doyle in what proved to be the last year of his life. He caught me scouting around the grounds of his hotel but I was too inexperienced at that time to make capital out of the meeting and have always regretted I did not pursue my advantage and get him to confess to a dislike of Sherlock Holmes. However, the brush set me thinking on the advantages of introducing our readers—until then fed on a stodgy diet of Council news, deaths, marriages, sales of work and local accidents—to the kind of celebrity who came seeking peace and anonymity in Devon's small sea-coast towns. I entered into a conspiracy with the proprietors of our prominent hotels and from then on was notified as soon as a distinguished guest arrived. Some very odd fish slipped into the net.

The first was Claude Hulbert, brother of the more celebrated Jack, at that time the most popular musical comedy star in the country. Claude was a specialist in silly ass roles, along the lines of characters portrayed by Ralph Lynn in the famous Aldwych farces. It was he on whom I sharpened my journalistic teeth, for I soon discovered that, no matter how acclaimed celebrities might be, they can always use more personal publicity; even in a local paper with a circulation of six thousand.

Claude supplied me with a crop of film and stage anecdotes and a photograph and from then on, throughout the period from Easter to October, the column 'In Town This Week' became a regular feature of the paper, bringing me into contact with many people who were the equivalent, at that time, of today's pop stars and sporting lions but are now, I suspect, half-forgotten.

One was Teddy Brown, the well-known xylophonist, a huge man who must have weighed around twenty stone, who moved around the country with a diminutive wife and a flock of children. I interviewed him in the family bedroom and it was like conducting the interview in a boiler factory. Another was Davy Burnaby, the most popular member of The Co-optimists, a show that began its run at the Royalty Theatre in 1921 and played fifteen hundred performances. Davy was another of those mountainous, genial entertainers and The Co-optimists symbolised the spirit of the age, an upsurge of lightheartedness that was specifically designed to exorcise the gloom of the '14–'18 period. Burnaby was known, at that time, as 'The Prince of Compères', and proved an excellent subject to interview. Nearly twenty years later, whilst myself compèring and presenting an R.A.F. revue at a camp in Northumberland, I met him again when he came round to the dressing-room to tell me how much he had enjoyed the show. The gesture was typical of show-business names in those days. They were, by today's standards, unsophisticated, but there was nothing wrong with their manners. Some of today's celebrities could learn a great deal from them, especially in the field of public relations.

George Robey, the Prime Minister of Mirth, gave me an interview and George, perhaps more than any other star, epitomised for all of us the old music-hall tradition, with his rubbery face and quick, simple humour. They were people, I suppose, who would not react very favourably to the modern studio interview, where victims are subjected to a half-cynical line of questioning, but they knew their jobs, they could give excellent off-the-cuff interviews in the act of applying make-up in their dressing-rooms, and once in front of an audience they seldom failed to produce belly-laughs, traditionally worth two hundred pounds apiece to the box-office.

It was an age of popular dance-band leaders and three I interviewed in this category were Jack Payne, Joe Loss and Mantovani. Mantovani has survived into the TV age and Jack Payne I re-encountered years later, when he financed *Where There's A Will,* a comedy I had written. We were able, during rehearsals, to reminisce over the hit tunes of the period, when he had been at the height of his fame.

I formed a personal liking for most of these entertainers. They were famous—as famous in their way as are the Beatles today—but offstage they conducted themselves like rational human beings and not one of them ever talked down to the press. The only one among them who slightly disconcerted me was Jack Buchanan, another musical star, who received me with his long legs stretched on the desk and a trilby hat set rakishly on the back of his head. He remained in that unconventional position throughout our half-hour discussion.

I did not succeed in interviewing two of our most famous women stars of the period, Jessie Matthews, then the darling of the musical comedy stage, and Gladys Cooper, the ageless actress, but I met both of them later and they underlined the claim that British women retain their beauty longer than women of other nations. These two were middle-aged when I met them but either would have passed for a woman in her early thirties. They had charming manners to match.

Interviewing stage personalities was an interesting and undemanding job and I never met one who was not prepared to co-operate. The only failure I had was in the realm of sport, after I was lucky enough to run down Don Bradman, who had gone into hiding to avoid publicity. He was recognised by an A.A. Scout on the road between Exmouth and Budleigh Salterton, and when the word was passed to me I traced him to the home of a maker of cricket-balls who lived in the area. I got into the house but Bradman was too quick for me. He locked himself in a room and shouted through the door that I was to go away, and that he refused to be interviewed by any pressman. He became quite excited about it and we stood there for ten minutes, bellowing at one another through the door of the cricket-ball manufacturer's lounge. I was thus able to write a more interesting account of a non-confrontation than would have resulted from a straight interview.

My prize nugget in the business of celebrity prospecting was George Bernard Shaw, then the most famous man in the world, who was far too wily a bird to give me the Bradman treatment. For all that, he was a difficult man to run down and if reporters descended upon him in a cloud, as they generally did whenever he made an appearance in public, he would make a show of bullying them and then beat a rapid retreat. He was a regular visitor to the Victoria Hotel, Sidmouth, just outside my beat, but I did not succeed in getting an exclusive interview until 1937, when he was a walking legend of eighty-one.

He had been playing hide-and-seek with the press for three weeks and I got the impression that he enjoyed the game enormously. I happened to approach him, however, on a day when he was in an indulgent mood and his reply to my 'phone message—that I was a married man with children, and would be fired if I did not get an interview—was, "Don't believe a word of it but wait there and I'll come downstairs."

He was one of those very rare celebrities who are not merely larger than life but far exceed the expectations of those nurtured on their eccentricities. In his pepper-and-salt knickerbocker suit he looked more Shaw than Shaw and his Irish brogue was so strong that it took me moments to adjust to it. I don't think he had expected to find anyone so young and awestruck, for I had sent up a *Daily Express* card and was obliged to admit that I only served Lord Beaverbrook as a local correspondent. This amused him and he led the way to an alcove overlooking the sea, methodically punching the cushions on my side as well as his before motioning me to be seated.

My experience with celebrities had taught me that it is as well to keep a notebook out of sight and conduct the interview on a trivial, conversational level. Celebrities talk far more freely if they are not being recorded and Shaw was no exception. He talked about everything. I asked him if he still championed the Duke of Windsor (who was marrying Mrs. Simpson, in France, that same week) and he said he did, but resented not having been invited to the wedding. He talked about the economy, the prospects of war, fashions, the theatre, Oscar Wilde, and Frank Harris, whose biography of himself he had obligingly finished after Harris died before it was completed. "I was very fair to Frank," he added, reflectively. "I not only left in all the unpleasant things he said about me but I added many additional ones."

One way and another it was a memorable afternoon. The interview lasted well over an hour and somehow we got around to the one subject where I could hope to compete with him on equal terms. The topic was Napoleon's First Empire and we soon found ourselves at odds over Imperial strategy at Waterloo. Shaw held that Napoleon sacrificed his chance of victory by launching Ney's splendid cavalry against well-posted infantry, but I maintained that his sole prospect of prolonging the campaign was to break the English centre before the Prussians assailed him in force on his right flank. The theory interested the famous Irishman and he called for a large sheet of paper and went down on his knees, sketching a recognisable plan of the battle as it had developed by early afternoon and proving his point (at least to his own satisfaction) by a series of curved pencil lines showing the direction of Blücher's advance. "Sure, he had plenty of time in hand," he argued. "If the silly fellow had supported Ney with infantry he could have pushed Wellington from the plateau." I stuck to my point, arguing that Blücher's divisions were already hammering at Plancenoit on the French flank, and that the Young Guard had been despatched to hold them in check, depriving the French of their strongest reserve. It was one of those fascinating historical 'Ifs' that defy a definitive solution but we both enjoyed the debate. Thirty years later I had the same argument at a literary dinner with Sir Arthur Bryant. We used knives, forks, spoons and salt-cellars for divisions.

When I left Shaw I at once wrote down as much of our conversation as I could recall and hurried home to hammer out a four-column feature entitled 'G.B.S. is Conversational'. I sent him a copy, never dreaming that he would acknowledge it but he did. By return of post came one of his famous postcards. It read, "Dear Mr. Delderfield. The interview was excellent. Few are. Many thanks, George Bernard Shaw." The despatch of that card has always seemed to me a very kindly act on the part of a man to whom a few columns in a local paper meant absolutely nothing, but I have since learned that it was typical of the gentler side of Shaw that he reserved, in the main, for nonentities. Since that day my work has brought me into contact with many professional writers. None have impressed me as did Shaw. He really was five times larger than life, and far more original.

2

Since I am occupied with namedrops I may as well jump forward a couple of decades and comment on impressions that have remained with me of stage celebrities I met when I was writing regularly for the stage and B.B.C. The most congenial show-biz lion I ever met was Maurice Chevalier, one of the few professional entertainers whose *joi de vivre* spills over into his offstage life. The most intelligent actress I met was Dame Flora Robson, whom I got to know well towards the end of the war. Most actresses approach their work emotionally but Flora, although a warm-hearted and excessively amiable person, uses an intellectual approach, without a tittle of that arty nonsense many professionals use as camouflage. Both Chevalier and Miss Robson have, as one might expect, a highly developed sense of humour and this, plus a quick brain, makes them delightful conversationalists.

One of the most likeable celebrities I met was Noël Coward and I was ill-prepared for the impact of his personality. I had been reared on the Coward plays, and I suppose I anticipated a certain amount of astringency in his approach. There was none, however, not a trace of that searing wit that characterises his comedies and is aimed, for the most part, at the pompous and the pretentious. He had that rare knack of making people feel they had known him for years and the only blanket adjective I can use to describe him is that equivocal word 'civilised'. Ivor Novello, whom I never met, had the same quality. Two very elderly ladies once paid a surprise call on his dressing-room during the run of *Perchance to Dream* and although he was tired, and badly needed the rest between matinée and evening performances, he ordered tea and spent the entire interval flattering them. That, to my mind, is evidence of star quality, the ability to treat every fan, no matter how inconvenient their presence, as a distinguished visitor and stars like Coward and Novello owe their reputations to this as surely as they owe it to their talents as entertainers. Happily I can name a stage personality of the 'sixties with the same discernment, Eamonn Andrews, whose TV affability is not bogus and survives the dousing of studio lights. To watch him handling nervous, elderly folk, in *This is Your Life*, was a rewarding experience. He puts as much into offstage preliminaries as he does into the actual show.

The most disappointing show-biz lion I met was Walt Disney and the dullest was George Arliss. I interviewed Arliss in my 'In Town This Week' days, when he was a world-famous film star, finding him polite but utterly unresponsive. To get him to say a firm 'Yes' or 'No' required considerable ingenuity. He was the first top-ranking film star I met and at the time I was astonished by his lack of originality. Later on, when I worked in films, I came to understand how much of a star's personality is padding, contributed by the director, the writer, the make-up department and the publicity machine.

This sense of disillusion seldom accompanies a personal encounter with stage actors or actresses, who are the most interesting because they are not products of a high-powered industry. John Gielgud struck me as a very modest and unassuming man but good company and a first-class after-dinner speaker. One of the few film stars whom I came to like as a person rather than a personality was George Formby, but he was basically a stage artist. Ronnie Shiner took me along to meet him when they were shooting a pub riot scene in the old Riverside Studios, and a few moments after we had been introduced one of the extras, acting under direction, hurled a rubber tankard at George who was standing behind the bar. It must have been a clumsily-designed stage property for it cut Formby's eye and raised a large bruise on his forehead. I was particularly struck, however, by the manner in which he went out of his way to make light of his injury in order to moderate the embarrassment of the extra who had inflicted it.

The most effervescent offstage actress I met in my theatre days was Cicely Courtneidge, who adores her work, and shares her spillover high spirits with everyone about her. She is a good tonic on any stage or film set, for when she is around one has the feeling that the end product of the industry is fun and nothing else. Another very amiable lady is Sonia Dresdel who told me, ruefully, that she was 'stuck with bitches'. "I played one very early on and was a great success," she said, sadly. "Ever since, when they're casting around for a bitch, they think of me. I *do* wish someone would give me a nice, cosy, endearing, motherly role!"

Middle-aged film and theatregoers will recall the late Gordon Harker, a square-faced Cockney heavy, who made a great name for himself in comedy-thrillers forty years ago. Gordon, offstage, was a quiet, thoughtful man but so was Ralph Lynn, possibly Britain's most celebrated stage-idiot. Theatregoers who meet comedians offstage are often surprised and disappointed by their reserve but there is a logical reason for this reticence on their part. Somebody wise once wrote that comedy is an exact science and that is why comedians are such sad dogs. In the main I have found this to be true. Ronnie Shiner approached his work with the seriousness of a classical composer and would not relax until every line was carefully set down and rehearsed. Occasionally, however, actors do sustain their stage reputations after the grease-paint has been removed, as I discovered in the case of Alastair Sim. An agent introduced me to Sim in a lift, presenting me, rather fulsomely I thought, as the author of *Worm's Eye View*. "Did you write *that*?" Sim asked, in deceivingly awed tones, and when I admitted as much he added, "God forgive you, my boy!" and strolled out of the lift with a resigned hoist of his famous eyebrows.

My encounter with the late Walt Disney was more chastening. At his representative's request I had travelled specially to London to meet him in the suite of a luxury hotel he was occupying whilst clearing the ground for a new film, based on a book. I had read the book and was there, presumably, to expound my ideas as regards its conversion to a scenario. Walt appeared blowing his nose, and announcing glumly that he had caught a heavy cold whilst in the company of the King of Sweden. I was sorry about this but it hardly excused him listening to my theories for one hour by the clock, without offering me a cup of tea. I could have sustained the one-sided interview better, I think, had it not been for the arrival of a squad of assistants, who filed into the room at irregular intervals, one by one, and each without uttering a single word. I have no idea what their function was, for they sat very still in a long row, with folded arms and blank faces, reminding me not so much of patients in a dentist's waiting-room but hired guns in a gangster film. I continued talking but my confidence began to ebb under their unwinking scrutiny, whereas Disney confined his comments to terse monosyllables and an occasional sniff he had brought all the way from Sweden. The interview finally fizzled out like a damp firework, wriggling a little before it died, and I left the suite without the least idea whether or not my ideas were considered practical or whether, in fact, my expenses would be paid. Disney died before I found out.

Walt Disney notwithstanding, I cannot but feel, when I reflect on the show-business personalities of the past, that much of the glamour of the stage has departed on the echoes of the electric guitar. These people, of whom I write, were more than entertainers in their heyday. They represented, for those of us bogged down in a repetitive job, a fairytale world just over the horizon, and a majority of them lived their parts both on and off the stage. Many would be thought inadequate today but it should be remembered that they entertained millions of people very successfully over a very long period, without the paraphernalia used by today's pop stars. Gracie Fields just stood there and sang. She did not walk about trailing yards of flex and buttress her performance with mechanical backing. Ralph Lynn only needed a finger-trapping toast-rack to get a belly laugh at the Aldwych. George Robey only had to mime a naughty word in order to create uproar in the cheap seats. George Formby's apparatus was limited to a ukelele. Entertainment was far more simply designed in those days and the stars, as a rule, were simple people, who worked tremendously hard and earned every penny they received. All had served long apprenticeships, going the rounds of Number Two dates in provincial theatres, and returning tired out to a cold supper at Ma's Digs. A few of those I met, or watched at their work, I came to admire, and, notwithstanding my subsequent disenchantment with show business, all of them have retained my respect as people who gave full value for money.

Tweedledum and Tweedledee

I

The British are an exceptionally conservative race. They display a deep distrust towards change in their national way of life and although their history is studded with eccentrics they are, at bedrock, suspicious of displays in public places. In view of this I find it extraordinary that so many of their Prime Ministers over the last century should have been clowns.

There was Palmerston, whose strident chauvinism was a nonstop harlequinade; Disraeli, who never once took his tongue from his cheek; Gladstone, who came to identify himself with an Old Testament prophet; and the donnish Asquith, who could find time to write a daily love-letter to a young girl whilst directing Britain's contribution to the bloodiest conflict in history.

Nearer our own times there was Lloyd George, possibly the most accomplished entertainer who ever trod Westminster boards, and after him Baldwin, who was rarely seen without a cherry-wood pipe, and liked to lean over a sty and scratch his pigs with a stick, concealing his astute political brain under the motley of a kindly, unimaginative English squire.

After Baldwin there was MacDonald, whose clowning took the form of kissing duchesses and making long, rambling speeches that not even the faithful could understand.

By then, of course, the British voter was aware of the inherent weakness in his political system and, accepting the fact that the real business of government was carried on by the Civil Service, resigned himself to buffoonery in high places, even bestowing an affectionate nickname on the reigning clown. Lloyd George became 'The Welsh Wizard', Baldwin 'Honest Stan', MacDonald 'Ramsaymac'. By the time Neville Chamberlain appeared, with his ragged moustache and his umbrella, one began to feel that these people should forgo election addresses and resort to circus-billing. "Roll up, roll up and watch the Umbrella Man vanquish the Ugly Sisters" would, I think, have been appropriate billing for the election that should have taken place around 1939–40 but was bypassed, the British electorate having rather more pressing affairs in hand at that time.

By then, of course, Churchill was in power, and in some ways he proved the most electrifying clown of them all. He cleared the ring of rivals, roared defiance at hecklers, went everywhere with a half-smoked cigar in his mouth, and wore a succession of funny hats. For years the British delighted in him and then, quite suddenly, they tired of the performance and longed for a bit of peace. That was how they came to elect a quiet little man like Clem Attlee, who had no pretensions whatever towards buffoonery.

In the period between 1938 and 1955 my work as an airman, journalist and dramatist brought me into contact with these two Prime Ministers, whose personalities were so opposed to one another. This contrast seems to me to reveal something fundamental in the British character, an assertion that compromise between two extremes is the only thing that is important in the art of government.

2

I met Attlee twice and had two conversations with him, one of them in private.

In 1937 he came to the West to rally the cause of Labour and as a pressman I attended a small private tea given in his honour. As there were no other journalists present I was able to talk to him for perhaps thirty minutes and from the first he made a deep impression on me, so that I never shared the public view that he was a nonentity.

I was aware of his record, of course, up to the time when he appeared in the lounge of a prominent local Socialist and sat sipping tea, looking like a patient Chinese mandarin presiding over a trivial lawsuit. I knew that he had fought on the Western Front as a tank officer at a time when the Top Brass regarded tanks as clumsy toys, and how, throughout the 'twenties, he had worked in the East End as a social reformer. He seemed to me at that time, and does in retrospect, the very best type of

Englishman, a man whose dominant characteristic was compassion and concern for the unfortunate, and who considered it a privilege to spend himself working for them, a man without personal ambition of the kind one associates with every professional politician, someone with deeply-rooted convictions based on Christian ethics but the good manners not to wave them like banners. I envied him his quiet but fluent command of the English tongue when expounding an idea or propounding a policy. He never raised his voice or allowed himself to be carried away and remained, in essence, a man of tremendous restraint. One knew, somehow, that he had never willingly misled anyone in his life, that he would make a good friend and a forgiving enemy. In this sense, I think, he was unique in politics, and Britain is the poorer for him not having taken office in the early 'thirties, when our leaders were first confronted with the menace of Fascism and responded to it with that most craven of all policies, non-intervention.

Ten years later, when he had grown considerably in political stature, I had the very real pleasure of meeting him again. He brought his daughter to see my comedy, *Peace Comes to Peckham*, on her twenty-first birthday, while the play was running at the Princes Theatre, and during the interval he came down into the foyer and told me gravely that he and his family were enjoying the entertainment. I asked him whether he would like a drink. After a brief hesitation he asked for a gin and lime, and we carried our drinks into the box-office, where I reminded him of the occasion we had first met. He recalled it in detail and this surprised me, for so much had happened in between, and it struck me then how lightly the years, and the fearful responsibilities that had pressed on him as Churchill's deputy, had dealt with him. He still looked like a kindly mandarin pondering a judgement. He still talked like the middle-aged man next door commenting on the headlines in the evening paper, the kind of chap whose hedge-clippers you would borrow on a Saturday afternoon. But on this second occasion I detected something new about him. Outwardly undistinguished, and without displaying any of the apparatus or shadow-play of power, he yet projected a kind of dynamism. One had the impression that he was possessed of an immense store of wisdom, emerging as commonsense. I was to see him once again.

3

I never met Churchill but I stood close to him on three occasions and these occasions, seen in retrospect, remain in my mind as three stages in a career of astonishing variety. They could be signposted failure, triumph, and death.

In the very early 'thirties he too came West to address a Conservative garden-party, at a time when he was in the wilderness, without the least prospect of finding his way out again. His long series of personal adventures were behind him but, far from trailing the glory of an imperial past, he looked as though he had already conceded defeat, accepting it with a crustiness that would have put any experienced reporter on guard, encouraging him to tread softly on Churchillian corns. There was nothing about Churchill's manner or appearance at that time to suggest that, in less than a decade, he would rank with Pitt, or that his name would pass into the language as the embodiment of dramatic leadership and truculent oratory. I am inclined to the view, however, that he was conserving his stupendous energies and, as time went on, and he warned repeatedly of the growing menace of Germany, he addressed a small part of those energies to the task of preparing the British electorate, particularly that part of it inclined to the left, for his assumption of power in the spring of 1940. If this was not so why did we turn automatically to Churchill after Chamberlain's egregious Hitler-has-missed-the-bus speech?

Churchill was in and about the Air Ministry all the time I was based there in the spring and early summer of 1944 and later, when the war was drawing to a close, but I did not see him again until V.E. Day, when I had the luck to walk into an office on the first floor that adjoined the balcony on which he was to announce the Allied victory. Naturally I remained there, despite the bleats of the officious civilian clerk on whose chair I was standing. By leaning out over the stone balustrade, and craning my neck to the right, I could see Churchill's famous profile a few yards away. It would have taken ten clerks to drag me away.

It was a tremendous moment. Down below, Whitehall and the adjoining square was densely packed with people, all staring upward, and when Churchill began, "This is *your* victory . . ." the roar that echoed across the capital was like that of a thousand jets breaking the sound barrier at treetop level. I remember thinking back to that sad, slightly sagging figure of the early 'thirties, and my father's wry comment, "He's been drinking brandy . . .", and wondering at the curious shifts in human destinies. For here was a man who had been written off by every political pundit in the world but had finally emerged as someone who could set London in an uproar with six syllables.

A few weeks later he was toppled and the quiet mandarin took his place, to occupy it for six years before their positions were reversed once more. Until then, I think, one had never credited Tweedledum or Tweedledee with such resilience, and the grandee must have been astounded to find himself shown the door by the mandarin. He was only the first to be astonished. Nobody, it seems to me, has yet explained how Attlee held together a team of lieutenants that would have daunted Cromwell. Bevan, Bevin, Herbert Morrison and Stafford Cripps were all big men in their own right, and there was unquestionably a galaxy of talent in the post-war government, but Attlee controlled them all effortlessly, without resort to the wiles of Lloyd George, the flattery of Disraeli, the thunder of Gladstone and Churchill or the butchery of Macmillan.

He slipped away in the nineteen-fifties without fuss, the way he did everything in his public and private life, and it was a very frail little man I watched mount the steps of St. Paul's one bitterly cold day in 1965, as one of his rival's pall-bearers.

. . .

Until that moment I had never seen Tweedledum and Tweedledee together, as so many people present must have done, but it seemed fitting that Attlee, whose walk was beginning to develop into a stumble, should stand there bareheaded behind the enormous coffin resting on the shoulders of six panting Guardsmen.

Almost everybody who had played a part in that curious wartime alliance was there to see Churchill honoured, as no Englishman has been honoured since Wellington was borne to that same spot more than a century before. At the rear of the cathedral, near the great doors that opened and closed to admit distinguished mourners, one's attention fluctuated between the arrival of the Royal Family, the Churchills, De Gaulle, Eisenhower and a score of others, including one reigning prime minister and a band of ex-prime ministers, of whom Attlee was the smallest. But it was Clement Attlee I watched as the cortège left and he followed it into the near-freezing atmosphere beyond the great doors. And here, approaching the steps, a rather touching thing happened, for Attlee did stumble and Eden, who seemed to be anticipating the falter, reached out and steadied the little man's elbow. It brought into focus the party truce of the war years and I wondered then whether the Tweedledum and Tweedledee routine is anything more than a game the British like to play between crises.

Some Well-meant Advice to Postal Wooers

The cosy practice of bundling, so long practised in Wales by courting couples pressed for time and separated by distances, is no longer in vogue. It had, indeed, been long discontinued when I had need of it.

They tell of young men working in remote country districts walking miles after laying down their tools to enjoy bundling sessions into the small hours, when, presumably, the hardy fellows would start back, to be on hand for work in the morning. It says a good deal for the ardour and steadfastness of the early Victorian Welshman. If he would go to these lengths to spend a couple of hours beside a girl sewn up in a bag, it is not surprising that his descendants had the strength of mind to take over the B.B.C., the British banking system, and most of the lucrative posts in the T.U.C. and the Parliament at Westminster.

Today, I imagine, the practice of bundling has been rendered obsolete, even in the remotest of districts, by the availability of the second-hand car and higher wages earned by couples contemplating marriage. Very little courting, I would say, is practised nowadays on foot. In the minds of the young mobility takes precedence over everything, including romance. For my part, I was lucky enough to be on hand for the earliest stage of the used car boom, but this did not solve the worst of my difficulties, the two hundred odd miles between East Devon, where I lived and worked, and South Manchester, where my fiancée, May, had her home. In any case, several courting years had passed before I acquired a battered Austin Seven and in the interval the only means available to effect a meeting was the London, Midland and Scottish Railway.

The fare from Exeter to London Road, Manchester, was thirty shillings and sixpence in those days. I remember this particularly, because, at the time of my first trips, I was earning thirty shillings a week and had to scratch around for the odd sixpence on Friday night before I could buy the return ticket. I always travelled to Manchester overnight, leaving at ten-twenty and arriving at London Road about six a.m., the journey including a longish stop at Crewe where I sometimes think I must have spent about a third of my life.

Occasionally, very occasionally, May would travel south to Exeter, but we eventually worked out an ingenious system of saving time and money by taking advantage of the numerous football excursions to London that started from Exeter and Manchester simultaneously and cost a mere ten and sixpence. On these occasions we would rendezvous at Euston or Paddington, according to the time of arrival of our respective trains, but London had little to recommend it as a trysting place for courting couples who were not resident in the capital. The parks were available, of course, but as we had both been travelling all night we found it something of a strain to spend an entire day walking the gravelled paths and as for privacy, the Welsh bundlers were far better off than we were, even in a two-roomed Welsh cottage. At least the parents below were in favour of the match.

We enjoyed those football excursions nevertheless. We would linger over innumerable coffees in one of the three Corner Houses, visit museums and art galleries, and take advantage of a seat placed opposite a celebrated mummy or a famous painting. And always, before the day was over, we took a tube to the Tower of London, the Bloody Tower and the Byward Tower being two places where a limited amount of privacy was available, particularly in the slack part of the day. The Beefeaters, I discovered, were far more tolerant than the park-patrolling Metropolitan policemen of those days, who seemed to have received special instructions regarding provincial courting couples. The Permissive Society was a long way ahead of us and policemen always scrutinised us as if they were trying to relate our faces to photographs in the police files.

On these excursions I sometimes approached the physical hardihood of the veteran bundler, cycling the twelve miles from Exmouth to Exeter, travelling overnight to Paddington, walking about the capital all day, travelling back to Exeter by night, and cycling home again at four a.m. on Sunday morning. May, for her part, showed equal determination. She made the two journeys by night and on her return walked four miles from London Road station to her suburb in South Manchester. Courting in those days was hard on the pocket. It was harder still on the feet.

This period in our lives lasted four years and during that time British railway stock must have taken a small, upward leap. We saw one another, on the average, about six times a year but on only eight occasions during that time were we able to enjoy one another's company for more than a few hours. This was when we went off somewhere for a holiday, to the Lakes, to North Wales where we met, or to a south-eastern resort, a daring thing to do in the early 'thirties. Finally, we got engaged on the battlefield of Hastings and I like to think that the shade of Harold, himself an extremely energetic traveller (he covered the distance between Stamford Bridge, in Yorkshire, and Pevensey, in Sussex, at an average speed of thirty-two miles per day) added his blessing.

When, in 1934, I acquired the Austin Seven, I mistakenly thought our distance problem was largely overcome. An early Austin Seven would do more than forty miles to the gallon, and petrol at that time could be bought for one and a penny a gallon, but the car was already elderly and it did not do to press her along. Whenever I did one of three things happened. Either the carburettor needle stuck, and I would have to loosen it and blow bubbles into the chamber until it cleared. Or I would get a puncture. Or, for some inexplicable reason, the horn would sound without my assistance and begin a long, high-pitched, uninterrupted note that must have infuriated hundreds of sleepy families in the villages of Gloucestershire, Worcestershire and Derbyshire through which I passed. I soon learned to take it leisurely and once, on a return trip, I was fifteen hours driving from Cheshire to the Devon coast.

It will thus be seen that we were obliged to do most of our courting through the medium of the Post Office. In the period under review, actually from autumn 1931 until we married in the spring of 1936, we exchanged an estimated total of five hundred and twenty-five letters apiece, that is to say, an average of about three each week, not including parcels and postcards. I am sure this is not a record. Some couples I knew wrote to one another every day, but all the same it was no mean achievement. With stamps at three-halfpence apiece we invested a further seven pounds in romance, a sum equivalent to fourteen football excursions.

There is a good deal to be said for postal wooing. It develops both the handwriting and habit of marshalling one's thoughts on paper. When you haven't seen your fiancée for months, and are still concerned with keeping her interested, you are required to exercise a good deal of ingenuity. As a professional yarn-spinner the correspondence was part of my long apprenticeship. In addition, it must not be imagined that an interminable exchange of letters is a tedious occupation, even for those who are not looking for marginal benefits. To begin with, it tends to reduce participants to a state of suspended animation, so that the very sight of the postman is an occasion, like the appearance of funnel-smoke off the coast of a castaway's island, or the sound of distant bagpipes heard by the besieged garrison of Lucknow, or was it Arcot? Moreover, in those days, there were three deliveries a day, even in country districts, and no nonsense about first and second class. The exchange of news and endearments was thus far more rapid than it would be today. A letter posted in Manchester by seven p.m. was virtually certain to drop through a Devon letter-box by noon the following day. This, I suspect, would be regarded as a minor miracle in an era of landings on the moon.

There was another enlivening aspect, a kind of game to be played one with the other. Tiffs were sometimes promoted by an ill-judged remark or omission and involuntarily prolonged, long after the heat had gone out of the exchange, the dispute being sustained by crossed letters. This, of course, added to the excitement surrounding the arrival of every new letter and sometimes the slightly counterfeit quarrel had to be terminated by a telephonic exchange.

We did not use the telephone as much as we might have done. May did not have one in the house (very few people did in the early 'thirties) and if we wanted direct communication it had to be done through a fixed call, booked to a call-box. A telephone booth is not the most comfortable place to wait on a winter's night in Manchester, so we usually reserved this means of communication for briefing each other on the estimated times of arrival of the football excursions, information concerning a rendezvous, birthdays and the like.

It is generally accepted that one enjoys hard-earned cash more than a windfall and this logic applies to those obliged to do their courting through the post. In other words, having each gone to so much trouble and expense to come within range of one another, postal wooers are not disposed to waste as much time in bickering as couples who live within bawling-out distance of one another. Every meeting is a great adventure, every parting a tragedy played on a low key. Marco Polo, embarking on an odyssey to Cathay, could not have been more braced and expectant than I when I lowered the misted carriage window and looked into a murky dawn, to discover that I had begun my vigil on a Crewe railway siding. Or when, rattling along at a steady thirty-two miles per hour, I passed through Matlock, saw a signpost to Cheadle or Stockport and realised that the long haul through the dark was almost over. Or, for that matter, when I passed the local railway station and noticed a poster advertising a ten-shilling excursion to watch Arsenal and West Bromwich Albion contend for the F.A. Cup. On these occasions I would tell myself that one day I would actually attend a professional football match.

In view of all this I feel qualified to give postal wooers of a later generation a few broad hints. If you are not in possession of private transport keep a close watch on British Rail announcements. By so doing, you can save yourself money, even nowadays. If one or other of you possesses a second-hand car, then in God's name, keep it serviced. Otherwise all manner of frustrations might beset you miles from nowhere in the middle of the night. If you are passing rich, and both of you possess private transport, then study the map of the British Isles very carefully and hit upon a halfway house, but if you do this be sure that it is set down in a depopulated area. Cities were not built with courting couples in mind. If, on the other hand, you are situated as I was in the first stage of the saga and limited, in the main, to dependence upon the postal services, then buy your stationery in bulk. If you exchange as many letters as we did over so long a period you might save enough for a down payment on the marriage bed.

The Left and the Right of it

I

Notwithstanding his colourful and exceptionally dominant personality, my father's fiery radicalism did not rub off on me and this was not because I inclined towards an alternative political faith. It was because, by the time I was about twelve, and Labour was making its presence felt at Westminster, my father's Gladstonian Liberalism petrified. By the mid-'twenties his views on how the country should be governed seemed as archaic as Peel's or Palmerston's.

Something like this happened to many of the old radicals who swept their party to power in the famous 1906 election. Most of the issues that agitated them were either settled by the time war broke out in 1914, or had become irrelevant under the fearful pressures of four years' nonstop slaughter. I see my father's political development as stopping in December 1916, when Lloyd George, until then his hero, neatly disposed of Asquith and took his place as leader. It was too much for my father to swallow in one gulp. He dropped away and was left floundering in a hotch-potch of outdated controversy composed of Free Trade, Irish Home Rule, Disestablishment of the Welsh Church, and all the other issues that bedevilled his generation. He distrusted the New Left as much as he distrusted Welsh Wizardry but his indoctrination against the Tory party in his youth prevented him from moving, even slightly, to the Right.

Right and Left were labels not often displayed in the shires until the early 'thirties and they emerged, strange to relate, not from the Slump, and the terrible social inequalities of the post-war period, but from the postures adopted by the Dictators in Europe. The real watershed in British politics was not the Spanish Civil War of 1936, as is generally believed, but the invasion of Abyssinia in the previous autumn, resulting in the collapse of the League of Nations, until then the Holy Grail of the British Socialist and Liberal. After that, consciously or not, almost every elector found himself or herself enlisting with one side or the other, and the interesting aspect of this from my standpoint was to see it happening on my own doorstep. For this was something quite new, owing little to the conventional political loyalties my neighbours had held throughout the 'twenties. For the first time, or so it seemed to me, provincials began to sense rather than inherit their political affiliations, and almost overnight the words 'Blimp', 'Diehard', 'Red' and 'Bolshie' lost their jocular approbrium. What really occurred, I think, was that the arrogance and menace of the two Dictators compelled the local Left to mature, and maturity on their part caused the local Right to take them far more seriously than during the seventeen years that had passed since the Armistice.

Something along these lines was happening all over the country at that particular time. Until then the small but always vocal Left of provincial Britain had been obsessed with domestic issues. Foreign affairs did not figure predominantly in their pamphlets and speeches. They had as much as they could do to broadcast their views on matters like bad housing, unemployment and, later on, the Means Test, whereas, deep down in almost every Socialist, was a furtive Imperialist, secretly proud of all that red on the map and believing implicitly in the infallibility of the British Navy. He never let his loyalty to the flag show and would inveigh glibly against Imperial exploitation on the part of the wicked capitalists, but it was there for all that, as was soon revealed when the Spanish Civil War caused the entire political scene in Britain to turn a somersault.

I have always seen this General Post as one of the most astonishing processes in the history of democracy as it evolved in Britain over a period of seven centuries. It was so sudden and so complete that it left most people breathless and bemused.

I make no attempt to describe it from the national standpoint. At that time I never spent more than the odd day or two far from my local beat, and I had very little opportunity to study the political scene as a whole. The nature of my work, however, gave me a grandstand view of how it affected all the people I knew, mostly by their Christian names, whereas, for my part, at the age of twenty-three, I could not help but be influenced by their apostasies.

Until then, until the autumn of 1935 that is, the small group of Liberals and Socialists on my beat were passionate devotees of the League of Nations. In addition, many of them were paid-up members of the League of Nations Union and the Peace Pledge Union, a group led by men like George Lansbury and Canon Dick Sheppard. Regularly, at least once a week, they attended peace meetings pledged to promote international fellowship, or distributed leaflets attacking men who trafficked in the sale of arms. Day after day they declared war on war, any kind of war, in whatever cause.

The local Tories, for their part, sometimes paid lip-service to the League but they did not put much faith in it as a means of settling international disputes and were contemptuous of more extreme forms of pacifism. As the 'thirties passed the halfway mark, however, the metamorphosis occurred. The local Right shed its traditional belligerence and became almost plaintive in the cause of peace. I attended, with poised note-book and pencil, most of these political or quasi-political meetings and was thus well-placed to notice what was happening on local platforms. Books published on the period have since confirmed that the same *volte-face* was happening simultaneously in every town and village in the land and a very curious spectacle it provided. By mid-1937, less than two years after the sad-eyed Negus had quitted his conquered realm, and come to lodge at the Ritz, political attitudes in the towns and villages where I peddled news were utterly reversed. The Left put on the costumes of Edwardian Jingoes, howling for arms and a bloody confrontation with Fascism, whereas the Right, the people one had always thought of as militant, flag-flapping reactionaries, were advocating policies of the kind local Socialists had used to build their platform five years before.

It was all very confusing and took a little getting used to. A man cannot suddenly come to terms with reckless extravagance on the part of the local miser, or the advocacy of milk by the town drunk, especially when he knows the miser as Fred and the drunk as Albert. One did get used to it, however, and by the time Chamberlain flew off to Munich, and Franco, with the active help of the Dictators, had conquered Spain, Left-wing militancy and Right-wing pacifism had become accepted local attitudes, fixed until the moment in 1940 when Churchill succeeded in polarising the two attitudes.

It is interesting, looking back, to isolate the events that brought about this all-change on the part of one's neighbours. I can recall some of them vividly.

The first, I think, was the burning of the Reichstag and the mock-trial of the Dutch half-wit Van der Lubbe. The second were newsreels showing elderly Jews scouring the streets of German cities, with armbanded young thugs looking on. A third was Hitler's Night of the Long Knives, that warned some people, even those living in remote Devon villages, that we were now confronted with a Continental Al Capone. A fourth was the murder of Dollfuss, the little Austrian Chancellor. Then came Mussolini's invasion of Abyssinia and the tacit acceptance of naked aggression by the democracies, and after that the outbreak of the Spanish Civil War and the policy of non-intervention.

It was at this point that shame began to invigorate the local Left. Meetings on behalf of the Spanish Republican cause were organised and some of the speeches made at them by former pacifists might have served Joe Chamberlain at the height of the Boer War, in 1900. The reverse was true at Right-wing meetings, where speakers hammered away at the theme that what was happening on the Continent was none of Britain's business, and that elected governments in Germany and Italy were at liberty to pursue any policy they chose so long as British interests were not threatened.

Statements like this, often made by responsible people, maddened the local Left who, by now, were convinced that the intervention of Germany and Italy in Spain was nothing more than a dress-rehearsal for the conquest of the world. This, in fact, soon became so evident, even to neutrals in the debate, that the local Right began to put it about that appeasement was a cunningly conceived policy designed to buy time in order that we could re-arm for the fight—if there was a fight. This justification for the craven behaviour of government did not fool any local Socialist or Liberal I interviewed during this hectic period. Their heroes were men like 'Potato Jones', a Welsh skipper who ran the blockade into a Spanish port with a cargo of potatoes for the Basques, and we even had a local celebrity, Dougal Eggar, who enlisted in the International Brigade, was taken prisoner by the enemy, and spent months in one of Franco's crowded gaols.

Things now took a more serious turn in and about the hustings. For the first and only time in my experience political violence erupted on the streets of the little town. A local Blackshirt group was formed and local policemen, hitherto occupied in checking on reports of adulterated milk and collecting cattle straying on the highway, were called upon to intervene between jackbooted Mosleyites, self-consciously standing on Chapel Hill with Mussolini glares and folded arms, and their less organised opponents of the Left, who pranced around the speakers, howling abuse and sparking off little scuffles. It gave one pause to see young men one had known throughout one's entire adolescence striking out at one another on their home ground, and accusing one another, over the shoulders of a sandwiched policeman, of using knuckledusters, but this actually occurred one summer evening and I wondered, rather wretchedly, where it was likely to lead; wretchedly because I felt myself, to some small degree, personally responsible for the sorry state of affairs.

I wonder how many peace crusaders of that period examined their consciences as attentively as I did as the Nazi menace across the Channel enlarged itself, in a matter of seven years, from malevolent dwarf to fire-breathing dragon of monstrous proportions? Perhaps a majority, for I was to encounter many ex-pacifists as enlisted airmen, sailors and soldiers in the next five years. Like me, most of them still felt a little foolish whenever they recalled their fervent convictions of the recent past.

. . .

The wave of violent reaction against war, as a means of settling international disputes, did not reach the remoter provinces until the end of the 'twenties and for my part I was not fully aware of the horrors of the Western Front until I read Remarque's *All Quiet on the Western Front*, in 1929. It was about then that the books of survivors of the holocaust in Flanders began to attract serious attention, ten years having had to elapse before the general public could brace itself to take an objective look at the years 1914–18. *All Quiet* made a very deep impression on British youth. For the first time the German infantryman was seen as a fellow victim and not as the baby-crucifier and rapist of wartime propaganda, but British and French writers were also trumpeting their abhorrence of war in plays and novels, some of which made a considerable impact on young people at that time. Aldington's *Death of a Hero* was one that impressed me, and Sherriff's play *Journey's End* was another vivid reminder of what had happened to the previous generation. Translations of the French novels *Under Fire* and *The Paths of Glory* told the same story and a popular newspaper made a unique contribution to the peace campaign by publishing a horrific pictorial record of the First World War called *Covenants with Death.* I joined the local League of Nations Union on the strength of these books and became a conscientious and rather smug leaflet distributor, alongside the local Liberals and Socialists. The fact that I was a member of the local Junior Imperial League at the same time does not imply that my convictions were suspect. The 'Imps', as the League was called at that time, was a social movement with mild Conservative undertones, so mild that few local members took them seriously. Some of us even attended local Co-operative Youth Group gatherings, determined, socially at least, to enjoy the best of both worlds.

In our area, however, where Conservatism was very deeply rooted, the Tories had practically cornered the youth market and down at the Imps headquarters we had high old times, so long as the local Conservative agent kept out of the way. Conservative policies were not discussed there. The talk was of dance bands, the recently arrived talking pictures, and who had the best legs among the new members.

By the time Hitler took office, however (it was shortly before my twenty-first birthday), I was forced to reconsider my position. Not long afterwards, in order to ensure that my renunciation of war went on record, I signed Canon Dick Sheppard's peace pledge, but it seemed to me, as it must have seemed to many young men at that juncture, that one could not really expect to have it both ways for much longer. Driblets of news concerning the concentration camps reached the town (I was subsequently amazed to learn that conditions in these camps do not appear to have been generally known in Britain until we captured Belsen, in 1945), and I interviewed several Jewish refugees who confirmed the frightful truth of what was happening in Germany after 1933. Then, with the failure of the League to stop Mussolini's invasion of Ethiopia, I moved over, resigning from the Junior Imperial League and writing for the return of my peace pledge card. It came, with a letter of regret, and I celebrated its return by joining Victor Gollancz's Left Book Club.

By now the pattern of Fascist intentions was becoming clearer day by day and after I had digested Koestler's *Spanish Testament* I no longer had any doubts about the future. I executed my private somersault. From advocating disarmament I moved on to write banal leading articles urging the policy of rearmament upon the dithering Government, and I did not blame some of my local Conservative friends from thinking me weak in the head. After all, I was in good company. All but one of my fellow pacifists in town had similarly recanted but we had little to boast about. We had bleated down the years, first to convert swords to ploughshares, then to convert the ploughshares back into swords, and the only excuse I can find for us is that we had grown up in the aftermath of the Somme and Passchendaele and had, in common with most of our generation, been the victims of a gigantic confidence trick. We had honestly believed that the 1914–18 war was a war to end wars. Nobody had told us that the Versailles Treaty was a blueprint for its successor. Yet I do not know that we were any more fatuous than the Americans, or our friends who held to the Right. The disengagement of the one, and the bad faith of the other, brought about the still-birth of the League of Nations at a time when it had a fair chance of survival, whereas the British Government's policy of appeasement was a direct encouragement to the men holding the world to ransom. It was a sorry picture and everyone involved (with the exception of Churchill, who never moderated his Jeremiad) could have been said to have made a contribution to the situation in which the democracies found themselves in 1938.

Yet perhaps I overlook one factor, at least as far as the British electorate was concerned. Perhaps there was something in the very air of Britain in the period between the Armistice and the end of the slump, that made the cavortings of Continental Dictators seem so grotesque that it could be watched for entertainment value alone. God knows, we had enough to occupy us, with three million unemployed, and over seven hundred in our town in 1931, a town with a working population of about four thousand. Aside from that, however, there wasn't one of us, high Tories included, who had not been touched in some way by the great liberal upsurge of ideas that changed the face of Britain in the last years of Victoria's reign and in the first decade of the new century. It was very difficult, growing up in an English shire, watching how our sober elections were conducted, and how an unarmed police force went about their work, to conceive of whole nations succumbing to hysteria on the German and Italian patterns. No one had ever knocked on our doors in the middle of the night and if, perchance, a neighbour was missing from his accustomed place without a satisfactory explanation, the entire district, supervised by polite policemen, joined in the search until he was accounted for.

I suppose, like everyone else in Britain then and now, I took social stability for granted until I had a conversation with a Polish student, a Jew over here on a short holiday in the spring of 1938. He happened to be with me while I was collecting information about a murder and a suicide in one of our surrounding villages, and the nature of my inquiries amazed him. "Why, in the name of God," he said, "should anyone want to murder or kill themselves in Britain?" He told me, shortly before his return to Cracow, that he was living on borrowed time. "I shan't live to be thirty," he said. "That man will come for us soon." I heard from him once in the summer of Munich and after that silence. Very few young Polish Jews survived the war.

I think of the Democrat's dilemma when I see today's demonstrations against the war in Vietnam, and watch films on the Russian rape of Czechoslovakia. Where, exactly, does one draw the line between the renunciation of war as an extension of policy, and tame submission to tyranny? That particular 64,000-dollar question is still unanswered.

2

I have said that international politics did not preoccupy us much in East Devon and this is true, at least until the mid-'thirties. For a majority it remained true until September, 1938, but Munich demolished the last parochial railings that had isolated us through the years, when I was growing up in the little sea-coast town of Exmouth. After the ecstatic post-Munich honeymoon (a brief and very uncomfortable interval for most of us) we knew, with complete certainty, that the roof would fall on us in one year or two.

So few people have been frank about their personal reactions to Munich that I intend to be, admitting that I shared in the general relief when Chamberlain stepped down from the 'plane, smiling his rabbit-toothed smile, and waving his famous piece of paper. I was relieved but by no means reassured. At best it meant a chance for someone to shoot Hitler. At worst it was a respite, one more spring and one more summer perhaps, for the history books told us that wars do not begin until the harvests are in. But when the town clerk asked for volunteers to make out billeting lists for children likely to be evacuated, when an exceptionally courageous local Liberal candidate named Halse stood up in our church hall within a week of Munich and told his audience that they had been duped, and that Hitler would occupy Prague in a matter of weeks, I think I resigned myself to Armageddon.

I had been writing plays then for ten years without ever having had one produced by professionals. That summer, the last summer of peace, I had two presented, one by the Birmingham Repertory, the other at 'Q' Theatre in London. Both were well received and I was offered eight hundred pounds for the film rights of *Printer's Devil*, to appear after the war as *All Over the Town*. I had broken out of the cosy circle at last but my timing could not have been worse. *Printer's Devil* was produced in July. In August the Hitler–Stalin pact was signed. On the first day of September Hitler went looking for that Cracow friend of mine, and Wardour Street, hub of the film industry in London, was evacuated. "It was so quiet," said a wit, "that you could hear the options dropping." Mine was one of them. On

September 3rd all the theatres closed and I started a new local column called 'With the Forces . . .'

I volunteered for the R.A.F. and stayed on the job awaiting a call-up until the spring of 1940, and bad as things were for everybody after that I don't think they were nearly as depressing as the eight months of the Phoney War. I would choose to relive any period of my life in preference to that interval of gloom, frustration, doubt and yammering boredom.

It was as though we had all died and were waiting in a blacked-out railway siding for the undertaker to come and bury us. Nobody who did not live through this period as a young and ambitious person could possibly imagine its overriding sense of futility, for all the time one had depressing doubts about the possibility of a new lease on appeasement and non-intervention. When, at last, the Panzers began to roll westward, when Churchill took Chamberlain's place and the epic of Dunkirk was followed by the Battle of Britain, everything was changed utterly. Then it was as though we had not survived a chain of frightful disasters, but had won a brilliant victory and in a way, I suppose, we had. The alchemy of Churchill, months of brilliant sunshine, and the whiff of Gestapo breath in our nostrils, fused Left and Right in a way that would have seemed unimaginable a year before. Middle-aged men who had been calling one another rude names ever since the invasion of Abyssinia nearly five years before shared an amiable cliff-patrol in the Local Defence Volunteers, forerunner of the Home Guard. Younger men, who had been dragged apart by policemen at the Blackshirt scuffle on Chapel Hill, joined the same unit and travelled in convoy to military depots. People hoped and people grinned. People didn't give a damn about standing alone and fighting it out on the beaches. And (with one exception) nobody I met that summer had the least doubt but that we should emerge not merely intact as a nation but cockier and more self-assertive than we had been for twenty years.

There was something else, too. Whenever I returned to Devon on leave I never once heard the words Left and Right bandied about. They cropped up again, of course, but not until around July 1945, when we all trooped off to the polls.

Kitchener's Manic Stare

I

The one-storey building, cramped between two modern office blocks, looked as if it had no business there. It was small, shabby and totally undistinguished. Some time, perhaps around the period Napoleon's invasion force assembled at Boulogne, it had been given its last coat of whitewash, possibly in readiness to house the balloon section of the Fencibles. Now it was being used as the recruiting centre of the R.A.F. and above the barred window was a large notice-board bearing a chalked legend that screamed, 'R.A.F. Drivers *Urgently* Needed! A few vacancies in other trades'.

Inside a sergeant sat at a trestle table covered with blank forms. The table, and the chair he occupied, were the only items of furniture in the room. It was very cold in there, colder and damper than standing in the queue outside and the sergeant seemed aware of this. He had turned up the collar of his greatcoat, put on a pair of frayed mittens, and pulled down the Balaclava flaps of his forage cap, so that he looked like his great-great-grandfather huddling in a trench before Sebastopol. Thus far had the pointing figure of Kitchener directed me, a belated victim of hypnosis induced by the manic stare of the victor of Omdurman, in 1898.

. . .

The memory of the poster was very clear in my mind on that cold November morning, notwithstanding the fact that it had been stripped from the hoardings twenty-one years ago. As a child it had mesmerised me, along with so many others, most of them to their ultimate ruin. The stern frown, the huge moustaches, the pitiless eyes and the accusing finger, combined to elevate the man to the status of God's Viceroy, so that I saw Kitchener, at that time, as the sternest of stern parents, the most merciless of birch-wielding schoolteachers, the He-Who-Must-Be-Obeyed.

So compelling was that frown and that finger that they could induce feelings of guilt in a six-year-old. Looking up at them I had a conviction I was shirking my duty by standing there alongside my mother in a butter queue. I should have been beating the charge on a parapet somewhere in Artois or Picardy, like the little drummer boys seen in battle scenes painted by Lady Butler.

Posters, of the kind used by big commercial houses to market famous products, had always fascinated me. They were the scenery of Central London and many of them acquired the status of old friends, eagerly greeted at the junction of streets or as one approached a familiar railway arch. The gay, pyjama-clad castaway, clinging to his huge bottle of Bovril; Grandma and granddaughter sipping Mazawattee Tea; the athletic old chap revitalised by a dose of Kruschen Salts and, as soon as I learned to read, the enigmatic Monkey Brand poster that announced, 'Won't Wash Clothes', thus informing you what the product would not do but remaining obstinately silent on what it would achieve.

Kitchener's manic stare did not belong in this jocund company. It was at once a menace and a challenge. It did not so much as hint at glory but demanded the uncomplaining sacrifice of all personal ambitions. And after all these years it had drawn me here, to a room that looked like a dungeon cell in the castle farther up the hill and a single gaoler, wearing a faded blue uniform with blue fingertips to match.

2

The queue outside reached all the way to the High Street, about three or four hundred young men already seeing ourselves as latterday Hell's Angels, rat-tat-tatting our way across Continental skies. And this in spite of persistent rumours that there were no vacancies for aircrew and were unlikely to be for months ahead. Despite this the notice was encouraging. R.A.F. drivers were needed. *Urgently* needed. And there were vacancies in some other trades. The man immediately behind me, introducing himself as Hitchcock, had worked this one out having, it appeared, already gone into training for the R.A.F. by taking a crash course in the new Service slang. "Got some gen," he muttered. "Don't think it's duff gen, either. Got to use the old loaf to slide into this outfit. A.G., that's my fancy. A.Gs sit in the turret and turrets roll away intact when a kite prangs. The rest of the crew fry but the A.G. gets off with a shaking. Pukka gen," and he underlined his advice with a savage nod.

I was not prepared to accept his information concerning the survival prospects of air-gunners but he was right about having to exercise our wits in order to join the R.A.F. at that time. In the autumn of 1939 influence of some kind, or a stroke of luck, was needed to enlist in most arms of the Forces but one required exceptional persistence to infiltrate into the ranks of the R.A.F., as the queue outside the depot demonstrated. Hitchcock continued, in the same confidential undertone, "Back door approach, old boy. They're screaming for tradesmen, catch on? Drivers, flight-mechs., riggers, armourers, even cooks and butchers, Christ help us! You sign on and remuster soon as you've done your square-bash. Stands to reason, doesn't it? I mean, there you are looking in from the inside, with the kites lined up waiting for you. Me? I'll take anything they offer, even A.C.H./G.D. at a pinch." I did not know what A.C.H./G.D. meant but I looked at Hitchcock with respect. Here was a man who had obviously done his homework. The rest of us had to rely on guesses and rumours. Logic was in short supply in the autumn of 1939 and there was a million unemployed to prove it.

As I say, Kitchener had done his part in getting me there but it was difficult to equate his frown and finger with what occurred in that forbidding little room when, at length, Hitchcock, myself, and about a dozen others crossed the threshold and descended three steps into the sub-zero temperature. Elation ebbed from all but Hitchcock, sustained by his easy familiarity with R.A.F. slang and his pukka gen. The rest of us were not so fortunate and advanced with caution, not so much because of the penetrating cold but on account of the crestfallen expression on the faces of the steady stream of rejects. The squat, muffled sergeant at the desk worked by the book. He interviewed, if that is the word, each one of us under the swinging electric bulb but he did not accept a single man. He was like an impatient landlady in high season turning away good money, and one had the impression he would rise at any moment and hang a card reading, 'Full. Try "Seaview" next door', at the window. Then he was confronted with Hitchcock and at once the scene assumed animation so that I forgot my purpose there and slipped into the role of observer. Suddenly it became terribly important to watch Hitchcock enlist. We saw him as the champion of democracy, taking on the forces of reaction and bureaucracy.

He said, gaily, "Put me down for heavy transport, Sarge—Queen Marys, crash tenders, fire-engines, anything you like," and the sergeant raised his head, so that I saw him clearly for the first time.

He was a hardbitten little man, small but thickset, overweight but not flabby. He had wary eyes and a ragged moustache that looked as though it had been gnawed a great deal, probably from frustration at having to redirect so much promising material to the nearest infantry depot. He said, blowing on his mittened fingers, "Full up. No drivers. Next," and I expected to see Hitchcock turn away with a grimace or a brave grin. He did not, however, but remained there, carefully extracting a packet of Player's from his pocket and offering it to the sergeant. The sergeant took a cigarette without thanks and lit it with a match struck on his thumbnail, in the manner of bad men in Westerns. "Okay, Sarge," Hitchcock said, "I'll settle for flight mech.," and he reached out to help himself to a form. The sergeant's hand got there first, pinning Hitchcock's to the table.

"Full up," he said. "Nex'."

Until then I had thought of Hitchcock as a bit of a blowhard. It goes to show that snap judgements should be made sparingly among the English, even during Phoney Wars.

"You've got a notice outside," he said, obstinately, "a bloody great notice that's attracted a bloody great queue. Some of us have been out there an hour."

"You 'ave?"

"Yes, we have."

"I'm cryin' me eyes aht," said the sergeant. "Nex'."

"It's stupid," Hitchcock went on, as though reasoning with himself, "I mean, to have a bloody great notice up saying you want drivers when you don't."

"Bin thinkin' the same all week," the sergeant said. "Now bugger orf, mate, I'm busy." But Hitchcock did not bugger off. Instead he stood quite still, drawing on his cigarette, as though testing the theory of an irresistible force meeting an immovable object.

"Suppose," he said at length, "suppose you go out and scrub that notice?"

The sergeant's chin came up so sharply that it was as though the Invisible Man had struck it from between his cramped knees. He seemed to have some difficulty comprehending the full meaning of Hitchcock's suggestion, as though it had been spoken in a foreign tongue.

"*Scrub it?*" he repeated at last. "You mean *me?*"

"You or us," Hitchcock said. "It don't matter who does it so long as it's done."

The sergeant began to rock, not bodily exactly but from the shoulders upwards. It was a rather curious movement and seemed to have been touched off by the impact of Hitchcock's words striking alternate blows on either ear. There was silence in the crowded room and a sense of terrible expectancy. We might have been watching a complicated high wire act in which, farcically, but also tragically, only Hitchcock and the sergeant were involved. I don't think we saw it as a direct confrontation between the civilian mind and the Service mind but the implication was there, and it was important to us all to see how it would resolve itself.

After what seemed a long time the rocking motion ceased and the sergeant spoke again.

He said, enunciating his words very clearly, "You mean *me* go out *there* and . . . and *rub* it off? Without orders? Without ser much as a chitty from S.H.Q.? On me own like?"

"Why not?" said Hitchcock, "it's wasting people's time, isn't it? Come to that it's holding up the war effort. No bloody future in a notice that doesn't mean what it says, is there?"

I saw then that Hitchcock was not so much a reckless man as an extremely insensitive one. Alone among the men crowded into that little room he was unaware of the enormity of his suggestion, of the sheer idiocy of applying the logic of a civilian to a man who must have sloughed it off years ago, when he was a contemporary of Lawrence of Arabia masquerading as Aircraftman Shaw at Uxbridge. Some instinct warned the rest of us of the impending explosion and we made what room we could for it, backing away from the trestle table and huddling together near the steps leading up to the street.

The sergeant half-projected himself out of his canvas-backed chair and lurched forward, supporting himself on spread hands. His body shook so much that the neatly-stacked enlistment forms cascaded inwards, burying his arms to the elbow. His complexion was that of a man in the throes of a seizure and I found myself looking at his moustache for specks of froth. He was obviously having the greatest difficulty in finding words adequate to the occasion for his lips moved soundlessly as he fought to regain a measure of self-control. Then years of training reasserted themselves and he lowered himself slowly, as upon a bed of nails. One sensed that he had won a great victory over himself and that he owed it to those years on the square, when he had so often come within a hair's-breadth of falling upon some luckless recruit and beating him over the head with a rifle butt. Everybody, I think, was aware of this, that is to say, everybody but Hitchcock. He still looked relaxed and chipper, puffing away at his cigarette whilst awaiting formal sanction of his strange conceit. When it did not come, when the only sound in the room was the intake and expulsion of the sergeant's breath, he just had to press his luck. He was that type of man, the sort of man who would ask someone just acquitted of murder how he had administered the cyanide. He said, "Let's get weaving then. Where's the bloody duster?"

I have never seen a man move more swiftly or witnessed a room cleared at such speed. One moment we were all standing there, watching the confrontation, the next we were all in the street, striking the head of the queue in a body and driving it down the slope so that it lost all cohesion and eddied the width of the pavement. Hitchcock disappeared altogether, blasted from the face of the earth one assumed, but I caught a fleeting glimpse of the sergeant dancing a kind of clog dance immediately below the chalked notice, and a word or two of his self-accompaniment followed me as far as the High Street, phrases one had always associated with enraged drill-sergeants.

. . .

A month later, when I returned to the little building, the notice was still there but the sergeant had gone. In his place sat a corporal with steel-rimmed glasses and a schoolmistressy expression that discouraged me from seeking information concerning his predecessor. The corporal signed us on as Clerks/G.D. and went through the ritual so impassively that it was ridiculous to identify him as the man to whom that pointing finger of Kitchener had directed us.

I never looked at a regular N.C.O. during the next six years without hoping to recognize that sergeant and buy him a beer, for somebody should have rewarded such scrupulous exactitude in the execution of orders. Soldiers have won medals for less, and a host of civil servants have harvested honours for doing precisely what he did as a matter of course. I never did meet him, however, and I never, as I half-expected, saw Hitchcock swaggering round a perimeter in his flying-boots distributing pukka gen. Perhaps, soon after their initial collision, they met and killed one another, but I think not. It is more likely that the sergeant had a stroke and that Hitchcock, troubled by the high rate of casualties among air-gunners the following summer, entered the diplomatic service.

The Far Side of Glory

I

It ought to be obvious that anyone enlisting in the forces of the Crown sacrifices his individuality but every generation has to rediscover this for itself. Just how complete this sacrifice is to an Englishman is not apparent until a day or so after he has taken the oath and donned the motley. He then discovers that it is far more absolute than joining a school or secret society, or, indeed, entering into a marriage contract with a wealthy woman, for not only is he required to exchange his name for a number, and place himself wholly at the disposal of superiors (many of whom are semi-literate) but sign a book, or possess himself of a little slip of paper if he wishes to remove himself from the camp for as much as ten consecutive seconds.

This yielding up of personal liberty takes a good deal of getting used to and an Englishman is less inclined to accept the strictures of his new situation than are his Continental neighbours. In countries across the Channel the male has been conditioned, over generations, to the straitjacket of conscription, whereas here a civilian at peace with the law rarely sees himself as a full-time soldier, sailor or airman, unless persuaded that his national existence is threatened.

Yet there are, for the observant and the moderately adaptable, certain compensations, apart from the glow of rectitude that comforts an enlisted man whenever he runs against a contemporary who had the sense to hang on to his individuality. Comradeship he takes for granted in a matter of days, one might almost say hours, and the Englishman is not much given to protestations of patriotism or the pursuit of glory. The real compensations, for my part, crept up on me during the first seven weeks of my service when I was square-bashing, or hanging about waiting to square-bash, and although unobtrusive they were insistent in attracting my attention, giving me a gentle nudge every now and again and saying, in effect,

"Imagine that! You're shut up in a vast and extremely diverting lunatic asylum-cum-gaol. You haven't done anything, and you're not insane, but here you are so make the most of it. Just look at that warder over there! He's far crazier than any of the inmates. Watch him and see what he does next. Is he going to pretend he's Napoleon?" Or, "What can be the real purpose of this bit of ritual? How did it originate? What kind of person thought it up and wrote it into a manual? He must have been further round the bend than the underlings he employs to teach it to newcomers!"

After a week or two this process of absorbing the impact of people and procedures becomes not merely engrossing but exhilarating, like a ride on a big dipper, followed by a visit to the hall of distorted mirrors. One does not know and cannot guess what will happen next. Or why. Or how it could possibly fit into the pattern of a war for national survival. It has, or seems to have, no possible relevance and no connection whatever with the apparatus of war, like tanks and dive-bombers and machine-guns. In a way it is like a waking dream that would soon develop into a nightmare were it not for the frequent bursts of laughter from all sides and an overall sense of taking part in an unrehearsed comedy presented—one dare not say organised—on a gigantic scale.

I do not suppose for one moment that my experiences during that blazing spring and summer—surely the sunniest of the century—were any different, or more wildly extravagant, than those of anyone else who joined the Forces in 1940. It was only that they seemed so because, for nearly twenty years, I had been prospecting for material to be quarried from an English scene and taken home as raw material for books and plays and stories. Because of this, I imagine, my senses were exceptionally alert to the bizarre and the ridiculous, to the eccentric, the madly farcical and the pseudo-dramatic, so that although I was to remain in the R.A.F. for the better part of six years, it is the first six weeks of that period that are more deeply etched in the memory than any period that followed. I was not closely involved with any of the men I met at that time and if I ever knew their names I have since forgotten them. The scene was changing all the time and the moment we passed out as recruits the men with whom I shared those initial experiences were scattered to the ends of the earth. For all that, I see them clearly after nearly thirty years, in ones and twos and batches, in good humour and ill, in moments of vexation, frustration, consternation and speechless indignation, and to me, taken all round, this vision was worth the sacrifice of individuality.

. . .

I was sworn in at Uxbridge, the camp where Lawrence had buried himself at the height of his fame and subsequently described in his book *The Mint*, withheld from publication until long after his death.

At that time, for my draft at least, it was not a camp where one learned the rudiments of military life, that was attached to volunteers like a porter's stick-on label and subsequently replaced by another sticker identifying him as 'R.A.F.-type'. Uxbridge, in May 1940, was a huge reception centre where a few hundred professionals, most of them promoted overnight to the rank of leading aircraftmen, corporal, sergeant and flight-sergeant, were endeavouring, God help them, to absorb the hundreds of thousands of men who had volunteered for 'the duration of the present emergency' (a subtly-worded phrase this) into what had been a small, highly-trained, extremely efficient service.

Regulars told me at that time what life had been like in pre-war days, before the absorption of more than a million amateurs. Everyone knew his place in the hierarchy, every man was a master of his craft, and the R.A.F. functioned like a well-ordered Victorian household, all the way down from Air Marshal Papa, who read morning prayers, to A.C. Plonk the scullery-maid, who carried cans of hot water up four flights of stairs before she had rubbed sleep from her eyes. I believe this to be true. The framework still existed when I was swallowed by the monster, but even then, less than nine months after the outbreak of war, the pre-war fabric had collapsed under the fearful strains placed upon it during the expansion period. Its victory that same summer, a victory that indubitably saved Europe from eighth-century barbarism, was more of a miracle than war historians would have us believe. Inside the R.A.F. it was generally assumed that the wartime expansion of the

Luftwaffe was accompanied by even greater stresses, and that we kept far enough ahead to win the Battle of Britain by a whisker. I spent the first few days of my service life at Uxbridge before moving on to Cardington, where I shared a bell-tent with nine others under the great hangar from which the airship R.101 set out on her fatal voyage to India in 1930.

Cardington at that time was like a large railway terminus, coping with half a dozen derailments, but Uxbridge was a veritable madhouse, where life alternated between short, crazy rushes and periods of bewildered idleness, shared by our N.C.O.s. These last behaved exactly like a pack of half-trained sheepdogs coping with an unfamiliar flock of sheep. Whenever they heard a whistle they ran in, prancing and barking, but soon they decided that the whistle was a direction for other dogs away across the camp, whereupon they stopped short, crouched and hung on our flanks, panting and rolling their eyes.

The first of them, I recall, was a tubby little man with hastily-tacked-on corporal's chevrons, who was required to swear us in and supervise our trade tests. I got the impression that both procedures were as new to him as they were to us. We shot about between marquees that contributed to the pervading Uxbridge smell, not unlike the West Buckland smell, inasmuch as it contained the same basic element of boiled greens but here it was laced with bruised grass, sweaty blankets and sun-bleached canvas. The corporal lined us up and pressed tattered New Testaments into our right hands, squealing that we were to repeat after him the oath of allegiance binding us to "protect the king anishairs". We were uncertain as to what we were pledging ourselves to protect but before we could discuss it we were deprived of our Testaments and hounded into a larger marquee where, on a trestle table, there rested an Oliver typewriter and a book on ornithology open at a page devoted to chaffinches. Shorthand-writers were then ordered to take down a dictated passage relating to chaffinches and type it on the Oliver typewriter. This was not difficult, for the corporal, having trouble with unfamiliar words, read very slowly, but when it came to typing it out the thing was quite impossible. The typewriter was so old and so clogged that Mr. Oliver himself would have had to borrow a Remington or a Smith's Premier in order to produce a legible typescript.

The corporal was aware of this and had, it seemed, insured against it. His job, as he saw it, was to produce qualified clerks at high speed and he did just this with commendable ingenuity. When the typewriter carriage stuck and the keys clubbed he pointed helpfully at a wastepaper basket crammed with fairly legible transcripts of the same passage. "Take one of them an' 'and it to me," he ordered, and we did, wordlessly, sometimes using a test-piece that the corporal had just returned to the basket. He then said, "Okay. Passed first class, all of yer. Congratulations, mates!", and we were herded out of the marquee at the double and into a pay-tent where we received eight and threepence apiece, representing three days' pay at two and ninepence per day. We went off to London and spent it at the Windmill Theatre, afterwards repairing to the Union Jack Club in the Waterloo Road.

At Cardington they were not quite so amiable. The tent lines under the hangar stretched away as far as the little railway halt and one of the N.C.O.s. placed in charge of our draft was another newly-promoted corporal afflicted, poor chap, with a slightly-twisted face as though, when a child, he had been confronted with some unimaginable horror, had blanched and had his features frozen in a singular expression. One of the less gentlemanly recruits in our tent said the corporal's face reminded him vividly of a cat's arse and after that we always thought of him as 'Catsarse', not because we did not sympathise with his difficulties but because he seemed only to know two English words. They were "On p'raaaade!"

He would appear two dozen times a day in the tent lines screaming "On p'raaade!" in a voice that would have rocked the airship R.101 at its moorings but there was rarely any purpose in the order or the resultant scramble from the crowded tents. When we had assembled and numbered we would stand about in the broiling sun for upwards of twenty minutes and would then be dismissed, so that I readily fell in with the suggestion of a red-headed recruit, already far gone in disillusion, to hide under the blankets when Catsarse issued his next order to muster outside. It was an unfortunate decision. This time the others were away a long time and when they returned each was possessed of a couple of treasury notes. All Ginger and I had succeeded in doing was to dodge the initial pay-parade and for me this resulted in complications that lasted until the following spring, when my name and number was finally added to the list in pay-accounts.

My fellow conspirator on this occasion interested me, at least, his sense of disillusionment did. He was like a bride who had taken the greatest pleasure in the preparations for the wedding, in the actual ceremony, and the reception but had recoiled from the moment of truth when she found herself between the sheets with a brutish husband.

Whenever he had gained the privacy of the tent he would begin to curse and mutter, his maledictions being shared between the R.A.F. and himself for being such a fool as to volunteer. Sometimes he would work himself up into a lather of self-reproach, searching madly for the hidden motives that had prompted him to commit such a monstrous folly and it was interesting to listen to him as he tossed and turned under his blanket, trying to find room for his legs without incommoding his comrades, or inadvertently striking the tent by dislodging the pole. He would mumble, like a deranged priest at his prayers, "Can't understand it . . . nobody pushed me . . . nobody twisted my arm. But here I am, trapped . . . finished . . . chivvied from arsehole-to-breakfast-time, and for what? That's what beats me. For what? For two and bloody ninepence a day!" Gloom finally got the better of him, his pessimism enlarging itself until it enfolded the entire nation and its present perils. "Point is we're going to lose," he would reflect aloud. "Nothing to stop that bugger now, that's for sure! We've had it, lads. We've really had it, you hear? He'll be over here in a week or so, paratroopers dropping right beside that hangar, and then what'll we do? Tell you what I'm going to do—run like hell!"

At this juncture in the war such wild talk was terrible to hear and began to alarm some of his tentmates. At first they reasoned with him, laying stress on our former triumphs, on the lamentable failures of Spain and France to invade us in 1588 and 1805, on the strength of the British Navy, on the possibility of a mass rising in Europe, but it was no use. He refused to be comforted and if ever there was a man seeking arrest under the new law prohibiting the spreading of alarm and despondency it was Ginger the Doomed. I often wondered what happened to him that winter, when the bombs were crashing down on British cities and the prospect of annihilation loomed large. Perhaps, like others whose patriotism overreached itself in the spring, he escaped from the Service through one of the less conventional channels, such as loss of memory or persistent bedwetting, or perhaps he managed to persuade someone to reclaim him to industry. I cannot believe that he ever became converted to the war or to his part in it. His prejudice was too deep for that and all the more outstanding because, at that time, he was the only person I met who gave expression to a perfectly logical fear that we would be beaten in the short run. Perhaps he became a detainee under Regulation 18B, and was given a comfortable cell alongside Sir Oswald Mosley. He would, I think, have adjusted to that. He could have sat out the war in Wormwood Scrubs, prophesying the collapse of the British Empire, whilst still probing into his own reasons for volunteering in 1940.

Before we left Cardington for Morecambe we discovered that we had misjudged Catsarse. He did possess a vocabulary larger than two words and exercised it for our especial benefit. It was the day we were bundled into stores and issued with our uniforms and were then so civilian-minded as to set up an exchange mart with the object of adapting them to our persons. Speed was so essential in those days that nobody bothered to measure our girth and we received greatcoats, tunics and trousers according to our height, ascertained by slamming each recruit against a wall and stunning him with a slide rule.

The results were extraordinary. Thin men, shrouded in voluminous garments, looked like carelessly assembled scarecrows, and fat men were unable to fasten more than the top button of any garment so that they wore tunic and greatcoats as cloaks, giving them the aspect of Corsican brigands. Glengarries were distributed with similar sang-froid. Some rested on biggish heads like little blue tents pitched on a boulder. Others, flung at narrow-headed recruits, came halfway down the face, as though the wearer was preparing to rob a passing stage-coach. Realising that we could not face the prospect of a long war in this sort of gear we began to swap and were well launched on the process when Catsarse appeared and demanded to know what was happening. His reaction was similar to that of the recruiting sergeant at the depot, when advised by Hitchcock to expunge the out-of-date notice. He saw the exchange not as a means of expediency but as a military crime that bordered on mutiny. He screamed and danced and ran about tearing garments from the backs of half-dressed men, and telling us at the top of his voice that we could each get a year in the glasshouse for taking such liberties with government property. It was useless to explain the reason behind the orgy of swapping. The harder we tried the more excited he became, so we spent the rest of the morning dodging about the tent lines in search of our original issue. Later on we did our swapping in private but I never did manage to exchange my tunic, a very curious garment indeed composed of two entirely foreign halves, one designed for a man about six feet in height, the other for a shortish, rather plump man. I cannot imagine how it was ever sewn together in the first place and can only suppose that the tailor was blind and sewed by Braille. The left flap projected two and a half inches below its fellow, and the breast of the right half bulged, as though it had been cut for a busty W.A.A.F. Nor was this all. For some reason, that had to do with the fibres in the cloth, the ends of the vent stuck out at right angles like the feathers of an amorous duck. I wore it for three years and eight months and finally came to terms with it in the way a housewife will sometimes cherish a handleless kitchen knife, passed on by mother, that she used to prepare the first meal after the honeymoon. I never succeeded in swapping my boots either and they were a singular pair. They turned up at the toes and did not look like boots but more like a clumsy pair of Oriental slippers.

On our final day at Cardington we were mustered on the up platform of the railway halt, not for the purpose of entraining but in order to establish our identities beyond all doubt, and have our names checked against a nominal roll. We looked directly across the line at Catsarse, who stood on the down platform alone, holding a sheaf of papers clipped to a board, and calling each name and number as his forefinger reached it in the column. As soon as his number was called the owner was required to jump off the platform and cross the line to the down platform, where he was at once dismissed, but as there were more than five hundred of us the process occupied most of the afternoon.

Little by little the ranks began to shrink until, at around 16.30 hours, I was alone on the up platform, wondering at my isolation, and beginning to think I was not properly enlisted. Then Catsarse tucked his board under his arm and glared across at me, enquiring, "You over there! Is your bleedin' name 'Daffodil'?" I told him it wasn't and explained who I was, but my words must have been carried away on the wind for, after re-examining his list, he said, "Number 925656?" and when I admitted to this, "Okay. Near enough. It's the number that cahnts. Dis-*miss*, A.C. Daffodil!" He then walked slowly away shaking his head, wondering perhaps if he was likely to encounter an A.C. Violet or Hyacinth in the incoming draft. Because of this I do not associate Cardington with hot summer days but with the promise of spring.

2

From Cardington we travelled by slow train to Morecambe, an eager, wisecracking, skylarking lot. We might have been excursionists getting our annual glimpse of the sea and secretly I marvelled at our high spirits. The man next to me kept singing snatches of 'Scatterbrain'. In July 1940, what, I wonder, did the English have to sing about? Was every man on that train exulting in his release from predictability?

We were billeted in one of the tall boarding houses on the sea-front. I was senior man of a group of twelve, wedged into three bedrooms, and we were not very welcome because the landlady (the prototype of Mrs. Bounty, in *Worm's Eye View*) regarded high summer as her seasonal peak and all she received for billeting us was one pound per man per week.

What genuinely astonished me about Morecambe at that time was its neutrality and in this respect the town was not unique. Blackpool, just along the coast, was no different in 1941, and some seaside resorts, far removed from the Channel coasts, managed to retain their resort status throughout the entire war. The week we arrived in Morecambe coincided with the opening stage of the Battle of Britain but nobody would have imagined, passing along the sea-front, or marching up and down the pier, that the nation was engaged in a war with a few hundred tribesmen in the Khyber Pass, much less the hordes of

Panzers and Stormtroopers who had just taken Paris and the Channel ports. I don't know whether Wakes Weeks were on but the town was crammed with holiday-makers wearing blazers and summer dresses, who gave us incurious looks as we stamped past their deckchairs, learning how to salute pilot-officers to the front and flight-lieutenants to the left. They were by no means hostile, and here and there one of them smiled, but they all seemed vaguely embarrassed by so much martial activity and I got the impression they would have been relieved if we had been kept away from the sea and the parks. Our landlady, Devil take her, had civilian visitors in the first-floor rooms and we did their washing-up when we came in from the streets. We never succeeded in coming to terms with this. Nor did anyone ever persuade us that all those holiday-makers, licking their ice-creams and nibbling their candyfloss, were war-workers enjoying a well-earned respite from factories in the North and Midlands. Neither were we successful in establishing friendly relations with our landlady, whose discipline was far more galling than that existing in any camp I occupied later in the war and who seemed, perhaps on account of lost lets, outraged by our presence. One of the bonuses of the nuclear bomb is that there can never be another war such as this, with one half of the nation under military discipline and the other living under a sign 'Business as Usual'.

From Morecambe, a month or so later, I moved down to Cosford, my first experience of a permanent Technical Training Camp that sat on the landscape like a vast town, north-west of Wolverhampton. Here I was set to work in an orderly room and soon came to realise that I should never have listened to that idiot Hitchcock about the prospects of remustering inside the Service. At Cosford I found myself bogged down as a clerk and it seemed to me extremely unlikely, short of a great stroke of luck, that I would be permitted to remuster to another trade as the war got into its stride.

The work was hard and very monotonous, a nonstop orgy of form-filling and typing daily routine orders, nominal rolls, personnel occurrence reports, chits of every description and it entailed long spells of night duty, without a compensating day in the open. We were in Technical Training Command, one of the five Commands existing in the R.A.F. at that time, and as always at this type of camp, where the intake of airmen taking specialised courses was continuous, the permanent staff was far too small to cope with basic requirements. Every so often armies of embryo flight-mechanics and riggers descended on us, with their accumulated needs and complicated personal problems. Avalanches of paper poured into the orderly room and spilled into our trays. Telephones rang every few moments and distant strangers asked us what they were to do with eighty-four flight-mechanics stranded in Edinburgh, or sixty-three riggers left behind in Dover Castle.

The peacetime administration system, devised I was told, by experts from Gamages, Harrods and Woolworths, was already breaking down under the strains imposed upon it, not because it was ill-conceived but because it had been swamped and we newcomers had been given no opportunity to absorb it, but if we worked hard even more was demanded of the nucleus of regulars. In addition to coping with the enormous amount of paper work they had to find time to train us.

The office equipment was archaic. Elderly Oliver typewriters, of the kind I had used to take my trade test at Uxbridge, were totally inadequate for the tasks expected of them and went sick one after another, so that I sent home for my portable Remington and used it all the time I worked in orderly rooms. The regulars were a splendid lot, invariably kind and patient, and genuinely grateful for what little help we could give them, but as the pace of the war hotted up, and the administrative needs grew and grew with thousands of men arriving to be trained for manning the airfields of Fighter, Bomber and Coastal Commands, the desks could only be cleared by working round the clock, fortified every now and again by mugs of tea served from a bucket.

A popular legend has grown up concerning the undue emphasis placed on paperwork in the armed forces during World War Two. I have seen film-shots of impatient squadron commanders of the Bader type, throwing files into the wastepaper basket as a gesture of contempt. I am sure Bader was far too good an officer to act in this way. He would have known that it took upwards of thirty ground staff to keep a single pilot aloft, and each one of those ground staff, 'wingless wonders' as safely entrenched civilians came to call them, had to be trained and clothed and fed. They had to be supplied with stores, tools and equipment of every kind and their manifold personal problems had to be investigated by M.O.s, padres, and legal and welfare officers. All these processes required detailed paper work and God knows, much as I hated it at the time, I soon realised that without that inflow and outflow of paper the R.A.F. could not have functioned for a week.

I was duty clerk at Wing H.Q. on Sunday, September 16th, when we got the invasion alert and I don't think I ever did a longer or more complex stint in my whole life. I was on the job two days and one night without a break other than for meals and only an occasional flash of that interval returns to me now. A gas-caped, tin-hatted flight-sergeant, stumping into the orderly room and saying, casually, "Well, chum, the bastards are landing. This is it"; a warrant officer, demanding the keys of the decontamination centre; a flying officer ringing from Crewe and demanding of me (with three months' experience) how he could get a trainload of flight-mechanics to the camp when the regular rail service had been suspended. But above all, the quiet voice of a Spitfire pilot, ringing from Duxford, begging me to find his brother who was serving on the camp. "Things are pretty lively down here," he said, apologetically, "and I'd like to have a word with the kid before I take off again."

By early autumn, when some kind of rhythm had been established and I had been upgraded to leading-aircraftman, I told myself that by any means short of desertion I must escape the claustrophobic atmosphere of that Nissen hut. For years now I had been free-ranging, making my own daily time-table and I found the immobility and repetitiveness of the job insufferable. I knew then that I had made a bad misjudgement and must start looking for a means to correct it, so I put in for a commission that necessitated volunteering for aircrew. At that time only aircrew rejects were considered for commissioning in another branch and the prospect of being shot to pieces in the sky seemed infinitely preferable to drowning under an avalanche of forms.

There was a chance that I would be accepted as an air-gunner but although I passed the colour test I was ultimately rejected on account of a defective right eye, and had to be content with the promise of the C.O. that he would put me forward for a commission as soon as I had completed a year in the Service. That was too long to wait so I tried to remuster to several other trades and at length took the desperate step of volunteering for their bomb-disposal squad but here I ran down the true source of the trouble. Clerk/General Duties, was Group III and it was a rule of the Service that no one could remuster downwards, that is to say, into Groups IV or V, embracing many of the trades practised in the open. Apart from this, I was a shorthand writer and we were in very short supply at that time. Stuck with clerking I decided to relieve the monotony of the endless days and nights by organising camp entertainments, starting with a revue and building up to a Christmas pantomime.

I have since met men in the entertainment industry who used camp entertainments as an escape hatch from routine work into an area where their talents were fully extended, but either I was unlucky or my talents were not sufficiently outstanding. The C.O., a blunt, ex-naval type, asked me how many acts pantomimes had and when I told him two he gave me two days off to write the script.

The pantomime, notwithstanding, was a success. It was expertly produced by a cheerful, fresh-faced bespectacled airman, who approached me one night and politely offered his services, telling me that he had played small parts in several British films. I accepted the offer gladly and he made a splendid job of it. His name was Ken Annakin, familiar to a generation of post-war filmgoers as the director of *Those Wonderful Men In Their Flying Machines* and many other successful films, including one I was to write, *Value for Money*, with Diana Dors in the lead. Incidentally, that pantomime, *Binbad the Airman*, was instrumental in saving the Birmingham Repertory Company part of its scenery. We borrowed a lorry-load for the occasion and when we returned it the theatre's New Street store was a smouldering ruin, having suffered a direct hit the night before.

In the late autumn the tedium of life in that scurrying place was relieved by the arrival of my wife and the issue of a living-out pass. It promised more than it offered. The only lodgings available to a couple living on an L.A.C.'s pay and a married allowance, together totalling about fifty shillings a week, was a small back room in a council house in a country town a few miles up the line, and rail journeys to and from the camp were complicated by endless delays caused by bombing. Another airman and his wife occupied the front room, the third bedroom being used by the landlady and her husband, a butcher who was dying of cancer of the stomach. His condition emphasised the hopelessness of that era, for us and for everyone around us. Each night, regular as clockwork, German bombers throbbed across the sky, showering the industrial Midlands with land-mines, five-hundred-pound bombs and incendiaries. The landscape of the approaches to the cities changed day by day. At night the blackout regulations were made ludicrous by the numerous fires. Towards Christmas our landlord died. A few minutes before he had asked me to lift him on to the commode and when I saw that he was unlikely to last the night I telephoned his daughter. The doctor came, signed a certificate and shrugged his shoulders. What was one death among so many? Coventry, only a few miles away, was in ruins.

In the New Year I was posted to Bridgnorth, the first of many spot postings that were to contribute to the frustrations of that period. Trained men, and I now regarded myself as a trained man, were constantly being uprooted and sent off in dribs and drabs all over the British Isles, often to no purpose, for when they arrived nobody expected them. It usually required about a month to settle to a new routine and that month was invariably wasted. Apart from this these blind, individual postings had, I am certain, an adverse effect upon morale. Sailors and infantrymen learned to work together as a unit, sometimes serving through the entire war in one another's company, but every cross-country train in Britain at that time carried airmen encumbered with kit, making their solitary way to yet another camp. In the period between May 1940, and December 1943, I was booked in at thirteen.

Every now and again the mechanical grab at R.A.F. Ruislip reached out and snatched a shoal of men for overseas postings. On one occasion I got as far as the boat and was struck off the draft, having been promoted, in my absence, to the rank of corporal. It was a mixed blessing, carrying another two shillings a day but at the rank of corporal the buck, as the Americans say, stops. It cannot be passed any further and perhaps this explains Corporal Hitler's determination to initiate orders instead of acting as longstop. In the capacity of corporal I once found myself in the unenviable situation of having to select a required number of tradesmen to fill a draft for overseas. I did it by lottery.

In the late summer of 1941 prospects suddenly seemed a little brighter. I was posted to Blackpool, then seething with airmen and May, who had been trekking round in my wake like a *vivandière*, found yet another back room in a seaside boarding house.

We had visited Blackpool in the piping days of peace. I always thought of it in the context of *Hindle Wakes* and the intriguing query printed on the playbills wherever the piece was presented—'Should Fanny Marry Allan?' Fanny would have had plenty of alternatives in wartime Blackpool, where something like thirty thousand airmen were billeted in the town and all the principal hotels were used as wing headquarters. May got a job here on the local newspaper and we then had sufficient money to eat if food could be found. One of the disadvantages of a living-out pass was that one was always hungry.

At Blackpool the curious schism of wartime Britain between serviceman and civilian was again evident. Town life was conducted on two levels. The resort was being used as a recruit training centre and all day long the voices of the drill instructors echoed in streets of late Victorian and Edwardian home-from-homes. But neither permanent staff nor recruits had much personal contact with the residents, who must surely have benefited from the enormous influx of Service personnel. Bickerings between the two sectors were frequent and often acrimonious. It sometimes seemed to me that we were not in England at all but on neutral soil, Swedish perhaps, or Swiss. Later, in French and Belgian provinces, I felt much more at home.

It was at Blackpool that I became aware of the continuing failure on the part of the R.A.F. to adapt to the pressures of expansion, stressed earlier in this chapter. By now hundreds of thousands of conscripted men were joining us, called by regulars and volunteers, 'The population of China', a term derived from their seven-letter service numbers and to anyone in a position to observe, the waste of manpower was appalling. Nowhere was this more apparent than in the hotel that housed the Non-Effective Pool, a place to which all the odds and sods gravitated.

Here were recruits whose initial period of training had been broken for one reason or another, through illness, accident, compassionate leave on account of bombed homes, recall to industry, and a dozen other reasons. By the autumn of 1941 the pool was a maelstrom and the N.C.O.s in charge of it were overwhelmed by the resultant muddle. Nominal rolls of strays were pinned to the walls and senior N.C.O.s running the Pool were expected to keep track of every one of them. This was clearly impossible, for the names changed every hour as men came and went, were posted, deserted, or just went into hiding in cinemas and cafés. It was a sobering experience to stand and watch the poor devils at work, darting round rooms that had housed generations of Lancashire holiday-makers and scratching out names with stubs of pencil. I thought I had seen the ultimate in paper avalanches at Cosford but work in that N.E. Pool was far more demanding than in an orderly room and sometimes it seemed to me that the senior flight-sergeant, and his temporary staff, were drowning under it and coming up for air every few seconds as a stream of runners appeared to wave more chits under their noses.

A more entertaining spectacle at Blackpool was to witness a swoop by military police on the known lairs of the scrimshankers, who were flushed out into the open like game and paraded in the street for a spot check of names and numbers, and an explanation of what they were doing watching a film at 15.00 hours on a winter's afternoon. No amount of punitive action, however, could contain them. They were too many and far too well versed in the tactics of evasion. Even while their names were being called they would bolt down alleyways like rabbits, or drift away and merge with groups of men having their tea break. Because they all wore identical uniforms it was difficult to isolate them and in the end the parade would shred away and the M.P.s would go into action again, like a posse in a Western film.

It was all part of the national mood at that time, a kind of limbo between the backs-to-the-wall period of Dunkirk and the Battle of Britain, and the flood tide of hope that began with El Alamein and extended to D-Day two and a half years later.

In the meantime everybody I met seemed to put their faith in the Red Army, battling it out in Kharkov and Sebastopol. A heady wind of enthusiasm for Communism blew through the billets and men began to refer to Stalin (as yet unmasked) as 'Uncle Joe'. I have always believed that the hangover of this brief love affair with the Russians had a good deal to do with Labour's unexpected victory in July 1945.

In the meantime, however, the urgency had ebbed from the war. Fear of invasion had lifted. Hitler became a joke again and service became a drudgery. A kind of disgruntled somnolence settled over the town, relieved only by newspaper reports of Russian heroism and this uninspired mood was strengthened by news, flashed on the cinema screens in December, of the attack on Pearl Harbour. With that Blackpool and its vast population of airmen seemed to settle down to wait for the invasion of Europe and the collapse of Germany.

The Hide and Seek Camps

I always thought of them as the hide and seek camps. Many of them had innocent, rustic-sounding, Good-Queen-Bessie names —Hinton-in-the-Hedges, Renscombe Down and Peplow-with-Hodnett, and the like, so that you tended to see them as green islands in the drab pattern of wartime England, with its near-perfect blackout, its pilchards, spam, clothing coupons, rationing and utility fixation. From a distance they seemed to hold the lost secret of peace but this was a mirage. They only appeared that way because they were a hell of a long way from anywhere else and all the signposts had been removed. By order; to confuse stormtroopers; who had been expected years before but had somehow missed the ferry.

When you arrived at a hide and seek camp you always had the impression that you were the second man to arrive, the first being the gate sentry who examined your identity card. There was never the least evidence of martial stir in and around the manor house, lodge, or farmhouse that did duty for S.H.Q. Smoke dribbled from a makeshift cookhouse that had been a barn or a shippon for several centuries, reassuring you that you would be fed if you were not looking for dainties but when you entered there was rarely anyone sitting at the tables inside and sometimes you could hump your kitbag and accoutrements a mile around the perimeter before you came across the odd airman spiking wastepaper with his pointed stick, or a shirt-sleeved W.A.A.F. hanging her smalls on a line.

Yet things happened in those camps, as you discovered once you had settled in and drawn your blankets and palliasse. All manner of things that seemed to have very little to do with the war raging outside but too far away to be heard. The Station Commander's pigs might escape, to be hunted through the woods by whooping personnel. A couple of aircraft—possibly the sole complement of a camp—might collide on take-off, to become the subject of a Court of Enquiry a year from now. The

N.A.A.F.I. might catch fire and it would be discovered that the fire-tender crew had gone on leave and taken their keys with them. Not the sort of things that usually happened behind the wire of R.A.F. stations but far more diverting than occurrences in the big pre-war camps like Uxbridge and Cosford. Perhaps this is why I preferred them.

Particularly memorable was my arrival at Hinton-in-the-Hedges, in the early spring of '43. It was so deep in the hedges that its presence could not be detected from a standpoint of ten yards. The runway, hemmed in with Northamptonshire timber, was innocent of aircraft but sported a fine crop of weeds growing between cracks in the tarmac. Not a soul was in sight and once I had turned my back on the gate sentry I might have been walking across a Constable landscape. I followed a petrol pipe that beckoned me towards an isolated building on the skyline and halfway there I met another corporal carrying a buff file and marching along very purposefully, as though he had an important mission to fulfil. I asked him to direct me to S.H.Q. and he said he would turn right about and accompany me there. It was the farmhouse, he said, reversing direction, but when I protested that I did not want to take him out of his way he opened the file and showed a dozen sheets of blank foolscap paper. "I'm not going anywhere special," he said, "I carry this file wherever I go. It's the R.A.F. equivalent of the Navy broom. Nobody ever challenges an Erk with a file under his arm. I carried this one all over Malta during the siege." It was a piece of camouflage anyone living in a hide and seek camp would be likely to adopt and I lost no time in getting one for myself.

The thing that staggered me about Hinton-in-the-Hedges was its hidden strength in personnel. I arrived on a Monday and the fortnightly payday came round the following Friday. In the interval I had assessed the camp's population at round about two dozen, including officers, but when I went down to the dining hall to draw my fortnightly three pounds, fifteen shillings, it was overflowing with airmen and W.A.A.F.s. At least two hundred stepped forward, saluted and bawled their last three numbers when the cashier pushed money across the table. Then, just as mysteriously, they all disappeared again and I never did discover where they spent the fourteen days separating two paydays. Was it on satellites over the horizon? Or in caves, where secret weapons were being assembled? Or, as I think more likely, in a private Arcadia behind the screen of woods?

It was at one of these hide and seek camps—I forget which—that my pay arrears finally caught up with me.

Ever since that ill-judged moment at Cardington, when I had hidden under the blankets with Ginger the Doomed, and missed my initial payday, I had been living on interim payments, dribs and drabs of sometimes as little as ten shillings at a time. I lodged a series of complaints and had interviewed innumerable pay-accounts clerks but I could never establish a case strong enough to lead to a settlement. Somewhere in that river of paper that flowed in and out of every one of these establishments was a chit with my name on it and one day, I promised myself, it would emerge, to my own relief and everyone else's astonishment. Finally it did, halfway through the 'D's at a trifling pay-parade.

I had only attended out of habit. The pay-sergeant called: "Dearden, double-o-six—one pound, seventeen shillings and sixpence; Delahaye, one-one-seven—two pounds, one shilling and sixpence"; snd then, after an understandable pause, "Delderfield, six-five-six—thirty-seven pounds, sixteen shillings." It was an odd sensation, to stand there open-mouthed with everyone staring in my direction, to step forward, gather up that wad of notes, step back, salute, and try to make myself invisible. I left the camp shortly after that and for once I welcomed a posting. I never could persuade anyone that I was not acting as an *agent provocateur* and was a disguised Group Captain planted among them to listen for careless talk that cost lives.

Providing you had a taste for rural seclusion, life on a hide and seek camp was infinitely preferable to life on an established base. Nobody chivvied you and you could sometimes go days without seeing an officer or even a flight-sergeant. Discipline was slack and crafty weekends were easy to come by. A family atmosphere grew up inside S.H.Q. and at every one of these camps tender friendships developed between airman and W.A.A.F., encouraged no doubt by the scent of wildflowers that came out of the woods, and the sensation of being one of a company of castaways not over-anxious to be rescued.

We made our own entertainments and they were usually an improvement on the occasional E.N.S.A. show. At Hinton I staged *Printer's Devil* (and ultimately got my commission on the strength of it) and at Peplow we formed a Pep Society that organised, not merely concerts and other entertainments, but outspoken debates on current affairs.

If you were partial to creature comforts the hide and seek camps were not for you. Sanitary conditions in some of them were primitive and the food, arriving irregularly by long haul from a distant parent station, and usually prepared by a single, grossly overworked cook, left a good deal to be desired, even in wartime Britain. At Renscombe Down, on the Dorset coast, we queued for one meal a day and ran two miles into Swanage every evening in order to be on hand for what was available at a voluntary canteen. We washed, hundreds of us, at a single tap in the yard, and every day more and more men arrived to find accommodation in or around the girls' school where the camp was pitched. I wondered sometimes what those girls did about calls of nature. Our privy was a communal one, crescent-shaped and screened with strips of hessian. It had a nice sea view and men would dally there on the six-seater, reading fragments of newspapers and discussing topics like the relief of Stalingrad and the destructive power of the new block-busters we were then dropping on Essen. I slept for a fortnight in a leaking patrol tent that provided some kind of shelter for eight of us but by then I was an old campaigner. On the fifteenth night, with rain bucketing down, I slipped out to make my own arrangements. S.H.Q. had taken over the school buildings and having prospected it by daylight I knew that it was already full to overflowing. I had noted, however, a disused radiator in a wall recess in the games room, and this I carted away and dumped in the yard, moving into the recess where I was tolerably comfortable for the remainder of my stay. Across the room, sometimes illuminated by a sliver of moonlight, was an honours board containing the names and school-dates of girls who were now, I imagined, the mothers and wives of airmen. The board was a pleasant reminder of pre-war decades, when the squeals of hockey-players would have penetrated here from the playing field where the tents were pitched. It always seemed to me evidence of a world turned upside down that here, where fifty men sprawled and snored, girls in pigtails had once indulged in a passion for the gym mistress. I wonder if it is a school again, and whether the owners were compensated by the Government for that radiator?

It is the hide and seek camps rather than huge, anonymous R.A.F. towns like Uxbridge and Cosford that I recall with a twinge of nostalgia after the passage of nearly thirty years, and it was of the hide and seek camps, in direct relation to their big brothers, that I thought when there was all that noise about the Royal Commission's decision that we should scrap our local councils and surrender our civic future to monster regional groupings. It would be good for us, they said. It would save us time and money all round in the long run. Would it? Welfare, as applied to the serving airman during World War Two, was generally very good. He could be sure of justice and compassion on any camp, providing he was patient and content to chart his case through the usual channels. But if he was looking for expediency he was far more likely to find it in a hide and seek camp, as I did, in the winter of 1942–43, after I had learned that my wife had been rushed into hospital after losing the child she was expecting.

I was very new on the camp. I had not even been assigned a unit and in a situation like this one needed contacts. I took a hut-mate's advice and went straight to the Station Warrant Officer, a hardbitten regular, who had battled his way up from the Boys' Service and taken twenty years to do it. He heard my story in glum, unblinking silence, an impassive, unemotional man I would have said, sparing of words, even in his cups. When I mentioned that we had already lost two children, however, he half-turned and threw back the hatch that linked his tiny office with the orderly room. "Corporal here needs a railway warrant to Devon," he said to the duty clerk. "See that he gets it straight away," and to me, "Train to Gloucester at six-seventeen. You'll make it if you put your skates on. Here's a 295 for a week. Wire or 'phone if you need an extension."

I began to thank him but he waved thanks aside, adding, with the faintest touch of embarrassment, "Good luck, chum. Regards to the missus."

I had never seen him before and I never saw him again, but

because of him I was at the hospital before it was light and that despite an air-raid *en route*. He was not untypical of the senior N.C.O.s one encountered in the R.A.F., particularly in the hide and seek camps. A commission did not mean a great deal in these places. The life of the station revolved around a handful of regulars who had left school at fourteen but had learned all it is necessary to know about the art of handling men in sun-blistered little patches east of Suez, on the decks of crowded troopships, in cheerless barrack blocks set back from a treeless plain, and in hideaway camps like the one where my W.O. friend was nursing officers and men alike.

I remembered these places with affection later in the war when I was attached to Air Ministry, and in touch with them by telephone and signal. The radio programme, *Much Binding-in-the-Marsh* had made them a national joke by then, and staff officers who had never spent an hour in one would sometimes make merry at their expense. A bell would tinkle and the officer, remembering Air Ministry's love of practical jokes, would say, "It's Little Butterwart-under-Edge on the blower, chaps. *Is* there such a place, or is somebody pulling my leg? Sling over the green book and let me check before I make a bloody fool of myself." They would give him the green confidential book that listed every R.A.F. establishment and he would assure himself that he was not the victim of a practical joke and listen to the respectful supplications of an adjutant at Little Butterwart-under-Edge. At times like this I would have been delighted to hear he had been posted there.

The Vivandières

The flapper went out of fashion around 1932, the breed being rendered obsolete by a preference, on the part of young women, for individuality. Girls became girls in their own right and ceased to practise the cult of what one might call collective-projection-of-come-hitherness. Ten years elapsed before the demands of total war promoted a somewhat similar demonstration of collectivism on the part of British womanhood. This was the sudden emergence of the Service Type, complete with uniform trappings, racy slang, and shame-the-Devil attitudes seen in the W.R.E.N., the A.T.S. and the W.A.A.F. God bless them one and all.

I use the word 'similar' advisedly. There was, in fact, little similarity (beyond a subconscious urge to conform to popular demand) between the Service girl of 1941–45 and her predecessor, the flapper of 1922–32. The flapper was essentially feminine, in some ways as feminine as the girls who wore the crinoline and poke bonnet. For all her insistence on personal liberation she was always prepared to defer to the male, whereas the Service girl embarked upon her career with a very real appreciation of sex-equality and was often at pains to prove it. Once initiated into the mystique she could be seen downing her pint of bitter with the best of us, could be heard swearing lustily when she was thwarted, and not only knew verse and chorus of all the bawdy soldier songs but sang them in mixed company, thereby giving civilians an erroneous impression of her moral standards. She had no use for the artifices of her grandmother, that the flapper was prepared to use at the drop of a lipstick if it could further her ends. Modesty, in the old-fashioned sense of the word, was not the Service Type's long suit, and if it had not been for her shape you would have had some difficulty in distinguishing her from her male counterpart when both were wearing battledress. Her uniform, once its newness had worn off, invested her with a new personality and an aspect of British womanhood not seen since the days of Boadicea. Indeed, there was something Boadicenian about the Second World War Service girl, particularly after she had swallowed a couple of draught Bass at the 'Mucky Duck' or 'The Cat and Fiddle' near her depot. Given the chariot she would, I feel, have made bloody inroads into any Nazi phalanx threatening her independence, and as for the amorous male, isolated for months at a stretch from loving wife and family, she could play him like a great, clumsy cod on the end of a line.

She was a comparative rarity until the war had run about a third of its course but after that, by 1941, she was everywhere, holding her own and sometimes calling the tune in port, in barrack, and on airfield. As time went on she even succeeded in instituting a class system that was quite foreign to the armed forces. It had nothing to do with rank but was governed by the Service in which she had enlisted.

At the top of the tier, socially that is, was the W.R.E.N., and at the bottom, representing a proletariat, were the girls of the A.T.S. In between, doing duty for a middle class, was the W.A.A.F., who thought of her Senior Service sister as 'toffee-nosed', and of her army counterpart as 'the tiniest bit scruffy'. At least, that was my impression, but perhaps it was prejudiced on account of the fact that I had no contacts with girls from the other two Services but was closely associated with the W.A.A.F. over a period of four years.

They were the best kind of company and I cannot imagine how we should have survived that grey, dismal era without them, for they were invariably cheerful, despite constant assertions that they were 'cheesed' and 'brassed off'. It always seemed to me that they adapted to Service life far more easily than did the male but this, when you think about it, is understandable. For a majority of them war was a welcome escape from shop-counter, office and household chore, and their Service disciplines, although occasionally irksome and pettifogging, were not maintained by the ultimate sanction of the glasshouse. For the really cheesed-off there were always two avenues of escape, a discharge on the grounds of being 'non-amenable to discipline', or the more popular exit known as 'Clause Eleven', a discharge through pregnancy. Few that I knew availed themselves of these desperate remedies. A majority were content with their lot and would not have changed it. They did not yearn, as we did almost to a man, for the cease-fire. They lived for the day, taking the frustrations and restrictions of Service life in their martial stride, often making very light of them, and finding in the anomalies of their situation sources of uproarious merriment. One of the few joyful sounds ever heard on a Service establishment in the stalemate years of 1941–43 was W.A.A.F. laughter. It was usually belly-laughter, with nothing in its note to remind you of the squeal of the flapper.

They made light of everything. Of their women officers, whom they arbitrarily divided into 'good sports', 'binders' and 'right bitches', of the regulations, like keeping their hair clear of their tunic collars, and of their standard issue, particularly their severely practical underwear, sometimes referred to as 'blackouts' and sometimes as 'passion-killers'. Under a male officer they were extremely industrious workers but under most W.A.A.F. officers they were inclined to sulk and slack off. Given tactful overlords they took their duties very seriously and became extremely proficient in a variety of skills and trades. By 1942 the R.A.F. could not have operated without them but their interest in the progress of the war, as a war, was negligible. Some of them, I suspect, were not in the least clear what it was all about, how it began, or who, apart from the British and the Germans, were embarked upon it. For all their come-day go-day approach, however, most of them had their eye on the main chance and here they were far more sophisticated than the flapper, whose attention was directed towards dance-steps and the June-moon-soon libretto of sheet-music rather than marriage. The flapper saw her male escort as a playmate but the Service girl was never averse to a little practical prospecting in terms of the future. She went about it in a very businesslike way.

Tucked away in every serving airman's documents was a large foolscap sheet a detailed personal record summarising his service, and all the entries save one were entered on this document in ink. The one exception was his status as a married man or a bachelor and this, for obvious reasons, was entered in pencil. An 'M' signified that he was married and an 'S' proclaimed the fact that he was still single.

Now the moment a closer-than-comrade association between an airman and a W.A.A.F. began to develop the latter would set about cultivating the documents clerk of the unit and it was not long before she brought herself to the point of asking him outright whether A.C. Blank's docs. were marked with a pencilled 'S' or a telltale 'M'. A man's documents, of course, were confidential. For some reason he was not even allowed to look at them himself, but regulations of this kind never inhibited the W.A.A.F. in her efforts to ascertain whether A.C. Blank's claim to be a bachelor was bogus. Alas, it so often was.

They would stroll into the orderly room on some fictitious errand and enquire, blandly, if they could "have a quick peep at Charlie's docs". If the documents happened to be in the charge of another W.A.A.F. their curiosity concerning Charlie's age, next-of-kin, and status was satisfied at once. The girls had a working arrangement to keep one another informed on matters of this kind. If the documents' clerk was male, however, the approach used was oblique. They would bring Charlie into the conversation and work around to his documentation in their own time, sitting on the registry table, swinging their legs and ogling the poor fellow, sometimes going so far as to make a direct appeal to his chivalry.

Once they were satisfied a man was safely married they could be very motherly, electing themselves wartime substitutes for absent wives in little matters of darning socks and washing shirts when his laundry went astray. I was once troubled by a persistent cough and a W.A.A.F., having observed that I made no use of a mixture sent from home, read the instructions on the bottle and thereafter made it her business to ensure that they were observed three times a day. "You don't want to go home on leave with that awful cough," she would say, measuring the dose, and holding a spoonful of the noxious stuff under my nose. "Your wife will be very worried about it if it hangs about much longer."

Their sex solidarity put the men to shame. I had been brought up to believe that women, thrown together *en masse*, are sure to get on one another's nerves, but this was certainly not the case as regards the climate in Waaferies that came under my observation. There was always more harmony there than in the male quarters, where bickering was frequent, and friendships between many of the girls I met on the camps outlasted the war.

I learned a good deal about the reactions of the enlisted girl to service conditions from Anne, who worked alongside me in the registry at Peplow through the autumn of '43. She was an exceptionally perspicacious girl, nineteen when I met her and crackling with intelligence and *joie de vivre*. As soon as she discovered I was a writer she took my education in hand, relaying to me useful titbits of information direct from the Waafery and declaring that I would never be equipped to write convincingly about women if I relied upon first-hand observation. I learned a great deal that was very useful from Anne, not least the fact that, once closeted in their quarters at night, the talk was exclusively of men. Never, she declared, did it shift to the abstracts that airmen would sometimes discuss between appraisals of the redhead operating the S.H.Q. telephone switchboard, the beautiful legs of the Section Officer Starbright, and the broad-mindedness of the blonde with adenoids in No. 3 Wing N.A.A.F.I. When, after speculation as to the meaning of God and how long Stalingrad would hold out, these cosier topics were resurrected, the talk, it was always said, had reverted to normal. According to Anne it maintained a consistent level of normality in the W.A.A.F. billets after the lights were out.

The most devastating W.A.A.F. within my experience was Betty from Birmingham, whose do-look-me-over smile would have stopped a column of men in their tracks, and whose husky voice on the telephone had the same effect upon the orderly room as the lute of Orpheus had upon the birds. Betty was only there to look at, however, and both she and I were grossly libelled by hutmates when we spent a week together locked in a section of the Admin. block and set to work on the course markings of a prodigious number of N.C.O.s. Our splendid isolation was not a mark of favouritism on the part of the C.O. but was in the line of duty, it having come to his notice that candidates had infiltrated into the orderly room in order to see how their averages were coming along. To put a stop to this prying he decided that the marking should be done under conditions of secrecy. I had no quarrel with this at all. Betty and I were ushered into the little room with piles of examination papers every morning, locked in and only released at specified times, a procedure that excited the sour envy of every man on the permanent staff so that I became known as "that jammy bastard who's locked up with HER all day". It helped to boost my flagging ego but it was all perfectly innocent, even when we overset two bottles of green ink on the papers and had to phone for extra blotting paper.

The most lugubrious W.A.A.F. I encountered was Gracie, who was employed as a runner on a satellite station set down in the midst of the dripping Shropshire plain. God knows she was game enough, plodding to and fro across the runways and cinder tracks that connected the widely-dispersed buildings, draped in a groundsheet from which water cascaded leaving pools wherever she paused, and wearing a crumpled cap that had lost all resemblance to the stiff-brimmed caps of girls who worked under shelter.

Gracie used to come into the Registry with dockets from the Engineering Officer, or the W.O. i/c Cookhouse or Equipment Stores, and hand them over in an almost pulped condition. All the time the steady Shropshire drip ploughed furrows in her face powder and formed little beads on her chin, but she only voiced a complaint on one occasion. Detailed to recross the airfield in a strong south-westerly just as it was coming up to N.A.A.F.I. time, she said, as a general expression of disgust, "What, *again*? All the way back *there*? In *this*? Well, I'll go, but I'll tell you something. The next time I go on leave, and me boy-friend asks me to give in, I will." We treasured that remark and I remember the chorus that greeted her reappearance among us after her next leave. In one voice everybody stood up and shouted, "*Did* you, Gracie?"

The most unrepentant W.A.A.F. I met around this time was Sandra, the girl who ran away with our cook and left us on cold rations until he was arrested for bigamy and a substitute could be sent over from the parent station. Sandra was dotty about that cook, who never concealed the fact that he was married and repeatedly pointed out that their idyll among the flour bins could never be regularised in the eyes of the law. This did not satisfy Sandra, who somehow talked him into going through a form of marriage during a crafty weekend and then publicised the event in the camp's Personal Occurrence Reports. The C.O., convinced that it was all a hoax, summoned the cook, flourishing his documents at him and demanding to know if he was aware that his assistant was posing as his wife.

The cook said, sorrowfully, that he was aware of it, and that in a way Sandra was his wife, for they had been married the previous Saturday in a registry office with a janitor and charwoman for witnesses. It was some time before the C.O. recovered the power of speech. When he did he asked the cook what had prompted him to commit such an act of folly. The cook was explicit. "She dared me," he explained and when pressed for details, added, "She kept saying I hadn't the guts to go through with it. You know how it is with a woman, sir." The C.O. denied that he did, and said that if a man could be that stupid he deserved two wives, and that the whole thing was out of his hands and a matter for the civilian police.

To the surprise of everyone present this handwashing on the C.O.'s part irritated the cook, normally the most amiable of men. He said, sourly, "Ah, that figures, *sir*! That's what I might have expected in this outfit—*sir*! Fight for your king and country they say so you do, dishing up a thousand meals a day, with no one to help but Sandra. But land yourself into a jam and what happens—*sir*? It's 'pass the can'—*sir*! It's 'Send for the civvy police and let those buggers sort it out'." For some reason he deleted the 'sir' from the final sentence of his protest.

His speech had a great effect upon the C.O. Far from exploding, as we had anticipated, he calmed down and asked, almost pitifully, "What *else* can I do? Bigamy is a civil offence. Just tell me what else can I do in the circumstances?" The cook was ready for this. He said, briskly, "Well, for one thing, you can get the R.A.F. Mouthpiece on the blower, sir. He'll know a way round it, won't he?"

Presumably he did, for the cook, although whisked away and lodged in Wormwood Scrubs (from which lodging he wrote me a touching letter beginning, "I am detained at the above address . . .") materialised at the foot of my bed very early one morning and having awakened me by shaking my foot, said, in a stage whisper, "I'm out, Corp. Probation. On condition me and Sandra don't see one another again. Where is she? Will I find her down the cookhouse?" But Sandra was out too, having been discharged a day or so before. Under Clause Eleven, naturally.

• • •

I see them now, a perfectly splendid body of busty, bright-eyed charmers, swinging along in their slightly clodhopping shoes, singing vociferously if not tunefully, their favourite ditty:

Roll me *o*verrrr,
In the *clo*verrr,
Roll me over,
Lay me down
And do it again.

But their bawdiness was no more than an outward expression of their unfailing high spirits, and I have a conviction that the war would have been lost without their help and encouragement. When the W.A.A.F. section, headed by its own band, marched by during the victory parade, a great company of W.A.A.F.s moved in step across my memory—parachute-packers, mess orderlies, plotters and clerks, cooks who dared men to marry them, and A.C.W. Plonks who plodded through the downpour with sodden bundles of chits and posting notices; investigators of airmen's documents, the washers of dirty dishes, and the dishers-out of dirty denims at equipment counters, a regiment of women for whom even crusty old John Knox would have found a more flattering adjective than 'monstrous' had he been wearing my size-ten boots for the duration.

No Peas on the Knife

I

Sinister rumours concerning the process of converting an airman into an officer had been circulating the lower ranks of the R.A.F. for years, passing from mouth to mouth with an accompaniment of nods and sly jokes, the way a village greenhorn might be prepared by friends for the marriage bed, or a novitiate warned of nameless indignities awaiting him on the threshold of a secret brotherhood.

We knew the standard procedures, of course. First the preparation of the multi-leaved form known as the 1024. Then the summoning before a board of wooden-faced selectors. And finally the testing period at the O.C.T.U., with the dreaded letters R.T.U. (Returned to Unit) poised like three boulders over the head of every cadet. But it was not the standard procedures that bothered us. Rather it was the implications hidden in them, along with the army of anonymous observers, waiting to pounce on the man who made a slip, who blotted his copy book be it ever so lightly, who was caught *flagrante delecto* with peas on the blade of his knife.

From time to time you met rankers who had pushed into the jungle but turned back, seeking the safety of the herd, and they would tell of their ordeal of standing like the boy in the picture 'When Did You Last See Your Father?', with a dozen pairs of eyes trained on them, a dozen rat-trap mouths probing their educational attainments, their political sympathies, their familiarity with fox-hunting packs and, above all, their family backgrounds. One or two candidates who had advanced even further into the unknown and yet returned spoke of top brass agents who mingled with O.C.T.U. cadets, like policemen infiltrating the underworld in search of evidence. What else, they argued, explained their summary rejection without an explanation, without a hearing concerning alleged inadequacies? And there was another school of thought that had many disciples. It was hopeless, they declared, to apply for a commission unless you were a Mason, for only Masons were allowed to complete the course, irrespective of qualifications. Yet some men who were not Masons did complete it, crossing the frontier from which no traveller returned, to be seen no more sipping weak tea in Two Wing N.A.A.F.I., or making use of the communal privy, so that to fill in a 1024 was the twentieth-century equivalent of seeking a passport to Cathay or Muscovy or the hidden cities of Tibet. It might or might not be issued but if it was the way ahead was beset with hazards and humiliations.

I knew as much as anyone about the rule-of-thumb procedures. As early as 1940 I had had initial interviews on units, and had since filled in half a dozen 1024s. But the interviews had been sterile and the 1024s had been swept away by one of the many cataracts of paper that flowed Londonwards from every station and satellite in the kingdom. When the wiseacres heard about this they shook their heads and reminded me of my Left-wing sympathies, my known and almost certainly recorded opinions that General Franco was a tyrant, and that the Russians would block the march of the *Wehrmacht*. It did not surprise *them,* they said, that the applications of a man of my calibre had been pigeon-holed after being marked, as was almost surely the case, 'No Action'. Besides, I was not a Mason.

On one occasion I half believed them. I came across one of the applications I had sent in but the words scrawled across it were not 'No Action'. They were 'Insufficiently educated to be an officer', and in the handwriting of an officer who had sought my advice in respect of a correspondence he was conducting concerning a lawsuit. Clearly the case had gone against him or the interests he represented.

By 1943 my skirmishes with the commissioning boards had enlarged themselves into a rather gentlemanly guerrilla war. It became a point of honour on my part to sustain the contest, not so much aggressively but persistently, a partisan probing the strength of the enemy he respects. I felt I owed it to myself to go on trying, if only for the fun of the exercise. Now and again I found allies among the officers of units in which I served, and less often I ran against a stonewaller, who set his face against any commissioning from the ranks. Invariably my allies were regulars, whereas the stonewallers were ex-civilians who had been pre-war members of the Volunteer Reserve. One of the latter, I recall, was a former sausage manufacturer. It was comforting to recall, on retiring, a dead loser, from my duel with him, that the Germans were said to live on sausages. There was another who, in peacetime, was identified as the pre-war owner of a pub on a popular holiday route. It was the pipedream of all the airmen who attended him to visit his pub after their discharge, order a pint, choke on the first mouthful, and accuse him of selling watered-down slops.

The presentation of *Printer's Devil* at one of the hide and seek camps enlisted the support of the C.O. and under his encouragement I filled in yet another Form 1024. This eventually resulted in an interview with the Commissioning Board and there was no element of third-degree in the questions put to me. Most of them were innocuous and during a polite pause a kindly old Wing-Commander engaged me in a long discussion on Roman fortifications in Dorset.

Nothing happened, however, and I soon came to look upon the interview as another skirmish from which I had emerged with honours even. The game had lost a good deal of its piquancy by then, however, so I withdrew to the hills to await my promotion to the rank of sergeant, due in a matter of weeks after thirty months as a corporal. Then something unlooked for occurred. I met an airman of my acquaintance who had a civilian friend employed in the Air Ministry department responsible for commissioning, and the civilian assured us that it was all a matter of papers going astray, and promised to look into my case personally. I did not place much hope on this promise and was therefore considerably astonished when, one damp morning in the late autumn of 1943, the adjutant sent for me and showed me a signal from the A.M. department in question. I recall its precise wording. It read, "925656 Corporal Delderfield, R. F. to proceed IMMEDIATELY, repeat IMMEDIATELY, to Officer Cadet Training Unit, Cosford, NOTHING, repeat NOTHING is to prevent this movement on the part of the abovenamed N.C.O."

I read the wire and the adjutant reread it. "Why the devil have you been column-dodging?" he inquired, petulantly, "a thing like this could involve all of us in trouble. Get cleared from the camp and go on down there this afternoon before the follow-up rocket arrives."

I left him feeling guilty. Clearly it was my fault that my stream of 1024s had gone astray.

2

It was like returning to the scene of one's childhood. Thirty-three months had elapsed since I booked into Cosford as a newly passed-out recruit, but it seemed much longer, more like half a century, back to a time when civilians carried gas-masks packed in little cardboard boxes, and people told one another stories about German parachutists descending on Kent disguised as nuns. War does this with time. The vista between the beginning and the end of a war is immense. Stepping down on to the platform at Cosford was like remembering the Boer War. A gate-sentry in a pith helmet would not have seemed out of place, and I recalled how a party of Czechs and myself had once outfaced a railway official here during one of the early air-raids.

We had emerged from a first-class railway carriage on to this platform, and offered him our third-class tickets. It had not mattered to the stationmaster that enemy bombs were falling down the line, that Paris was occupied, or that we were down to our last three fighter aircraft. The English are magnificent in this respect. They allow nothing to disturb the order of their priorities. Seven airmen had emerged from a first-class compartment with green tickets that should have been white. He called hoarsely for the guard and only when the Czechs met his accusations with incomprehensible protests, did he let them depart. There remained myself, with shoulder-flashes that were indisputably British. I took the only course of action that suggested itself. Knowing no word of Czech I recited the first verse of '*Au Clair de la Lune*', learned in childhood. With a growl of "Bloody country's swarming with Dagoes", he gestured me to follow the Czechs.

Nostalgia followed me to the Equipment Stores. The clerk to whom I surrendered my equipment was the man who had issued me with kit-items at that identical counter in 1940 and I contemplated him with respect. Alone among us, possibly alone among the two million men and women comprising the air arm, he had succeeded in evading postings for thirty-three months, a prodigious feat unless his father was an Air-Vice-Marshal and this seemed unlikely, for he was still an L.A.C. While he attended me I observed him closely, noting that he was sleek and fat, and that his expression was serene. Immobility, of course, was responsible for this, for only the static can arrange their lives in wartime. In three years, and with all those racks of equipment at his back, he must have established close personal links with the Cookhouse, the Military Police, the Orderly Room and the Transport Section, thus ensuring a plentitude of sausage and mash, freedom to pass in and out the gate without let or hindrance, the certainty that his leave applications were placed on the top of the pile in the adjutant's office, and free rides to and from the town any time he wanted to take the air. He gave me my denims and a look of sympathy. "O.C.T.U. Course? In this weather? Jesus, I'd sooner you than me, Corp." It was the voice of experience, of a man who had long since come to terms with the Service and knew where the true sources of power were situated. What did he want with a commission when he could swap a frayed tie for a late supper and hand over a buttonstick and a towel in exchange for a blind eye at the gate?

. . .

The going was rough, a good deal rougher in the physical sense than we had been led to expect. The Admin. types were at an initial disadvantage. Not only were they out of condition but years had passed since they had marched in step, swung a rifle, or executed a knees-bend on the square. Rank was at a discount, a cadet flight being a great leveller. Chevrons and badges were stripped off at the first parade and warrant officers and flight sergeants were at one with corporals and L.A.C.s, a convivial, desperately watchful bunch, all trying to make the grade. I was lucky at last and was given gratuitous advice the night I arrived. Once again I ran into David Floyd, the airman who had been instrumental in exhuming my papers from an Air Ministry pigeon-hole and Floyd (who subsequently went as a Secretary to the British Embassy in Moscow and is now Russian Correspondent on the *Daily Telegraph*) had the makings of a diplomat. He himself had just completed the course and summarised it for my enlightenment. "You'll find most of it archaic," he said, "but go along with it and play it their way. If you have to laugh do it behind your hand. In a curious way it's fun, and even if it isn't what's another six weeks' bull in a war that's in its fifth year?" It was sound advice and was to stand me in good stead.

Our instructors were neatly tailored types, reminding me of the more conventional among the prefects I had met at school. In their book there was no place for individuality. You reversed a precept you had learned as an airman and junior N.C.O., volunteering for absolutely everything. You were a keen type, to whom bullshit was mother's milk. You were a parade-ground fanatic, to whom drill was poetry in motion. You were a man who would rise an hour before dawn to ensure that his buttons shone. The Canadian drill-sergeant's approach to us on the square was a judicious mixture of gentle bullying and ironic respect, so that his rebukes emerged as "For God's sake lift your feet when marking time—*sir*!" Floyd was right. In a way it was a kind of game we were all playing with one another and sometimes, looking up at the threatening sky, I half-fancied myself back on the Exmoor plateau, wheeling and cavorting with the O.T.C. in the mid-twenties. Yet even school did not seem so remote as the winters I had spent news-gathering in the Devon lanes. Or as far away as the hide and seek camps of the day before yesterday.

My luck held. I had the good fortune to be allotted to a squad commanded by a former professional actor, who at once recognised me as the author of *Printer's Devil* and *Twilight Call*, and this indicated that I was halfway home at take-off. Notwithstanding this it would have been fatal to relax, to take anything for granted. Nobody could take anything on trust at an O.C.T.U. Cadets fell away week by week, until one felt rather like a determined survivor on a life-raft. My one grievous error occurred when I was taking my turn at commanding the squad. Waiting overlong in order to ensure that I gave the command right-about-turn on the correct foot, I lost the squad in a fog lapping the edge of the parade-ground but luckily we had an emergency measure for catastrophes of this sort. The squad turned about of its own accord and re-emerged in perfect formation.

The weather was foul, sleet, snow-showers and persistent east winds, but perhaps this was just as well. It may have encouraged the legendary spies to confine their activities to the mess-hall, and here we were careful to eat sparingly, rejecting any peas that were set before us. It was very curious to see rows and rows of flight-sergeants, sergeants and corporals nibbling rather than eating their way through a meal.

The end came with a subdued flourish of trumpets, blown the day we all trooped into Wolverhampton to be measured for our uniforms, and on Christmas Eve we were sent on leave as fledglings, warned that our commissions were subject to revocation during the period we remained temporary pilot officers. My luck still held good. I was posted to Cranwell, allegedly the Sandhurst of the R.A.F. where, it was said, they dined you under old masters to the strains of a military orchestra. It was difficult to picture myself in these circumstances after years in the hide and seek camps. I saw myself as Ko-Ko, translated overnight from County Gaol to the post of Lord High Executioner.

Chairborne Division, Writer Command

They called it Chairborne Division, Writer Command, a bunch of a dozen assorted professionals, stowed away out of sight and sound on a narrow shelf composed of landings that ran around a sixth-floor skylight of the Air Ministry building in King Charles Street, off Whitehall. Another stair led to the roof from which you could look down on the Cenotaph, across to Inigo Jones's banqueting hall, with its plaque commemorating the execution of Charles I, or half-right to Big Ben and the Houses of Parliament. Every time Big Ben struck the hour our rectangular shelf trembled and all the glass in the skylight and west-facing windows vibrated.

Our function was specialised propaganda, with the emphasis on reminding Russia and America of the fact that the R.A.F. was also involved in the war. Foreign journalists were tending to overlook this at that time, and most people outside Britain seemed already to have forgotten the interval between the fall of France and the German onslaught on Russia a year later. One got the impression, in 1944, that whenever our Allies were reminded of this, it was viewed as a re-enactment of the defence of Rorke's Drift, in 1879.

Up here, perched on the gallery, each with his desk, typewriter, and reams of foolscap paper, were some of the most amusing and interesting men I have ever met. To be one of them, for a period of almost two years, was a rewarding experience, more than compensating for the drabness of the preceding four years. Their humour and vitality, their tolerance and expertise, was infectious and stimulating, and I think of them all now not merely as war-comrades, whom one met and came to like after a chance encounter, but as friends and mentors, whose several personalities made the adventure of World War Two worthwhile from my point of view.

I did not join them straight away. My first two months as an officer were spent at Cranwell, in conditions of cushioned splendour, and on a course at Stannington, in Northumberland. I was very happy at Cranwell. Here was none of the hurly-burly of earlier camps, large or small, but an air of dignified calm, as though we were engaged in a gentlemanly war run on eighteenth-century lines in which belligerents exchanged courtesies, and went into winter cantonments during unseasonable weather.

I had but two distressing moments here on the Lincolnshire plain. One was when, whilst inspecting the cookhouse, a dozen exasperated airmen rose and shouted "Yes–*sir*!" in reply to my rhetorical question, "Any complaints?" The other was when the C.O. deputed me to take the names of fifty officers of senior rank who were playing billiards or reading magazines in the ante-room when they should have been elsewhere. Apart from those occasions Cranwell was a convalescent home compared to places like Cosford, Moreton-in-Marsh, and Hinton-in-the-Hedges.

In late January I was sent on the Admin. Course to Stannington, where two hundred newly-commissioned officers were housed in what had been a sanatorium. From my standpoint, with years of orderly room experience behind me, the course was what airmen would have described as 'a piece of cake', and I loved the wild, snow-covered Northumberland countryside, dotted with old inns and castles, and looking very much as it had looked when moss-troopers rode south on a cattle foray and the Percys and Dacres went out to contend with them.

It was while I was away up here that my Cranwell roommate, a middle-aged World War One veteran called Abrams (he was to become a prototype of Pop, in *Worm's Eye View*) noticed an appeal in Air Ministry Orders for men with newspaper experience to serve in the Public Relations branch and submitted my name without reference to me. It was the most fortuitous good turn anyone ever executed on my behalf. On my return to Cranwell I was at once despatched to London for an interview, and gently quizzed by Wing-Commander Lord Willoughby de Broke, an engaging man with the natural courtesy and quiet humour of the country-based hunting squire who has his own special place in English fact and fiction. Willoughby de Broke, then Deputy Director of Public Relations at Air Ministry, had a pleasing habit of reducing Service routines to easily-understandable sporting terms. When, at a conference, he was informed that an article on a confidential subject had been three weeks going the rounds of the Admiralty, he exclaimed, "Three weeks, you say? Gentlemen, it's time we put a ferret in!"

Passed by Lord Willoughby, I joined the staff of Wing-Commander Dudley Barker on the gallery, and was introduced to the other writers perched up there. They included, among others, Geoffrey Harmsworth, the impish and very likeable nephew of the press barons, Rothermere and Northcliffe, John Pudney, the novelist and poet (who had produced my first feature on B.B.C. several years before), Vernon Noble of *The Guardian* (then *The Manchester Guardian*), F. W. Walbank, a Yorkshire schoolmaster who later wrote some delightful essays on the English scene for Batsford's famous publications, and H. E. Bates, the novelist and short-story writer, whose books on the air war, notably the famous *Fair Stood the Wind for France*, were then enjoying a great success in Britain and America.

Half a floor below us, and connected by a spiral iron staircase, was the photographic department, and among the well-known professionals down there was Stanley 'Glorious' Devon, ace photographer of the *Daily Sketch*. Later on we were joined by Eric Partridge, the lexicographer, who was already well-known as an etymologist and subsequently published a number of standard works on slang.

The circumstances of Partridge's absorption into our company provide a typical example of the friendliness prevalent on that gallery throughout the years 1944 and 1945. He came to us unannounced, a lonely, avuncular-looking A.C.2, set down among a dozen commissioned men, and nobody told us who he was, or why he had been attached to us. He had served through World War One, had re-enlisted and got as far as the Western Desert before being discharged and sent home by Monty in person, because he was well over age, and had then joined the R.A.F. as an equipment clerk. He sat there unmolested, modestly puffing his pipe, until Geoffrey Harmsworth asked him to make a précis of the weekly Moscow telegram and went on to explain the nature of the job, not forgetting to define the word 'précis'. In the meantime, Vernon

Noble, recollecting the name Partridge in connection with his work on the *Guardian*, looked him up in *Who's Who*, to discover that Partridge had a long list of scholarly books to his credit, among them, I believe, *The Art of Précis Writing*. Vernon arrowed the entry in blue pencil and left the book open on Geoffrey's desk. It is characteristic of the man that, on learning Partridge's identity, he went straight across to him and made a handsome apology. Partridge remained an aircraftman until the end of the war but was accorded respect by all the men in the section holding senior rank. P.R.3, as it was officially called, was like that, a kind of Writer's Club, where rank counted for nothing, providing one could contribute to the flow of features and the racy conversation that emerged from the shelf.

The work itself was absorbing, the only absorbing work I had ever been given in the R.A.F., and it took members of the team all over the country and, after D-Day, all over Europe and the East. My first job was to publicise the airborne lifeboat, designed to be dropped to ditched aircrews, but there were many stories to be covered that Fleet Street would designate 'human'. There were also certain regular features on the progress of the air war and one of these, a weekly summary known as 'The Fraser', was syndicated to all the Hearst newspapers in the States, and cabled across the Atlantic each Tuesday.

'Wing-Commander Fraser', the alleged author, was a fictitious person, his rank being added to give the writer of the piece the necessary authority, and all newly-joined officers did their stint as Wing-Commander Fraser, cited in newspapers all over the world as Britain's Number One authority on tactics. To gather material for the Fraser broadsides I penetrated all manner of unlikely establishments, including several known by code-letters, and regarded as 'top secret gen. shops'. Here the vast and infinitely complicated pattern of the aerial attack on Germany, and the nonstop pre-D-Day bombing offensive, was revealed to me like pieces of a slowly-assembled jig-saw, and it struck me, not for the first time, that it represented a miracle in national recovery since the days when every major city in Britain was under attack by the *Luftwaffe*. By then, of course, we had air ascendancy in Europe and victory, although still distant, was assured.

I recall going to immense pains one weekend to assemble statistics on the bombing of the Italian railway system north of the Gothic Line, and then seeing my researches made obsolete by the landings of June 6th in Normandy. To my way of thinking this was easily the best-kept secret of the war. The Allied attack, of course, was scheduled for that summer, and rumours concerning its probable date and location had been circulating for over a year, but I was in and out of some of the vital keypoints of the Invasion throughout the whole of the preceding week and no hint reached me that the landings were imminent. Indeed, gathering material on *Pluto*, the pipeline that ultimately supplied the bridgehead with fuel, I got the impression the invasion would not be mounted until the end of July, or early in August, and that it was likely to be launched across the Narrows.

My work took me, on occasion, to places like the headquarters of S.O.E., responsible for liaison with the French, Belgian and Dutch Resistance movements, and also to the headquarters of the Tactical Air Force at Stanmore, where I was told that we had the privilege of being housed in a building that was the venue of Lord Nelson's dirty weekends with Emma Hamilton.

The coincidence of D-Day with the weekly despatch of the 'Fraser' summary put me in a quandary. Overnight Italy had become a sideshow, and I had to get some up-to-the-minute information concerning the air aspects of the landings, and cable it off before the deadline set at 11.00 hours that same morning. Geoffrey Harmsworth's innumerable contacts helped and I went across to the Houses of Parliament, where I located Hilary St. George Saunders, later to write *The Green Beret*, the story of the Commandos. Hilary gave me the necessary facts, plus a glass of House of Commons sherry. Stimulated by this I made the deadline with a few minutes in hand.

Long before then, however, I had settled in and my life was shaping a course entirely contrary to the aimless drift of the last four years, so that it seemed I had at last found a road that led somewhere and was not likely to degenerate into a farm track. May and I had, by then, adopted our first child, a baby girl, and in a matter of six months I had been rocketed from the rank of corporal to that of flight-lieutenant, skipping the rank of flying officer on the way up. I had also, almost absent-mindedly, written an R.A.F. comedy and sold an option on it to Basil Thomas of the Wolverhampton Repertory Company, completing it in three weeks whilst fire-watching on Air Ministry roof and on my weekly day off in Hyde Park and the gardens of Hampton Court. It did not seem to me significant at that time for, by then, I had a dozen plays going the rounds. Yet it was to change my life far more dramatically than the commission and the transfer to Air Ministry.

We were aware, of course, that soon, very soon perhaps, we would be scattered, but throughout the spring and early summer of 1944 we all took pleasure, I think, in the community of interests offered by that tight little group, skylarking and discussing the plays and novels we intended to write after the war, searching out odd angles of the war and sending the results all over the world, sometimes to see them appear in newspapers and periodicals in languages that were strange to us. But before we dispersed, before the great eastward surge of the Allies began, we were to share a collective adventure. On the night of June 13th the flying-bomb attack on south-east England began.

Miss Colyer and the 'Oh-Thems'

I

A good deal has been written, and even more shown on film, concerning the morale of the Londoner during the period of the authentic blitz, that is to say, the nine months linking September 1940 and May 1941. Less well documented is the period between June '44 and the early spring of '45, when a rain of flying-bombs and rockets fell on the capital.

The two onslaughts have little in common, so little indeed that they might almost have been incidents in two separate wars. The first was conducted as an all-out terror campaign, with a sporting chance of gaining victory for the aggressor. The second was hardly more than a prolonged gesture of desperation on the part of Germany. Seen in retrospect it could never hope to do much more than confuse and dismay.

Its effect on the civilian population, however, was disproportionate, and several reasons account for this. It came at the end of a long period of strain and malnutrition, when Londoners were justified in assuming that their long ordeal was almost at an end. In addition it was a nonstop attack, without the daylight lulls that attended its predecessor. But, above all, its impact was psychological inasmuch as flying-bombs could be seen approaching and seemed, indeed, to be making up their minds, as they bumbled across the summer sky, where to descend. Even the short-sighted were given a brief interval to decide which way to run and what cover to seek but this was a mixed blessing. It put the responsibility of staying alive on you and not on the missile. It deprived you of the chilly comfort of fatalism.

By and large the authorities made light of its effect upon morale, trying to treat it as a kind of sustained nuisance, like the activities of an unpleasant neighbour, or the descent of a swarm of wasps at a picnic, but this was a deliberate policy on their part. Both they and the public were very much concerned with this form of attack, and at one time it looked as though the rain of flying-bombs would achieve what the blitz never did succeed in doing—compel evacuation of all but the essential services and population.

Authorities and public alike hated and feared the flying-bomb and found the few moments between its appearance, cut-out and ultimate dive, an interval of horrid suspense. In the early part of the attack, until the defences had succeeded, to a degree, in containing it, hysteria was never far below the surface of the public mind in London and I saw little evidence of the we-can-take-it spirit that characterised the sustained bombing of '40–'41. London was a weird place to live during that final summer of the war. A million and a quarter of its population had gone and those who remained stalked rather than walked from point to point, showing in their expressions the effects of irritation, prolonged anxiety, and loss of sleep. People were afraid, and ashamed of fear; by late July, when flying-bombs seemed to be racketing in from the south-east at the rate of about one every five minutes, nerves were ragged and blitz humour, the ultimate safety-valve of the Cockney, had departed to the country with the third wave of evacuees.

Herein lies my deep respect for at least one Londoner, Miss Colyer, my Holland Park landlady, in whom resided all the good qualities of the British and all the characteristics that have made the Londoner, over centuries of good luck and bad, a byword for self-reliance and resilience. For Miss Colyer met the onslaught of the doodlebug with the same contempt and courage that she had deployed against every other weapon the enemy had used in attempts to confound her. I saw her then and I see her now as a justification for that delightfully insular line that appears in the verse of our national anthem. She had every intention of frustrating the knavish tricks of the King's enemies. Nothing the most fiendishly inventive among Continentals (whom she thought of, quite unconsciously, as a disreputable assortment of Dagoes, Wops, Squareheads and Frogs) could daunt or dismay her. Not for an instant. Not for the time it took a doodlebug to cut its motor and begin its long, swooping descent. For me, during that trying summer, she was far more than she appeared, a dignified, rather angular spinster, exercising a benevolent despotism over an assorted bunch of lodgers. She was the embodiment of a thousand years of London's history.

2

Notwithstanding the evacuations and the brief but lively February blitz, it was difficult to find lodgings in London in 1944. Thousands of houses had been demolished or made untenable and thousands of landladies had gone into the country but hundreds of thousands of Allied servicemen and servicewomen were looking for digs situated within easy travelling distance of their Greater London bases.

I found Miss Colyer through one of those shop-window advertisements, a grimy envelope gummed to a stationer's plate-glass by its flap, announcing a room vacant at Number Seventeen, Clarendon Road, Holland Park, a twenty-minute 'bus ride from the Air Ministry. My room was on the first floor front of a tall, mid-Victorian building, of the kind the Forsytes built about 1850, perhaps on the site of an earlier dwelling. Its proprietor was very dignified but daunting until you got to know her, a tall, slim, extremely active woman in her late sixties, with clear, uncompromising blue eyes and the complexion of a country girl in her teens. She looked much younger than she was, partly because of her complexion but also on account of her upright carriage and the astounding but carefully conserved energy she showed ministering to her assorted lodgers, distributed about the three floors. She and her favourite lodger, known as 'Mr. P.', occupied the basement.

I never did discover how many people were assembled under that roof. Numbers seemed to vary. Sometimes about ten would assemble for breakfast round the mahogany dining table on the ground floor, but other times there would only be me, Vernon Noble, a fellow officer who joined me later, and an elderly woman I thought of as The Garu because she was devoted to Yoga and health foods. Mr. P., a genial man about Miss Colyer's age, did not breakfast with us and rarely appeared above stairs, but the nature of his relationship with Miss Colyer was carefully explained to me the first day I settled in. "Mr. P.

has been with me a long time," she said, holding my gaze with the unwinking steadiness of the Ancient Mariner, "and he lives in the basement front. *But there's nothing funny about it, you understand?*"

Of course I understood. There was not, there never had been and there never would be, anything 'funny' about a single aspect of Miss Colyer's conduct, or her rigid adherence to the code of behaviour prevalent when she was a girl in the eighteen-eighties, but I would not like to convey the impression that she was prudish, or even old-fashioned in her outlook. She was just Miss Colyer, of Clarendon Road, who kept a boarding house, stood on her own two feet, and was the most self-contained and fully-integrated human being it has ever been my good fortune to meet. She was the British spinster at her best. You could picture her as the unmarried sister of a professional soldier, caught up in the siege of Lucknow and busying herself with the wounded in bombarded cellars, or as someone like Betsy Trotwood, who could be relied upon to mother David and Mr. Dick and keep the donkeys from her lawn. There were also elements about her that recalled Grace Darling, Florence Nightingale, Mrs. Pankhurst and Amy Johnson, any one of whom would have been improved by lodging with Miss Colyer.

She interested me from the beginning, a spare, tireless, indefatigable woman, reserved yet communicative, aloof but frigidly maternal, uncomplaining concerning the strictures of war and somehow managing to convey that what was happening across the Channel was a degrading street riot in which a few sober citizens, herself included, had become embroiled, and from which they would shortly succeed in extricating themselves.

Sometimes I would endeavour to draw her out about the war and extract from her conclusions about its impact upon a Londoner who had seen it through, as she had, from the beginning, but I was never very successful. She had fixed opinions regarding Hitler and Mussolini, whom she thought of as a couple of vulgarians, whose bottoms should have been tanned once a week throughout childhood, but she seemed to have no special animus for the German and Italian people, lumping them together with the French, the Spanish and the Russians, as inter-related families of coolies, whose lack of spirit had reduced them, perhaps deservedly, to the status of primitives in need of British missionaries to teach them hygiene and a few simple stories from the Old Testament.

Her approach to the Führer and the Duce was more personal and based upon deeply-rooted prejudices. She said of them once, "What can you expect, Mr. D.?" (she called all her lodgers by the first letter of their surnames), "what can you expect of two men of that sort? That Italian keeps a mistress, a Clara Someone, who looks old enough to know better, and that man Hitler bites carpets when he runs into a little set-back. I don't believe all I read in the papers but I believe that. I mean, people of that kind, keeping loose women, and biting carpets just because they can't get their own way, are bound to come a cropper sooner or later, aren't they?"

Her powers of understatement hypnotised me. Anyone who could refer, without irony, to Hitler's débâcle at Stalingrad as 'a little set-back', or see Germany's border states as put-upon neighbours in a suburban crescent, was unlikely, I thought, to be driven to cover by high-explosive. And in this, as things turned out, I was right.

When the flying-bomb blitz got into its stride, when the damned things began to crump down all around us at the rate of one every few minutes, I felt naked and exposed up in her first-floor front. Contemptuous of anything 'those hooligans' could achieve, Miss Colyer had not even bothered to plaster her large window overlooking the street with adhesive tape and one night, convinced that it was my last, I took refuge with Mr. P. in his basement two floors below. Together we weathered it out and were still there, dozing fitfully, when Miss Colyer marched in with our tea at seven-fifteen. Not a hair on her grey head was out of place. She looked fresh and vigorous and held herself as erect as a hollyhock stalk, so that we felt very sheepish in her presence and mumbled something about it being 'a bit of a night'. She looked surprised at this and said, addressing me, "Is *that* why you're here? Is that why you came down?" I could only admit shamefully that it was and Mr. P. spoke up gallantly, saying he had been glad of my company, whereupon Miss Colyer seemed at last to comprehend the reason for our disarray. "Oh, *them*," she said at length, "those buzz-things! Well, I wouldn't let *them* come between me and a good night's rest!"

and she marched out to carry The Garu's tea-tray up four flights of stairs.

One of the strange by-products of the doodlebug blitz was the wanderlust it induced. Under the old blitz conditions the besieged perfected a routine and adjusted to it jovially and almost happily over the months, but nothing like this occurred in the summer of 1944. For my part, and I know others who reacted similarly, I could only seek relief in roaming about from one end of London to the other, sometimes spending seven successive nights on seven different perches, as though seeking to confuse the mindless things and induce them to concentrate on worthwhile targets, like the Houses of Parliament and the Albert Memorial. Vernon Noble and I, in search of cover, spent one night under a billiard table at Highgate, and several nights in Air Ministry alcoves, where half a dozen stone floors interposed between us and the sky. After that I took refuge in the lighthouse-type home of the actor Walter Hudd, who kept blaming me, as a man enlisted in the Air Force, for the maddening persistence of the attack. Once I wandered out as far as Norbiton to say with my friend Ken Annakin, and then back to Troy Court, in Kensington, that received a direct hit when I was on duty in Whitehall. But all the time one had a feeling of being hunted and in the end I crept back to Holland Park to shelter under the splendid indifference of Miss Colyer, who did not vary her domestic routine by a single second and moved among her shrinking band of lodgers like Queen Elizabeth reviewing poor-spirited troops at Tilbury.

You could not call her performance magnificent because it wasn't a performance, merely a continuation of a placid, non-stop chore that had been the mainspring of her life ever since she put up her hair a year or so before Victoria's Golden Jubilee. And gradually, without being aware of it, we began to draw courage from her, and feed a little of it to each other, so that finally I settled for my first-floor front and lay there listening to regular explosions that slowly widened the plaster cracks in the ceiling. I was still uneasy but much comforted by the thought that no doodlebug, not even a demented one winged by ack-ack or fighter fire, or deflected by a balloon cable, would have the confounded impudence to single out a house where Miss Colyer was going about her business.

3

The extremely rapid deployment of British defences against the flying-bomb attacks is an aspect of the war that has, I think, been overlooked by historians. When the onslaught was about ten days old I was sent down to the Sussex coast to report on the counter-measures and I was very impressed by their imaginativeness and overall efficiency.

The defence was organised in depth, with what amounted to four protective belts stretching in the path of the bombs from the Channel to the Downs. Along the coast, and just inland, was the gun-belt, some of the guns being operated by mixed crews of men and girls, and immediately behind this the R.A.F. balloon barrage, with its crews tucked away in coppices and patches of gorse. Over the Channel and again, behind the barrage, fighter aircraft patrolled, so that a flying-bomb had four gauntlets to run before it reached the southern perimeter of London.

The success of this system, moderate at first, increased as time went on. Between June 13th, the date the attack opened, and the middle of July, two hundred and sixty-one were brought down by the gunners, nine hundred and twenty-four by fighter pilots and fifty-five by balloons, but enough got through to keep the Londoner on the jump. I witnessed several tragic incidents but the only bomb that came close to killing me was the one that dived on the Royal Military Chapel at Wellington Barracks, soon after eleven on Sunday, June 18th. I was on duty on the P.R. shelf under the glass roof when it glided down and it seemed to pass within hailing distance a few seconds before impact, killing or seriously wounding seventy-eight civilians and one hundred and eleven Service personnel attending Morning Service.

Down in the defence zone, where flying-bombs were passing over or being shot down far more frequently, one felt much safer, probably owing to the openness of the ground, and the size of the target area. I lay on my back on Romney Marsh early one morning and watched a Tempest V fight a successful duel with one of them, and was on Biggin Hill Airfield when a winged doodlebug sent everyone diving for cover between cut-out and impact. The course of damaged flying-bombs was often erratic. I saw one hit by ack-ack fire a few hundred yards out to sea, between Eastbourne and Folkestone, but although it swerved it pressed on, passing over at about two hundred feet, heading due north. Servicemen, enjoying a bathe in the shallows, scrambled out of the water and fled up the beach but seconds after disappearing inland it reappeared still losing height, and finally exploded fifty yards south of the tideline. No one was hurt but from then on one was apt to regard damaged missiles as more dangerous than those travelling on course at three hundred and forty m.p.h.

I spent an exciting and interesting week down here in the defence belts but when I returned Miss Colyer was unimpressed. When I told her that the defences were accounting for upwards of fifty per cent of the bombs (this rose, in the last week of August, to eighty-three per cent) she said, "Ah, so that's where you've been? Down at the seaside! Well, I hope you've been sleeping better down there than you did up here. Mr. P. can't seem to get used to the noise at all. He's looking very peaky and I've been telling him to see about a tonic. Iron. That's what he needs." It was the last thing, I reflected, that Miss Colyer would ever need. She had been born with a surfeit.

I grew so fond of her that when I went to France I made sure of retaining my room by paying her two months' rent in advance and promising to make up the balance if I was away longer. She accepted the money but said, querulously, "France? What are you going there for? Those hooligans won't last much longer. It's hardly worth the bother, is it?" I said I would like to be on hand when the hooligans were put down but it was never the slightest good attempting to explain to Miss Colyer that war involved movement, apart from movement to and from the kitchen, and up and down all those stairs.

In the new year I was back again, with tales to tell of the liberation of France and Belgium, but Miss Colyer was dubious about the wisdom of using British taxpayers' money to push one tribe of barbarians from another tribe's territory. "All I can say is I hope they appreciate it," she said, glumly, "for if you ask me it's six of one and half a dozen of the other as regards foreigners. Somebody told me once we had to pay so much a mile to run hospital trains in France in that other war. Did you ever hear of such a thing?" I told her I too had heard of it and that it was true, but that it was unlikely to happen on this occasion because we were now broke and would be reduced to borrowing vast sums of money from the Americans.

"There's another lot," she said, emphatically, "shameless they are! Kissing girls in the street in broad daylight when I went out for the rations yesterday. Saw them at it!"

She perked up a little when the newspapers published those revolting pictures of Mussolini and his mistress Clara, hanging upside-down from a bracket in Milan. I thought the pictures would shock her but they didn't. "You see what comes of keeping loose women," she said, piously, and then, "God bless my soul, what a way to go! I'm sorry for her, mind you!" 'Her' was not, as one might have assumed, the erring Clara. Miss Colyer's sympathy was for Mrs. Mussolini.

She still had the power to surprise me. Soon after V.E. Day, when things were reverting to normal, she appeared in my room one evening and asked me diffidently if I would come down and meet an old friend of hers. "She tells fortunes," she said, "and I want her to tell yours."

It seemed out of character somehow, Miss Colyer hovering with bird-bright eyes, whilst her friend peered into a tea cup, or gazed down at the Ace of Spades. I would have imagined that Miss Colyer would have regarded fortune-telling as a very frivolous occupation, of the kind practised by Hungarian gipsies and girls like Mussolini's mistress, but it was not so. She believed fervently in every prophecy her friend made, particularly the one concerning the trouble Mr. P. was going to have with his leg, and the move The Garu was destined to make in the near future.

When it came to my turn the fortune-teller predicted a big success in the theatre and when, jocularly, I told Miss Colyer that if the prophecy proved correct I would give her a present to commemorate our association, she spoke up very saucily and said, "You will? Very well, I'll have a portable wireless set. I've always wanted a portable wireless set. Don't you forget it, will you?" I said I wouldn't. She deserved something for all those early morning cups of tea she had brought to my bedside while the hooligans were having their final fling.

You could never be quite sure how Miss Colyer would react to a given set of circumstances. She surprised me yet again that summer when I brought a friend home, a gunner from Devon, who had been flown back from a P.O.W. camp after five years of captivity. It was very late when I brought him in so I made him a bed of cushions and rugs on the floor and Miss Colyer, appearing with the tea at seven-fifteen, only just avoided falling flat on her face when she opened the door.

Feeling some explanation was necessary I told her the full circumstances, how my friend had been wandering the streets, and had begged me to put him up for the night before he could catch his train home. She said, sourly for her, "Disgusting! That's what it is, downright disgusting! Here you are, feather-bedded up at that Air Ministry for a year or more, and that poor boy has been shut away with those hooligans, and where do you put him to sleep when he finally gets home? On the floor! Under my feet! And you snug between the sheets on a flock mattress!" She drove her point home by giving the gunner my tea.

I said goodbye to her when I was demobilised in November and never expected to see her again, but when the success her fortune-teller friend had predicted came with *Worm's Eye View*, I felt obliged to go out and buy her the portable radio she coveted. I had an uneasy suspicion that if I failed to keep a promise of that kind I would be classed, in her mind, with the hooligans, and she would come to equate me with Continentals who made a habit of welshing on promises.

I met her on the porch, carrying her string bag containing rations for the leftovers of her wartime clientele. It included Mr. P., who *was* having trouble with his leg, and The Garu, whose move had not yet materialised. She said, unsmilingly, "Ah, *there* you are, Mr. D.! Well, my friend saw it coming, didn't she? She read about you in the papers and was round here all out of breath the same night. What's that you've got? Is it the portable wireless set?"

I said it was and she thanked me gravely. "That'll come in handy just now," she said, "for Mr. P. can't get about and he likes a bit of music to help the day along."

We went down into her basement kitchen and drank tea while Mr. P. tuned in the set and got us a news bulletin that included items relating to measures the new government were setting in train concerning the Welfare State. Miss Colyer, of course, dismissed the entire experiment as an exercise in mollycoddling workshy layabouts. " 'From the cradle to the grave'," she quoted, scornfully. "Spoonfed everyone is nowadays, and where will it end? That's what I'd like to ask that Cripps and that Bevan! They're no better than the hooligans! Well, I've work to do, I was in the middle of my spring-clean when you showed up . . .", and she marched out, erect as a beanpole, carrying her mop in one hand and a bucket of water in the other. She managed the ascent to the top landing without a pause.

I said to Mr. P., "She must be turned seventy. How long does she intend keeping this up?" and he said, grinning, "Not all that long. We're going to put together and buy a cottage in the country. She's always wanted a cottage in the country. Somewhere down your way, Wiltshire, Somerset or Devon."

They got their cottage, a year or so later, and lived out the remainder of their lives there, very peacefully I believe, right alongside the main railway line connecting London and the far west. They liked watching the trains and perhaps, when an express rushed by in the small hours, Miss Colyer would stir in her sleep and dream fleetingly of the whoosh of the 'oh-thems' that had kept the population of London awake for nights on end but had never cost her a wink of the rest she needed to minister to all those lodgers and climb all those stairs. Over the past twenty-five years I have often listened to wiseacres advancing complicated theories as to why we won the war. If they had known Miss Colyer TV viewers might have saved any amount of waffle.

The Agincourt Trail

Wingco Dudley Barker, kingpin of the section, occupied a desk at the far end of the shelf, flanked right and left by the rest of us. Pale, alert, bespectacled and always amiable, he reminded me sometimes of the host at a literary banquet.

Dudley never behaved towards us like any C.O. in my experience. He was a sieve for ideas, an advisory editor who filtered our coverage of the air war and kept us in touch with our markets. He was also the originator and organiser of our dashes to and from the various theatres of war. An intelligent if somewhat enigmatic man I sometimes saw him as a youngish headmaster, concerned exclusively with an unpredictable but enthusiastic Sixth. He wrote a good deal himself, but whenever he was immersed in a piece he would retreat into a literary purdah and could stare at you for minutes at a time without being aware of your presence alongside him.

One morning, early in September 1944, he came up the spiral staircase and stood musing for a moment beside my desk, where I was struggling with a Fraser article about the defeat of the German counter-attack at Mortain. He said, perkily, "They tell me you've never set foot on the Continent, Del? Is that really so?", and when I admitted that it was, and that, prior to my enlistment, I had had neither the time nor the means to make so much as a day-trip to Boulogne, he said, "We've got to send someone to Le Havre. It's a bit of a shambles I believe and *They* want to know what's going on. I'll fix it up. You had better start this afternoon, for God knows when you'll get there." He smiled, a little patronisingly, I thought. "You really ought to satisfy yourself that France is really there, old chap! I'll lend you my revolver but I would ask you to remember it's never been fired in anger."

'They', in Dudley's mind and ours, were the exalted ones who lived on what was known as The Second Corridor, the place where the big decisions were made regarding the conduct of the air war. One walked very warily along the Second Corridor, notwithstanding the complete absence of 'bull' at Air Ministry. It was not unusual to bump into Archibald Sinclair, the Air Minister, or 'Bomber' Harris, destroyer-extraordinary of Germans and German cities. I remembered then that Le Havre had been one of those enemy pockets left behind by the eastward surge of the Allies across the Seine, after the Caen hinge had given way and the general advance began. There were many such pockets, fortified and well-garrisoned zones awaiting mopping-up, but most of them lay along the western coast of France. Le Havre, it seemed, had just been stormed by troops of the 51st Highland Division, after an extremely heavy air-raid, and rumours concerning the devastating results of the attack had crossed the Channel. The Second Corridor wanted an air observer's report on the situation.

I was given Dudley Barker's revolver and allocated a photographer, none other than the famous Stanley 'Glorious' Devon, who turned out to be the exact opposite of a layman's conception of a cynical Fleet Street photographer. He was a mild-natured, very deliberate man, who somehow combined a genial disposition with a built-in pessimism and a distrust for foreigners that equalled that of Miss Colyer, my landlady. "Wouldn't trust some," he warned me, as we climbed into the belly of a seatless Dakota at a Home Counties airfield that same afternoon. "Seen most in my time and some rum ones among them!" He had seen them, too, having secured photographic scoops of disasters, riots and revolutions all over Europe, as well as covering stories like the loss of the *Thetis*, the initial speed trials of the *Queen Mary*, and the birth of the St. Neots' quads. After the war I edited a small book on his work and we called it *These Clicks Made History*. It would be difficut to survey the history of the period without coming across one or more of Stanley's pictures.

It was an uncomfortable flight, about a dozen of us crouched between the struts of the Dakota, flying low over the littered beaches of Avranches that were even then becoming as dated as the field of Waterloo, although less than three months had passed since D-Day. That much had occurred between June and September. We came down on a landing-strip made of wire-mesh near Bayeux, where a shattered church steeple showed above the trees and tents had been pitched along the hedges of a meadow. Stanley Devon's distrust of Continentals extended to cows browsing nearby. "Don't go near 'em," he said. "You can't trust 'em like you can English cows."

There was no means of getting to Le Havre save by hitch-hiking, so we spent the night on a couple of stretchers on the airfield and set out early next morning, when the countryside would have looked its best under a clear sky and a warm sun had it not been for all the hardware left behind by the retreating Germans. Debris of all kinds littered the landscape. Paris had just been liberated and a stream of vehicles was heading for the capital but our direction lay north-east in a wide curve that would take us over the Seine, so we had to wait for a jeep that was heading for Rouen. We found one at length, piled high with spare tyres, and driven by an R.A.F. corporal. An hour later we were passing through what remained of Caen.

The devastation was frightful, far worse than I had grown accustomed to seeing in British cities during the blitz and the Baedeker raids. Every section of the old town looked like the site of a V.1 incident and only a narrow track had been cleared through the rubble for the passage of vehicles. Water and sewage systems had ceased to exist and the place stank of death and decay but the French civilians had their tails up, waving and smiling at Allied vehicles weaving between notices warning of the presence of mines and great piles of debris that threatened to subside and block further progress.

I remember vividly the first two civilians I saw, a white-haired old man and his little granddaughter, the child standing on a table supported by the old man. They called out to us, giving the 'V' sign and the child kissed her hand. Amid that desolation the gesture was moving and significant. It was the first indication I had of the esteem in which the British were held by people who had sacrificed their homes to be rid of an occupying power. Later on, when I moved over the whole face of France and Belgium, I became increasingly aware of the tremendous opportunity Britain had at that time of assuming European Leadership, in a way she had never been able to achieve in the past. The opportunity, as everyone knows, was thrown away, never to reoccur.

The blue of the R.A.F., I soon discovered, was accorded a special welcome. For four years the R.A.F. roundel had been a symbol of hope to these people. In the country districts (although not in Paris and some of the larger towns) the British serviceman was seen as a pledge that the long nightmare was over, and that life could begin again. In most parts of Normandy, and in nearly all the north-easterly, central and south-westerly departments, the destruction of factories, monuments, bridges and rail services, inevitable as a prelude to invasion, was accepted as the price paid for liberation, but it has since puzzled me to discover how these poor devils survived the severe winter that followed. In all the areas I visited in the next few months the machinery of life a Western European takes for granted had broken down under the impact of war. There was no fuel, no electricity, no drainage, no bridges across the many rivers, few usable roads, and practically no food. No items of clothing or household linen could be replaced, no petrol bought, and there was an absolute dearth of necessities like soap. The part of France I crossed on that first journey was half a desert, littered with abandoned lorries, self-propelled guns, wrecked aircraft and burned-out tanks. The temporary graves of some of the men who had cleared the area of Germans were marked by roadside crosses.

We got as far as the Seine that first day and spent the night in the pretty riverside village of Les Andelys, staying overnight in the house of a woman whose furniture and effects had been carted away by Germans she had billeted for a lengthy period prior to the invasion. This was the first instance I encountered of the curious double standards of the enemy. "Their behaviour was very correct all the time they were here," the Frenchwoman told me, "but on the morning they left I saw them loading everything of value into lorries parked in the courtyard. When I protested they were still correct in speech and manner but they went on loading. They even took my sheets, blankets, and carpets. All they left was what you see, a clean, empty house." The next morning we pushed over the Bailey bridge and turned north for Rouen, Bolbec and Yvetot.

Le Havre, as we approached it, was still burning, and long columns of German prisoners were coming out of the town. After Caen I had been prepared for destruction on a grim scale but the aspect of the port stunned me. Hardly a building remained undamaged, reminding me of photographs of Ypres and other Flanders towns I had seen in pictorial records of World War One. Every civilian I met wore black. And all walked the littered streets with their eyes fixed on the *pavé*.

We found accommodation at an inn near the harbour and whilst Stanley Devon got his pictures of the half-submerged shipping and U-boat pens I began my investigation. It was a depressing task. The air attacks, it seemed, had not only shattered the town but had cost the lives of an unspecified number of civilians and that night, hearing that an R.A.F. officer was in town, a deputation of citizens called on me to discuss compensation. I had no brief whatsoever to discuss this topic with them and said so, adding that, not only had I arrived without a franc in my pocket, but had not eaten since leaving the Bayeux air-strip. The landlord of the inn, hearing this, cooked us some meat that we ate by candlelight and it seemed the toughest beef I had ever sampled. Watching me struggling with it he admitted that it was horseflesh. There was, he said, no other kind of meat in the town.

I collected a number of first-hand accounts of the raid from survivors, some of whom assured me that it had been unnecessary, for the German garrison had been willing to negotiate and had, in fact, advised the civilians to move out to neighbouring towns like Yvetot. I could only conclude, at that stage, that the bombardment of Le Havre had been a tragic mistake, likely to sour Anglo-French relationships for a long time to come. I talked to a large number of people but none expressed the view that military necessity had played any part in the strike, and I have no doubt but that I should have returned to Air Ministry with a very one-sided account of the incident had I not located, on the second day, a young infantry subaltern, who had taken part in the attack on fortifications just outside the town. He drove me out there in a captured German Volkswagen, speaking enthusiastically of the bombers who broke the morale of the German garrison shortly before the assault. The fort-like structures on the ridge south of the town were shattered by direct hits and in the fields around, just beyond three lonely graves of infantrymen killed in the assault, were dead cattle, their bellies bloated, their legs pointing to the sky. In thin rain that began to fall it was a dismal sight.

The subaltern drove me back to the former *Luftwaffe* base to meet his commanding officer and it was from him that I obtained my first account of the credit side of the air attack. "Without it," the C.O. told me, "we should have incurred God knows how many casualties. Don't go back to London without putting that in your report and you can quote me as saying it. I wouldn't like the R.A.F. to get the wrong idea about what happened here. The enemy occupied strong positions and would have held out as long as they could." I mentioned what I had been told about the German Commander's offer to let the townspeople evacuate and he said this was true, according to his information. But he added something new. "As soon as the offer was made the Resistance people posted up notices saying it was a German excuse to make looting easier. Some people went in spite of this but a majority stayed on. That's why the civilian casualty rate was high."

The C.O., learning we were without rations or money, invited us to dinner, seating me at his right hand at the head of a long table, with about two dozen officers of the regiment. The food, captured with the building, was good and the wine was better, *Luftwaffe* officers having laid down an excellent cellar during their long stay. We were served by Italian prisoners captured during the Highlanders' previous campaign, and with the cognac the pipers arrived and paraded round the vast room. It was rather like attending a regimental dinner behind the picquet lines at Torres Vedras or Balaclava.

I told the colonel that it was essential I returned to London as soon as possible and he apologised for not being able to take me more than a mile beyond the town boundary, the limit of his territory. The subaltern arrived with the Volkswagen and Stanley and I, together with his bulky equipment, stowed ourselves into it and were driven at about four miles per hour over open country where I could see no sign of a track. The subaltern addressed his whole attention to the task of steering and seemed to me to weave about a great deal, even when there were no potholes to avoid. I put this down to his unfamiliarity with the gears but when we arrived at the ridge he said, with a smile, "Sorry about that. That stretch is still mined. Wait here and you'll be sure to pick something up going towards Rouen." He then turned the vehicle and drove slowly back the way he had come, this time in a fading light.

Stanley Devon had made good use of his time down in the docks area. He had located a stray American PX depot, staffed by a couple of naval ratings. He had cigarettes, soap, candy and two towels. It was the first new towel I had seen since 1939 and I kept it for years as a souvenir. It was almost dark now and there seemed no prospect of getting to Rouen that night. "Countryside's probably swarming with Jerry deserters," observed Stanley, with gloomy satisfaction. "Ordinarily they wouldn't bother with us, of course, but it's odds on they'd shoot us for my gear. It's very good gear, not the usual junk." Like all professionals he was very particular about the equipment and would surrender a comfortable seat on any vehicle in order that his cameras could be spared bumps and jerks.

In the final glimmer of light a jeep came speeding up the road and we flagged it madly. The driver, a British infantryman, braked so sharply that he went into a skid and then stopped and leaped out, advancing on me with a grin. "Ronnie Delderfield, I presume!" he said, in the best H. M. Stanley tradition. He was the proprietor of a toyshop in my home town of Exmouth.

We got into Rouen after a series of lifts and found two top-tier bunks in a transit camp but sleep was impossible. All night long the bunks rocked and the roof shook with the passage of heavy aircraft. It was the dawn of the Arnhem assault and our billet appeared to lay in the route of the air armada.

The next day, by flashing my Air Ministry pass, I cadged a lift home in an ancient Harrow aircraft. This proved the most hazardous part of the journey, for someone had seen fit to stow a damaged motor-cycle in the belly of the aircraft without securing it to the structure. Because of this I spent the ninety-minute journey to Hounslow clambering out of its way as the Harrow banked and the motor-cycle slithered in pursuit. By the time we touched down I was spattered with oil and bruised about the hands and knees. I arrived back at A.M. six days after setting out and the report, according to Dudley Barker, proved the highspot of the morning conference, a circumstance that seemed to amuse him for he said, in the ironic tone he employed when commenting on our comings and goings, "You see, Delder, you've picked up a bonus. You've not only satisfied yourself that France is really there but you've got Air-Vice-Marshals saying 'according to Delderfield'. That's not bad for a flight-lieutenant!"

An Auster Odyssey

It was now clear that the war in Europe would last through the coming winter and probably the summer of 1945. Hopes of an earlier collapse on the part of Germany, encouraged by the near-success of the July bomb plot, faded when Montgomery's plan for a direct drive on the Reich was dropped in favour of Eisenhower's broad front approach, so that someone down on the Second Corridor came up with the eccentric idea that the bomb tonnage required to flatten Germany could be worked out (presumably to the last half-ounce) by a review and assessment of the damage to French and Belgian targets prior to the D-Day assault in June.

The originator of this scheme, whoever he was, must have substituted clairvoyance for arithmetic. The object of the R.A.F. air onslaught on France, in the period between January and June 1944, had two specific objects. The first and most important was to isolate the Normandy coastline. The secondary and subsequent object was to strike at the launching sites of the flying-bombs and rockets. For years now the air attacks on German cities had been mounted with the object of reducing her war potential and there was absolutely no way, at that time, of assessing their effectiveness with any degree of accuracy. However, the Second Corridor wanted that set of facts and figures and possibly my report on Le Havre encouraged Dudley Barker to name me as the man to collect them, not as a lone observer, with a single ground-to-ground photographer, but as C.O. of a small flight made up of three pilots flying Austers, a P.R. photographer with experience of air-to-ground photography, a ciné-cameraman, a driver and a fifteen-hundred-weight van.

Briefing was sketchy. I was to command whilst the flight was on the ground and the senior pilot was in charge once we were in the air. I was given fifty-six major targets in France and Belgium and told to visit them all, collect detailed information on the effectiveness of the bombing, secure corroborative film and pictures, and send back the data as I assembled it. My secondary instructions were to contact and interview people of the Resistance Movement who had promoted the escapes of large numbers of R.A.F. personnel during the last four years, to look out for propaganda angles with an R.A.F. slant, and generally show the flag in all the places I visited where the British had not yet penetrated.

When I raised the vulgar question as to how I was to keep the team fed in areas remote from Allied bases they said, gaily, "Oh, you live on the country, old boy," and gave me an impressive-looking pass signed by Eisenhower and expressing his earnest wish that, as one of his investigators, "I would be given aid and comfort by all". I was very flattered to represent the Supremo in all the areas of by-passed territory, and I liked the phrase 'live on the country'. Somehow it smacked of a Napoleonic advance down the valley of the Danube in the year of Austerlitz and Trafalgar. I was less sanguine, however, about extracting aid and comfort from the civilians I had seen during my recent trip to Le Havre.

The senior pilot and myself went out to have a look at the aircraft set aside for our use. They were Mark I Austers and I said they reminded me of the flying machine Blériot used on his epoch-making cross-Channel trip in 1909. The pilot, an Ulsterman, was more forthright. He flatly refused to fly the aircraft and demanded Mark III Austers. Fortunately for all of us he got them and whilst we were awaiting their delivery I visited various underground headquarters in A.M. to examine the reports of Lancaster and Halifax crews who had struck at one or other of my fifty-six targets during the last few months. The tonnage of bombs dropped was impressive, and all the attacks looked as though they had been pressed home, but there was no real evidence available of what had been accomplished in terms of destruction.

We set out from Hawkinge one grey October afternoon and came down at Ghent to find out where we were. There was little, we had been told, to fear from enemy aircraft. The R.A.F. and the Ninth U.S. Army Air Force had now obtained complete mastery of the sky over the Continent. "If you should meet a stray enemy fighter," one well-wisher told me, "you're on a good wicket! Those Austers can only do a hundred and ten m.p.h. flat out, so all you have to do is to keep turning and hedge-hopping, and the slowest fighter plane in operation will overshoot you." I was to ponder this when we were cruising a lonely course over the old battlefields of the First World War, and to recall Dudley Barker's cheerful parting remark concerning our sole armament. "Look after my revolver, won't you, Del?" he had said, "And remember, it's never been fired in anger!"

A Group-Captain we met some time later was horrified by the set-up. Not, I gathered, because we were flying unarmed, but because we had flown Austers over water. "Dammit," he said, "any fool can crashland an Auster on the ground but you wouldn't stand a dog's chance if you ditched one. Besides, they haven't even issued you with Mae Wests!"

I was never a man to stick my neck out, and had already gone to some pains to ensure surviving the war, but the elements of risk attending the expedition did not bother me then, as they did when we were home and dry and I could view it in retrospect. At the time I was tremendously exhilarated with the prospect of having the freedom of Western Europe, with no one to shackle me with orders and advice. In a way, it was a welcome return to the old, free-ranging days on the *Chronicle*, with enough stories lying around to satisfy the greediest reporter. I liked my senior photographer, a stocky Flying Officer called Bernard Bridge, who had been a photographer on the *Blackpool Gazette* after opting out of his father's funeral furnishing business. Berni was a cheerful, uncomplicated soul, who had been present, in his official capacity, at both the Sicily and D-Day landings, and was sometimes prepared to take foolish risks to get good pictures. He was madly devoted to the ballads of Robert Service and was fond of quoting Yukon verses at uncomprehending Frenchmen. I came to like one of the pilots too, a phlegmatic Canadian boy called Huck, and generally flew in his aircraft, learning how to chart our progress as we moved from section to section on the maps. We flew low over the battlefields of innumerable Continental wars, all the way from Zutphen to Passchendaele, cruising at ninety m.p.h., but the Auster tanks only held about ten gallons and our hops were necessarily brief. Often enough we were almost dry when we came down in a field or on a strip of heath, for it was never easy to find a safe landing ground within reach of target areas. For one thing the Germans had staked all the likely fields and the obstacles had not been removed. For another, much of the available ground was being used to graze cattle and, to make things worse, whenever French or Belgian civilians saw an R.A.F. aircraft on the point of touching down, they would converge on it from all directions. It was attempting to avoid some scampering children that caused our first crash at Mons. The Auster was a write-off and the ciné-cameraman was badly cut about the nose. From then on we worked with two aircraft.

It took a little time to evolve effective methods of gathering the material Air Ministry was seeking. Officers attached to Second Tactical Air Force gave us some useful, large-scale maps and we began covering centres like Louvain, Courtrai and Malines whilst based on Brussels. In areas like this the main bombing attacks had been concentrated on the railway stations and goods yards and the wrecked station was usually the first port of call. I spoke French indifferently, my principal trouble (apart from tenses) being a strong and apparently guttural accent that led me, on two occasions, to be mistaken for a *Luftwaffe* officer on the run. Our uniforms were not dissimilar and an old lady, watching a friendly railway official take me firmly by the arm, cackled with glee and said something that embarrassed my guide. Pressed to interpret he said, with a smile, "She said, 'I see you've captured another of the swine. Are you going to shoot him?' " Something similar occurred at a country hamlet much further south. Seeing me step from van to farmyard two venturesome farmworkers leaped down from the loft aperture, shouting abuse and brandishing pitchforks, and this despite Dudley Barker's revolver that had never been fired in anger. On that occasion I discovered that I could speak French fluently and once I had identified myself we all three shared the joke over a glass of Pernod.

The Belgian railways were in ruins. At Malines locomotives and rolling stock were piled in pyramids of twisted steel and splintered woodwork. Turntables and repair shops were shattered but nestling in the heart of one pyramid of wreckage was a tiny engine displaying a plaque saying it had been made in

Britain in 1835, and sent to Belgium as the pioneer locomotive of the State railway.

At Mons everyone hastened to remind us of the British links with the town, beginning with the Expeditionary Force's first battle, in August 1914, and ending with the recapture of the town in November 1918. The Belgians, it seemed, could not distinguish between airmen and infantrymen and always called us Tommies. One mountainous old dame nudged me slyly and said, with a wink, "Ah, Tommee! How good I knew your father!"

I soon arrived at two conclusions. One was the deadly accuracy of R.A.F. bombing, resulting in very little damage to civilian houses and almost no civilian casualties. American bombing, carried out mostly by daylight, and usually from a great height, was less accurate but the French civilians libelled both of us. "When the French aviator bombs," they said, "he hits the target. When the British bomb they hit the town. When the Americans bomb they hit the department." The other conclusion concerned the heroism of a sizable minority of the people who had lived under the Nazis since 1940. Many of them had performed prodigies of valour. Railwaymen, who carried special passes that enabled them to move about at night, were obvious recruits for the Resistance Movement and once the Allies had landed in Normandy the local saboteurs, always enterprising, redoubled their efforts to harass the enemy. Near Louvain a German ammunition train was driven a mile out of the station and deliberately wrecked in collision. Another was driven through the station at ninety m.p.h. and deliberately overturned. Forged railway passes were issued to a network of skilled saboteurs in order to beat the curfew. Food, rifles and money was stolen from stationary transport, and sixty pounds of dynamite was used to blow up a third train in this area. It was at Mons St.-Ghislien, however, within a hundred yards of the spot where the Old Contemptibles inflicted so many casualties on Von Kluck's legions in 1914, that the most dramatic incident occurred. Here a German supply train was held up by masked highwaymen at the station, driven a mile down the track and then headed into a prepared gap caused by a dismantled bridge over a sunken road. It was still there when we arrived, a locomotive and tender upended in a chasm between two embankments, and a pile of shattered waggons blocking the track behind.

The Belgians paid a high price for these courageous acts. On All Souls' Day I visited the Tir National in Brussels, the building where Nurse Cavell was shot in 1915. It was used as a place of execution for Belgian civilians who were shot in the rifle range. In the gardens behind, close to the desecrated memorial to Nurse Cavell, were rows of graves, each with a rain-sodden photograph of the victim attached to the cross, and all that afternoon parents, widows and orphans paraded past, many of them in tears. I saw one woman throw herself face foremost on a grave and I think of her, and others like her, whenever a stream of advice concerning how Britain should shape its destiny reaches us from Bonn.

As the days passed, and the weather worsened, the work sorted itself into a pattern. The first, and pre-eminent priority was to keep the flight mobile in areas where there were no depots from which we could draw rations and petrol. We had very little money, and no prospect of getting any, and sometimes it was very difficult to keep the aircraft and the van in service. We found billets on the *lodgement militaire* system, seeking out the mayor at every place we visited, and demanding beds on the strength of our passes. As for food, we lived mostly on American 'K' rations, tins of self-heating soup and canned vegetables cadged from stray U.S. units, and cooked in utensils loaned to us by cottagers.

Then there was the investigation itself that soon resolved itself into a standard procedure, beginning with introductions, and a series of bewildering interviews with stationmasters, factory managers and civic officials concerning the effect of raids on specific dates, and ending with a clip of ground-to-ground, air-to-ground and film sequences of the havoc caused by the bombs. This was interesting but exhausting, partly on account of the Continentals' propensity to talk and gesticulate in chorus. Very few of the people I interviewed spoke English and often they violently disagreed with one another concerning important factors of the attack, so that acrimonious arguments would sometimes ensue with me as the referee. A more absorbing aspect of the job was my enquiries into Resistance activities and interviews with families who had lived under Nazi rule for four years. It was then that one began to get a real understanding of what the Occupation had meant in terms of oppression, and what it would have meant to the British if Hitler had launched a successful invasion in 1940.

People approached me shyly, pressing little notes into my hand addressed to airmen whom they had hidden and passed on to the Underground between Holland, in the north-east, and the Pyrenees, in the south-west. One young man I met in a town called Joigny, had concealed two British airmen in the back bedroom of his house whilst German officers had been billeted in the front room. At night, when the Germans retired, they would knock on his door and wish him good night. He finally organised an escape by dressing the airmen as railwaymen and sending them down the track to join a repair party, after which they were 'claimed', redirected, and passed on to the local distributing centre. The young man's nerves were still ragged and all the time he talked his hands shook. His mother, an elderly woman, was bedridden as a result of a visit by the Gestapo.

I met another young man, thin as a wand, who crept out of some bushes near a flying-bomb site in the Forest of Nieppe. He handed me a letter addressed to a flight-sergeant who lived at Harrow, whom he had dragged from a wrecked fighter-plane in 1941 and hidden for several days in a woodshed. The airman got away safely but suspicion attached itself to his rescuer and he spent a long period in a prison camp at Lille. A third man, in Arras, told me that he owed his life to an R.A.F. attack that had wrecked telephonic communications and prevented a check on his forged papers the night following his arrest. In the subsequent confusion he was released with a caution.

I met several families who described to me wholesale arrests and random executions of hostages and further south, in the Limoges area, I questioned the photographer who took the first pictures of the Oradour sur Glane outrage, where the entire population of the village was shot or burned in the church on June 10th, four days after the Normandy landings. Years later I had the satisfaction of reading that some of the perpetrators of this French Lidice had been traced and executed. The French told me that the Vichy police were more to be feared than the Gestapo and most of the people I talked to expressed a fervent hope that Laval would be caught and shot, as indeed he was as soon as the Third Reich collapsed.

As we moved about the Flanders plain, and down into the central areas of France, I was constantly reminded of older wars in which the English had been engaged. Flying over Vimy Ridge at about five hundred feet one clear, autumn morning, I saw the zig-zag lines of the Western Front trenches in the patterns of discoloured earth. The same patterns showed on the surface of filled-in shell-holes. Nearer the coast, just visible on the northern skyline, was a forest of crosses, marking one of the many British war cemeteries.

In the Loire area it was of feudal wars one thought, for here, unmarked by bombs, were châteaux stormed and occupied by the armies of the Plantagenets and something of the freebooting past remained in the attitude of isolated farmers with whom we sought lodging for the night. Down here we were neither friends nor enemies but *les soldats*. One got the impression that a long line of the farmer's ancestors, reaching as far back as Caesar's Gallic campaigns, had been forced at swordpoint to entertain detachments of military adventurers passing through the locality, and that one war had merged with its successor into a complex of quarrels that was no concern of farmers who had more important work on hand.

I remember one such family near Blaye, where we sipped thin potato soup while huge hams, reserved for the market, hung from the roof beams. The family retired to bed at seven p.m., to rise at four and go about their work on the farm. The sons slept in a hayloft. Living with the family was the inevitable French grandmother, a frail little woman trailing clouds of black serge. She spent all her time making pieces of blackened toast on an oil-stove, telling us they were *pour le malade. Le malade* was her husband who had died years before. War or no war these people lived frugally, as frugally as mediaeval peasants. In the morning, when we were filling the petrol tank of the van from a jerry-can, a few drops were spilled by a gust of wind. With a shout of joy the patron threw himself in the snow and crawled under the van to catch the trickle in a cup.

Perhaps the most surprising feature of this long haul into the central provinces was the discovery of stray English women, who invariably wept when they heard an English voice and would go to extraordinary lengths to be of service to us, offering to wash our shirts and socks, and making a tremendous fuss when we accepted their hospitality.

The first I met was in the Breton village of Sable sur Sarthe, where we stayed a night with the widow of a King's Messenger, who had spent the first part of the war in an internment camp but had been released, despite her refusal to surrender her British nationality. Her elegantly-furnished drawing-room was lined with bookshelves containing works by George Eliot, Seton Merriman and other English authors, and she told us that she had billeted German officers until the arrival of the first U.S. troops in the area. They too, it seemed, had behaved 'correctly', and one lodger had carried her bag to the station on one occasion. When she complimented him on his gallantry, however, he said, with Teutonic candour, "We have been instructed to behave correctly, madame. If we had been instructed to cut your throats we should do that!"

We met another Englishwoman in Bordeaux, the wife of a French aristocrat serving with the Artillery in the war that was still going on between the Free French and pockets of Germans holding out in Biscayan ports. She had some hard things to say about the panic of 1940, when she had made her way down to Pau from the far north-east. Water, she said, had been sold to thirst-maddened refugees at two francs a glass. She told us something of the black market, without which most of the French would have starved. Towards the end of the war prices for necessities were astronomical. Her husband told me that he spent four hundred thousand francs on food alone since the collapse of France.

The most touching encounter I had with an expatriot was in Saumur, on the Loire, where we took the first photographs of the extremely successful attack on the main railway line, including the Saumur tunnel, demolished by the famous Dambuster Squadron with the first of the R.A.F. 'earthquake' bombs. One bomb had penetrated right through to the line, leaving an immense crater and this raid was instrumental in stopping the arrival of a Panzer division *en route* for Normandy.

We walked out of the tunnel and straight into a wedding reception in the town, our arrival resulting in my most embarrassing moment of the war. The guests at once joined hands and formed a ring around me, singing 'Tipperary', a song that many French think of as our National Anthem. Afterwards the bride advanced into the centre of the ring to embrace me. The guests then drank my health and gave three cheers for King George VI and three more for General de Gaulle. A young French ambulance driver, who spoke very good English, volunteered to be my interpreter during our stay and that same night she offered to take me to the home of an Englishwoman who had been stranded in Saumur since 1940. I went to an apartment near the Loire bridge and advanced to shake hands with a middle-aged woman standing near the fireplace. Hearing my voice she at once burst into tears and was unable to control herself for several minutes. She said, at length, "That was stupid of me but yours is the first English voice I have heard in four and a half years." She asked me where I lived and when I told her in Exmouth she began to cry again. She had been born and raised in Sidmouth, nine miles along the coast, and we had many mutual acquaintances.

By no means all the goodwill extended to us was from stranded English people. Some of the French people in the remote provinces were exceptionally kind and helpful, and all were generous with the little they had at their disposal. A watchmaker in Poitiers went to a great deal of trouble to obtain an egg for my supper and later the following day, when I happened to reach into my valise, I found another. Written on the shell was 'Long live the R.A.F.'. This man, incidentally, had listened to B.B.C. bulletins throughout the entire war, using a home-made wireless set about the size of a cigarette packet, that he kept hidden in his cellar. At Angoulême, a little further south, I experienced another instance of the French provençal's enthusiasm for the R.A.F. Trying to make one drink last the evening in a café on Christmas Eve I was presented with an excellent bottle of wine from an anonymous donor. A note attached said, "From an old Free Frenchman. Happy Christmas to you, Englishmen."

By then we had worked our way down into the south-west, hundreds of miles from the nearest Allied supply depots and were living on our wits. It was bitterly cold and one of our Austers iced up and became unserviceable, so we had to abandon it and push on with one aircraft and one pilot, plus a van with a deadbeat battery. Every morning when we set out I would recruit a team of French civilians to push the van a hundred yards in order to get it started, so that our departures were always an occasion for civic clamour. These were matched by our arrival in the next area so far unvisited by the Allies. As soon as the van or aircraft appeared the entire community would stop work and run towards us, embracing us, shaking our hands, and demanding autographs. Huck, the Canadian boy, was unimpressed by these demonstrations. "Guess I could do with less flap and more grub," he would say, for rarely, in any of these out-of-the-way places, was there a bite to eat, except a little goatsmilk cheese and a few slices of salami. There was usually, however, plenty to drink and occasionally one or other of us was a little the worse for wear after breaking new territory.

At Bordeaux we were accorded the honour of liberating the Mouton wine-cellars, owned by the Rothschild family, and were persuaded to sample vintages as venerable as our guide. The sergeant and I were down in that cellar several hours and our emergence into the street coincided with the march-past of a column of French troops, on their way to invest the German Naval Brigade, still holding out at the tip of the Gironde peninsula. Seen through a rosy haze of alcohol it was an impressive scene, detachments of troops, including Colonials and units of the Foreign Legion, swinging along under the command of a white-haired old colonel sitting a huge, unclipped grey. The colonel saluted us gravely and we returned his salute, steadying ourselves against the wall of the vaults. We were obliged to remain there, propped at attention, until the long column had disappeared.

Life was rarely as convivial as this. Down in Toulouse, where we spent Christmas, we went hungry until I managed to sell my boots for five hundred francs and buy one small tin of turkey and one tinned Christmas pudding on the black market. The two tins did not do much to satisfy five sharp-set men and by noon on Boxing Day we were on the prowl again, having pooled a couple of hundred francs to pay for a communal meal if one could be found. In the late afternoon we found a downtown café, of the kind used in film sets dealing with French low life, and the woman in charge said she could provide us with a rabbit stew if we were prepared to wait whilst she cooked it. We waited. We would have waited all night, and eventually a large tureen appeared, holding enough stew to satisfy all five of us. It was highly flavoured with garlic and rather sweet to the taste, but we enjoyed it and congratulated ourselves on having found the café. I went into the kitchen, screened by a heavy curtain, to pay the bill and here, on a chopping block, lay half a terrier. The front half.

There is something revolting about eating a dog, even if it does taste like rabbit, and I wilted at the thought of those bowls of stew we had just emptied. The woman, however, was not abashed. She stared at me unflinchingly, holding out her hand for the money, and having recovered somewhat I tottered back into the café to unload my secret on the others.

It was interesting watching their reactions. Huck, after sitting still for a moment, gripped the edge of the table and said "Jesus!" uttering the name softly and reverently. The photographer and the sergeant clapped handkerchiefs to their mouths and ran into the street without a word. Johnny, the driver, mused for a moment, sniffed the half-empty stew-pot and began to bark.

The next day Johnny and I had better luck. In search of information we drove south-west of the city and found an abandoned camp, with its gates open and its sentry-boxes unoccupied. A spiral of smoke rose from the cookhouse and scenting food we drove there, to find a lonely R.A.F. corporal making tea over a petrol stove. He was the only inhabitant of the place and I never did discover what he was doing there, or how long he had been isolated from his unit. He was waiting, he said, to be collected by some Americans, had been in France since D-Day, and had since been so mobile that he had not had a chance to write to his mother. There was no food in the camp apart from tea, tinned milk and a sack of brown sugar, so we sat with him all that afternoon brewing pot after pot of black, syrupy tea. Just before we left he asked us if we wanted cigarettes and we told him we could take as many as he could supply, cigarettes being currency all over Europe and could produce anything from a litre of petrol to the services of a harlot. He unlocked a cupboard and exposed shelves stacked with cartons of Chesterfields and Lucky Strikes. "Guess they won't miss four hundred," he said, casually, and presented us with a carton apiece. We were so grateful that we asked him to name a favour we could do him in return. He said, thoughtfully, "You'll get home before I will. Here's my Mum's address in Highgate. Give her a tinkle and tell her I'm okay." About a month later, when I was back in London, I 'phoned his mother, describing the circumstances of our meeting, and how grateful we had been for her son's tea and cigarettes. "Ah, that's our Ken," she said. "Give his soul away, Ken would."

We had another interesting encounter down here that Christmas. One evening a Resistance fighter arrived with a priest and a car, and asked us if we would care to dine at a remote convent in the Pyrenean foothills. We agreed very readily. We would have accepted an invitation to dinner from Goering and Goebbels at that juncture. We drove south in the teeth of the mistral until we stopped outside a fortress-like building standing on a rocky ridge in complete isolation.

It was not a convent, we learned, but a château being used as one, and the Mother Superior was a Scotswoman who had settled on the Continent in 1930 and refugeed south-east in the great exodus of May 1940. Since then the château had been a staging-post for fugitives crossing into Spain by underground routes and among the men who took refuge here were Allied airmen and F.F.I. Intelligence officers on the run from the Vichy police. The Germans often raided the place but caught only a single English agent, who was taken to Toulouse and died under torture, without revealing the names or whereabouts of his colleagues. She did not know his name and could only describe him as a very gallant man. His body, she thought, had been thrown down a well in the locality. A large number of civil and military fugitives, she said, had escaped over the Pyrenees into Spain at this point. The Germans and their Vichy allies could not watch every pass and among their ranks was a spy who kept the organisation informed as regards which routes were to be watched on a particular night.

One of the most interesting observations the Mother Superior made that night concerned the fears she and her friends had entertained regarding the possibility of an invasion of England, in September 1940. She asked me to describe the mood of

Britain at that time and I told her that there had been no panic on the part of the public and that most people found the idea of a successful landing in Kent or Sussex unacceptable in view of our naval strength. "Then we were more afraid than you," she said, with a smile, "for to us an invasion seemed perfectly feasible and the continued resistance of Britain was our sole hope of a future." I added her name, the name of the priest, and that of the F.F.I. officer who had brought us here, to my list of people I felt should be thanked officially for their contribution to the Allied cause and on my return I handed in the list with a suggestion to this effect. I never heard whether or not they were contacted by the Services. Perhaps they did not look for acknowledgement, facing the risks of a firing-party, or transference to a concentration camp, in the knowledge that they were making the only contribution available to them of defeating Hitler. They came from all walks of life. Among them were men and women of wealth and social position, who could have come to terms with Vichy, and lived lives of moderate comfort throughout the war. There were others, a majority, who had nothing to gain by loyalty to the Allies but stood to sacrifice their lives if they came under suspicion of helping a fugitive airman or cutting a telephone wire on a moonless night. I have never seen any official figures of the strength of the Belgian and French Resistance movements at any one time but it must surely have amounted to hundreds of thousands who played a greater or lesser part in campaigns of sabotage in one form or another. I talked to a hundred of them and also a few of the men they had smuggled back to Britain. I think of them now as the most courageous people I have ever met.

Their spirit, perhaps, is epitomised by the women of the village of Wizernes, a rocket-site in the Pas de Calais area. A British bomber had crashed here, ploughing into the woods just short of the village, and all five of its crew were killed and buried in the local churchyard. The women of the village came to lay flowers on the graves but were driven off by German troops. They returned shortly afterwards, broke through the cordon and placed the wreaths. The graves were still covered with fresh flowers when I arrived in the area.

Snow fell as we worked our way northwards to Bergerac and Limoges. At Bergerac a frantic husband called on me and told me his wife was running a high fever after childbirth. She was, he said, a niece of General de Gaulle, and her doctor was in desperate need of penicillin. There was no penicillin to be obtained in Bergerac so he begged me to drive over to Bordeaux and see whether I could obtain some. We were desperately short of petrol, and the countryside was flooded, but I did not have the heart to refuse him and Johnny and I set out, the journey taking a full day. Authorities on whom I called spent hours telephoning Paris and asking for a supply of penicillin to be sent south but I never found out whether they were successful or not. It was a wretched experience to have to return to the husband empty handed.

Stage by stage we moved back into the Paris area, the job almost completed, and only a few of the target areas on my list remaining to be covered. To the north-east the Battle of the Bulge was raging and we had been lucky to miss the *Luftwaffe*'s swoop on several of the airfields we had used. Good photography, in the weather conditions obtaining, was impossible, so we crossed off four targets in the east and one in the west. The western one was a factory or port installation on the coast, Air Ministry having omitted to tell me that it was still in German hands. I should have paid a call on them had it not been for the watchfulness of a sixteen-year-old F.F.I. sentry, concealed in a hedgerow outside Pauillac. He jumped out and flagged us as we approached a crossroads and stood there shouting and waving his arms, a wild, piratical figure, dressed like a Corsican bandit, with billowing cloak and a belt stuffed with weapons. I have often wondered since whether the German garrison would have surrendered to a single R.A.F. officer prepared to bluff it out. It would have been pleasant to return home to Dudley and Geoffrey with a thousand Nazi prisoners in my train but the boy who stopped me said the road ahead was swept by machine-gun fire, so I took his word for it and reversed.

I met many German prisoners during my travels about France and Belgium that winter and was always impressed by their punctilious respect, and their general desire to please. In an American P.O.W. camp at Compiègne I was about to lift a mug of coffee to my mouth when a young German stepped forward, saluted smartly, and warned me that the coffee was too hot to drink. The incident seemed at odds with the arrogance of these men at the time of their easy conquest of Europe.

One of the last places I visited was the French Military Academy at St. Cyr, near Versailles. It had been almost completely destroyed and anyone who knew anything of the French military tradition could not but feel despondent at picking over the ruins and treading underfoot photographs of groups of cadets of pre-1914 classes who must have died, almost to a man, at the Marne and Verdun. Near the gate I stumbled over what I thought was a boulder. It was the decapitated stone head of General Kléber, the man who took command of Napoleon's army in Egypt when Buonaparte returned to France soon after the battle of the Nile. I would very much liked to have taken Kléber's head home as a souvenir but it weighed a hundredweight. Every barrack block around the central courtyard was a charred shell half-filled with debris but the magnificent equestrian statue of General Marceau, who led the armies of the First Republic, was unscathed. A bomb, however, had smashed through the chapel floor and opened the grave of Madame de Maintenon, the favourite of Louis XIV who persuaded him to expel the Huguenots, among them my own ancestors.

Years later, when revisiting Versailles, I heard a guide describing the British destruction of St. Cyr as an act of vandalism. I am not given to arguing with professional guides, a very unrewarding occupation, but I did challenge this one, telling him that St. Cyr, at that time, was being used as a German radar station.

Near Périgueux I came across an example of the terrible tensions an occupying army produces among civilians, and how that tension persists after the conquerors have departed. Approaching an isolated farm to borrow a saucepan I noticed that the door showed signs of having been battered, probably by rifle butts. When I went into the kitchen a young woman and an old man stared at me with expressions of terror, as though I had walked in flourishing Dudley's revolver, and the old man's agitation continued, even after I explained that I was British and came in peace. Suddenly the poor old fellow began to quake and tears streamed down his face, and so he continued all the time we were there, despite gifts of cigarettes and a slice of Sunlight soap. His daughter told me that, not long before, a skirmish had taken place close by between Germans and Resistance men and the farm had been searched by the enemy, who smashed in the door and interrogated the old man concerning his non-existent associations with saboteurs. His nerves were shattered by the experience so that the mere sight of a man in uniform was sufficient to reduce him to a state of gibbering terror.

By mid-January I had done all that could be done and sent our sole remaining Auster on to Brussels where it ultimately collided with a balloon barrage cable. The chief pilot survived to push on into Denmark and receive the surrender of the German troops stationed there in May. Berni, the Blackpool photographer who had accompanied me on most of the trip, had been withdrawn by then and posted, much to his indignation, to the Far East. I shared his disgust. He was older than me, had survived a hard war, and would have been due for early demobilisation shortly after the German surrender. As it was he was killed when his Dakota ran into a violent storm over the Indian Ocean. He is one of the many old friends I recall with affection when idealistic young people of a succeeding generation dismiss the Second World War as one more instance of their fathers' muddleheadedness. If I learned anything during that seven-thousand-mile journey across Europe it was that this particular war was a just war on the part of all who opposed German Fascism. Wars may be unfashionable, and undoubtedly most of them in the past have been unnecessary, but World War Two is a clear example of the necessity to fight to the last gasp under a given set of circumstances. The victory that came a few weeks after my return to Britain does not seem to have brought us much beyond a succession of almost insoluble economic and social problems, but this is beside the point. Defeat would have reduced us to a state of wretchedness beyond the realm of thought.

Bullseye: Or, Don't Ring Us, We'll Ring You

I

The old town looked smaller and shabbier than I remembered, and very still behind a veil of violet autumn mist, draping the leafless chestnuts and elms where the road climbed east to the frontier of The Curry, otherwise known as Budleigh Salterton. Lower down the hill that glimpse of the estuary I had always looked for, linking two parallel blocks of Georgian houses, would be just visible in the half-light, a steel sword laid across a blur of woods on the Haldon shore, but the overall stillness of the place surprised me a little. It was the day before Guy Fawkes Day, and in the 'twenties and 'thirties impatient little boys set fire to one another's hoarded bonfires and then discharged a rip-rap or two to celebrate on the 4th or rather the 5th of November.

I humped my valise and the large cardboard carton full of free-issue civvies down the station approach and took the road for home. That evening was all of twenty-five years ago but I can remember what I thought. "Catch me north of Bideford or west of Taunton from here on and you can shoot me!" Something on those lines.

It had been a day for new beginnings, or so H. E. Bates declared as he pranced about the Demob Centre at Wembley in his squadron leader's uniform, topped by a loud coster-type civvy cap, and looking as incongruous as a pantomime comedian in Ascot rig. Bates and I had been two of the first P.R. men in the queue, scoring heavily on the points system that controlled demobilisation. He was forty and I was thirty-three, with five and a half years' service, so we said our farewells and bundled down the spiral staircase to the lift, schoolboys on the last day of term. On the way out somebody stole my flying boots, the legacy of a pilot killed near Vanderville.

We had passed our medical check a day or so earlier, standing behind a pilot with a half-healed back injury that threatened to delay his return to Civvy Street while he convalesced. The M.O. pointed out that any pension claim on his part would be jeopardised by precipitate demobilisation, and that if medical advice was set aside the pilot would have to sign papers absolving the Board from responsibility. The pilot's voice rose an octave as he shouted, "I'll sign anything, *anything*! Just let me *out*!" I knew just how he felt. For the past month now a sense of panic that threatened to develop into hysteria followed me wherever I went. The war in the East was over, and even the blackout curtains had been burned but I felt more nervous and insecure than at any time during the last five years. Something, I felt sure, would come between me and demobilisation at the last minute.

The feeling of unease left me at Wembley Stadium where they fitted us (with rather more care than they had demonstrated on enlistment) for our civilian issue. Bates was so cockahoop that he decided to make an occasion of it. Exchanging his coster cap for a trilby he drove me back to Soho and stood me lunch in one of our favourite cafés. He was, by then, well established as a novelist, one of the best short-story writers in Europe, and by far the most authentic and gripping of his generation in aerial warfare topics. He spent that lunch, I recall, giving me good advice concerning subject matter, but I discovered that a good deal of the itch for success had gone now that I had my ticket. It no longer seemed very important to have my name on a gilded board outside a theatre in Shaftesbury Avenue. I was prepared to settle for less, a good deal less. There was home and there was the weekly paper, jogging along all this time under the shiftless eye of temporary reporters and unpaid subscribers. Sometimes they sent me copies but I soon gave up reading them. It irritated me to see so many wrong initials and misspelled place-names, and the strict paper rationing enforced at that time gave the *Chronicle* a wan, anaemic look. Its information was stuffy and lacked punch. No sense of fitness was apparent in the relative space allocated to funerals in the residential section and funerals in terrace-house blocks. Wedding reports omitted to devote a single line to the dress worn by the bride's mother. Accounts of sales-of-work and the local dramatic society's productions were scamped.

2

There was a light over the door and May was waiting on the step. Veronica, eighteen months now, was awake and stared up at me unwinkingly. I shut the door, remembering as I did that there was no seven- or nine-day limit on the time I would spend here now, and that I carried no pass with a date stamped on it. It was like being born again.

The feeling soon passed. In a week or two it seemed as though the last six years belonged to the period of early childhood. I made the same calls, went the same rounds, asked the same questions and used the same typewriter to reduce the answers into paragraphs. I saw the same faces and identified them with the same causes—the British Legion, the Bowling Club, the National British Women's Total Abstinence Union, the Caged Bird Society. A great part of Europe was in ruins and the dead lay in shallow graves from the Caucasus to the Pyrenees, but down here, despite the odd gap torn by a hit-and-run raider, Councillors continued to debate the relative advantages of a new rockery or a parking-ground. The names on the stored-away beach huts were unchanged—'Upsidonia', 'Farenuff', 'Restawhile', and 'Yrtiz', but I did not quarrel with this. It seemed to me just as it should be. After all, that was what the war had been about, the right of people in small communities to live their lives in a way that suited them. But for me things were not the same and never would be again. Within seven weeks of my demobilisation the first of my stray chickens came home to lay an egg on the doorstep I had re-crossed so thankfully. Before the new year was a month old *Worm's Eye View* was a smash hit.

. . .

It came out of a clear sky, so suddenly and dramatically that I had to rethink the entire structure of my future, all but overlooked in the excitement of the Auster odyssey, the furore of the peace, the July election, and the weeks leading up to the day of demobilisation. I don't know why I should have been so surprised. The summer that had passed, from a professional viewpoint, had been promising. Basil Thomas, of the Wolverhampton Repertory Company, had staged *Worm's Eye View* in October 1944, when I was in France, and it had been bought by a Midlands industrialist called Barlow, who sent it out on tour the following spring. It played six dates and at three of them attracted packed houses but when the tour ended all hopes of bringing it into London faded. It proved impossible to book a theatre, the company dispersed, and I had resigned myself, philosophically, to the passage of another false dawn. I returned the R.A.F. uniforms and props to store and reposed what hopes I had of a West End production in another play, dealing with the post-Crimean life of Florence Nightingale. It was called *The Spinster of South Street*, and I had written the first draft in Blackpool billets and the second in my room at Cranwell. Since then it had featured in the York Drama Festival, with Jean Forbes-Robertson in the lead, and Flora Robson had shown some interest in it. From time to time I had letters about it but so many promises regarding plushy productions had been made to me through the post and over the telephone during the last thirteen years that I was not in the least surprised when this proved another non-runner. I had a third play almost completed, a Cockney comedy, concerning a family split by evacuation, entitled *Peace Comes to Peckham*, but now I wrote largely from habit, like an energetic, town-bred terrier enlarging a rabbit warren from which the rabbits had long since moved away. I had a wife, a child, a second-hand Ford and a job I enjoyed. It was enough to get on with, more than many of my wartime contemporaries had once their gratuities had been spent. I was happy to sit back and await my post-war credits. They would come in handy for a holiday in the nineteen-seventies.

But, as Ernest Raymond says, you never can tell what a piece of writing is doing out there in the dark. Tony Bazell, the actor who had played 'Duke' in the tour, mentioned the play to Tony Hawtry, then running the Embassy Theatre at Hampstead. By Christmas it was on and Beverley Nichols had written of it, "This play made my ribs ache." By January it had transferred to the Whitehall, wartime home of Phyllis Dixey, whose curves I had admired every time I walked past the Horse Guards to Trafalgar Square. By February it was packing them in and netting me more than five times the salary I earned as a journalist. I gave it a run of several months and Ronnie Shiner, who had always shown unshakeable faith in the play, gave it a year. We were both pessimistic. Its run, after beating the current record set by *Chu Chin Chow*, lasted five and a half years.

I remember reading an article written by R. C. Sherriff, the author of *Journey's End*, on the subject of how a man adjusts to success in the theatre. He said the general view that an author was buried up to his neck in money was a mistaken one. It never happened this way. The money came in dribs and drabs, subject to all kinds of deductions and penal taxation. For every shilling grossed, eightpence slipped between the floorboards. In my case there was ten per cent for the agent, ten per cent for the Wolverhampton initiators, a backlog of outlay to be recovered by the promoter, and several expensive trips to town to attend to various matters arising out of the production. All the same it was far more money than I had ever thought to earn and I set about spending it. Before the run was two months old we adopted another child, this time a week-old boy. We bought a better car and began attending country house sales and replacing all our furniture with antiques.

I knew very little about antiques at that time, my interests in that field being confined to arms and armour and pre-Raphaelite paintings, but May had a tremendous flair for the business and what she did not know she soon learned from books. Our three-bedroomed house on the outskirts of the town was soon crammed with French commodes, porcelain figures, clocks, oil-paintings, eighteenth-century English pieces, prints and hundreds of books that made it difficult to enter the tiny room where I had worked before the war. We began to give parties, usually for old friends who were filtering back into the town from the Services, and that summer we bought a second-hand Daimler that gave us both a sensation of trundling in the wake of film-stars who owned houses with swimming-baths. One day, feeling madly reckless, I put a pound each way on the Cambridgeshire. My highest stake up to that time had been half-a-crown on the Derby. When the horse won at fifty to one I almost ran to the Post Office Savings Bank with my winnings.

In the autumn we bought a detached house on the cliffs at

Budleigh and commissioned builders to do extensive repairs to it, the Americans having occupied it during the war and burned doors and banisters to keep themselves warm. Cautiously our lives as well as our possessions began to expand.

We enjoyed it all immensely but success, and the relative affluence it brought, had disturbing undercurrents. I never had felt and never learned to feel at ease with theatre folk, except when interviewing them as a journalist. I did not see them as real people. To become one of them enlisted me, against my will, in a band of gipsies, who lived from hand to mouth, selling their skills like clothes pegs and painting their faces in anticipation of riotous assembly round the camp-fire. In habits of thought, and standards of social conduct, they were foreign to all the people I had known and consorted with over the years. Their gaiety was as brittle as their promises and I saw their frequent bouts of melancholy as unconscious rehearsals for parts they might be called upon to play later on. Their comradeship was lightly bestowed and as lightly discarded. Above all I had learned the hard way not to believe a single word they uttered, even when they were sober.

This was one thing, but another was more fundamental and had to do with our future habitat. Were we to up stakes, and go and live among the gipsies? Or would we be better advised to do what Warwick Deeping and his wife did when the overnight success of *Sorrell and Son* engulfed him in the 'twenties, that is, sit down and pretend that it had never happened?

For it was in these terms that I began to see myself, not as a creative artist, with some undefined role to play in the theatre, but as a stay-at-home entertainer, someone who turned out three- and one-act plays much as a cabinet-maker makes something practical from a stock of seasoned timber. I saw playwriting as a kind of extended journalism, better paid certainly, but not nearly so interesting or so vital because it was contrived and made to fit a pattern imposed on it by custom and fashion. I had always thought of everything I wrote as worth the passing attention of an audience but I had not (and still have not) an urge to compose moral symphonies, or to project fashionable or political themes over the footlights. I have never had much sympathy with the notion that the theatre should be used for any means other than diverting people, and this is not to say that I was obsessed with comedy. A play, to me, was a prolonged charade. If one sought enlightenment or mental enlargement then one went to a book and turned the pages slowly, pondering the wisdom therein. It was this detached approach to the stage that determined my course from 1946 onwards. I stayed where I was, among the people I knew and liked and trusted, and on terrain with which I was thoroughly familiar, continuing to write plays—a whole spate of them—but never letting them engage more than the surface of the mind and thinking of them, always, as a means of livelihood and nothing else.

It is not surprising that this attitude soon brought me into conflict with dedicated professional associates, none of whom could ever understand why I shied away from rehearsals and set my face against rewrites and the turmoil that surrounds each new production. In the chapter, 'The Sad Truth About Me and the Theatre' (that appeared in the first volume of these memoirs), I wrote lightly of my disenchantment with the stage, confining myself to the more amusing aspects of the situation in which I found myself after the success of *Worm's Eye View*. In fact, it went much deeper than that, the pull of divided loyalties wrenching me this way and that, sometimes so violently that I do not look back on that decade with much pleasure or satisfaction. Professionally that is, for my private and personal life was full of interest and excitement. The two children were growing up and more than compensating us for the disappointments we had suffered in the past. I learned to ride and rediscovered the Devon countryside from the saddle. May succeeded in teaching me a degree of discrimination concerning antique furniture, and although I worked regular hours, and sat at a desk six hours a day, I still seemed to have as much leisure time as I needed.

One of the more amusing aspects of this period in my life was that of looking at local functions through the reverse end of the telescope. For eleven years preceding the war, and for a period of fifteen months after it, I had watched the world from the press table but now, to my continuing surprise, and sometimes to my embarrassment, I had stepped forward to take my place beside the mandarins. I found myself crowning carnival queens and addressing Rotary Clubs and Women's Institutes.

I judged fancy-dress parades and opened bazaars. And sometimes, hearing myself utter familiar clichés, I would glance uneasily at the press table, where a group of old friends would be scribbling into notebooks, and then my presence on the dais would seem quite absurd, as though I was mounting a practical joke at my own expense.

From time to time people I hardly knew staged plays I had written in London and the provinces, and although none were as successful as *Worm's Eye View* they all paid off, either on tour at home and abroad, or in the repertory circuits, or among the amateurs, and sometimes in all three of these areas. In the late 'forties I had plays running at the Whitehall, the Princes and the Playhouse, but I stayed away from them whenever possible. I could never listen to them without thinking how easily they could have been improved. I wrote an occasional film script and found this exercise extraordinarily dull and when television became popular, in the early nineteen-fifties, I sometimes wrote a play for that medium, having already written a number of pieces for radio. I preferred radio work to TV writing. It is more interesting, from a creative point of view, to tell a story by sound only and I have a theory concerning the surprising lack of impact made by a majority of television plays. It revolves around the enormous number of options open to the originator. The limitations of a radio play are severe and this, I think, demands a great deal more thought and selectivity on the part of writer, cast and director.

I did many other things apart from write. For more than two years I ran a small farm, learning how to milk cows and rear pigs, fowls and ducks. May became an expert at making Devonshire cream and butter and we ultimately acquired a T.T. licence from the Ministry of Agriculture. Later on I ran a brace of antique shops but all these activities, I soon realised, were no more than field work in preparation for what I really wanted to do. On January 1st, 1956, almost exactly ten years from the time *Worm's Eye View* began its run, I cut the painter and did it, settling down to write the first section of *The Avenue Story*, a long saga that aimed at projecting the English way of life in a London suburb from the end of World War One to the reconstruction period of the late nineteen-forties.

The abrupt change of direction involved us in considerable

financial readjustments. I had published three or four books by then but the theatre had claimed by far the greater part of my time. In that first year as a novelist my income dropped seventy per cent, but so did my expenses and once the backlog of taxation was paid off I was no worse off. Although my standard of living fell, and we moved from house to cottage, I enjoyed a sense of liberation that had evaded me since the day H. E. Bates and I drew our civvy kit at the Demob Centre. At last I could write what I wanted to write and not what fashion and the advice of professional actors dictated.

In the next decade I completed three two-volume sagas, four histories of aspects of the Napoleonic Empire, and half a dozen shorter novels. The three plays I wrote during this period were historical dramas, specially written for Pitlochry Festivals. Everything I knew and felt and had experienced over the past forty-odd years went into the characters I created and came to like as they grew from a few sentences on a blank sheet into three-dimensional, flesh and blood men and women. In most cases I used the West Country backdrop, where the sky and seascape are never the same for more than ten minutes and the landscape, apparently unchanging, puts on a brand-new costume for each of the four seasons. From going to London once a fortnight I went there about twice a year, and after half a dozen brief and very depressing expeditions to the Continent, I threw the travel brochures in the waste-paper basket and settled for more familiar scenes, the Welsh hills, the Lakes, the moorland country of the North Riding, the Cheviots, and, above all, the pine, bracken and granite outcrop country of the West. I can never be absent from Britain for more than twelve hours before I begin to suffer the pangs of homesickness and the older I grow the more mulishly insular I become. One of the post-war trends that continues to amaze me is the annual summer trek to countries like Spain and Italy where, as I see it, a majority of people are still grappling with social and political problems solved by British liberal governments in the late nineteenth century. They may have more sun, and they may be temporarily solvent, but they are amateurs in the essentials of democratic practice, particularly those of maintaining public order and sharing what there is to be shared. Some day, I hope history will acknowledge this.

Which brings me, more or less, up to date, a balding, unrepentant, stay-at-home, content to sit here weaving home-grown garments, at peace with most people (except gibbering enthusiasts who strap men and monkeys into capsules and send them spinning round space), and content to accept at its face value the farewell tag stage directors toss at young actresses after an unsuccessful audition—"Don't ring us. We'll ring you!"